Julia Quinn started writing her first book one month after finishing university and has been tapping away at her keyboard ever since. The No. 1 *New York Times* bestselling author of more than two dozen novels, she is a graduate of Harvard and Radcliffe Colleges and is one of only sixteen authors ever to be inducted in the Romance Writers of America Hall of Fame.

She lives in the Pacific Northwest with her family.

Please visit Julia Quinn online:

www.juliaquinn.com
www.facebook.com/AuthorJuliaQuinn
@JQAuthor

By Julia Quinn

The Rokesby Series:
Because of Miss Bridgerton
The Girl with the Make-
Believe Husband
The Other Miss Bridgerton
First Comes Scandal

The Smythe-Smith Quartet:
Just Like Heaven
A Night Like This
The Sum of All Kisses
The Secrets of Sir Richard
Kenworthy

The Bevelstoke Series:
The Secret Diaries of Miss
Miranda Cheever
What Happens in London
Ten Things I Love About You

*The Two Dukes of
Wyndham:*
The Lost Duke of Wyndham
Mr Cavendish, I Presume

Blydon Family Saga:
Splendid
Dancing at Midnight
Minx

Agents for the Crown:
To Catch an Heiress
How to Marry a Marquis

Bridgerton Series:
The Duke and I
The Viscount Who Loved Me
An Offer from a Gentleman
Romancing Mr Bridgerton
To Sir Phillip, With Love
When He Was Wicked
It's In His Kiss
On the Way to the Wedding
The Bridgertons: Happily
Ever After

The Lyndon Sisters:
Everything and the Moon
Brighter than the Sun

*The Ladies Most
(written with Eloisa James
and Connie Brockway):*
The Lady Most Likely
The Lady Most Willing

JULIA QUINN

THE BRIDGERTONS:
Happily Ever After

PIATKUS

PIATKUS

First published in the US in 2013 by Avon Books,
An imprint of HarperCollins, New York
First published in Great Britain in 2013 by Piatkus
by arrangement with Avon
This edition published in 2021 by Piatkus

13 5 7 9 10 8 6 4 2

A CIP catalogue record for this book
is available from the British Library.

ISBN 978-0-3494-2980-9

Printed and bound in Great Britain by Clays Ltd, Elcograf S.p.A.

Papers used by Piatkus are from well-managed forests
and other responsible sources.

Piatkus
An imprint of
Little, Brown Book Group
Carmelite House
50 Victoria Embankment
London EC4Y 0DZ

An Hachette UK Company
www.hachette.co.uk

www.littlebrown.co.uk

For my readers,
who never stopped asking,
"And then what happened?"

And also for Paul,
who never stopped saying,
"What a great idea!"

Contents

The Duke and I: The 2nd Epilogue   3

The Viscount Who Loved Me: The 2nd Epilogue   47

An Offer From a Gentleman: The 2nd Epilogue   83

Romancing Mister Bridgerton: The 2nd Epilogue   121

To Sir Phillip, With Love: The 2nd Epilogue   165

When He Was Wicked: The 2nd Epilogue   197

It's In His Kiss: The 2nd Epilogue   241

On the Way to the Wedding: The 2nd Epilogue   279

Violet in Bloom: A Novella   321

Dear Reader—

Have you ever wondered what happened to your favorite characters after you closed the final page? Wanted just a little bit more of a favorite novel? I have, and if my conversations with readers are any indication, I'm not the only one. So after countless requests, I revisited the Bridgerton novels, and gave each one a "2nd" epilogue—the story that comes *after* the story.

For those of you who have not read the Bridgerton novels, I would caution you that some of these 2nd epilogues might not make much sense without having read the accompanying novel. For those of you who have read the Bridgerton novels, I hope you enjoy reading these short stories as much as I have enjoyed writing them.

Warmly,
Julia Quinn

The Duke and I

Midway through *The Duke and I*, Simon refuses to accept a bundle of letters written to him by his late estranged father. Daphne, anticipating that he might someday change his mind, takes the letters and hides them, but when she offers them to Simon at the end of the book, he decides not to open them. I hadn't originally intended for him to do this; I'd always figured there would be something great and important in those letters. But when Daphne held them out, it became clear to me that Simon didn't need to read his father's words. It finally didn't matter what the late duke had thought of him.

Readers wanted to know what was in the letters, but I must confess: I did not. What interested me was what it would take to make Simon *want* to read them . . .

The Duke and I:
The 2nd Epilogue

Mathematics had never been Daphne Basset's best subject, but she could certainly count to thirty, and as thirty was the maximum number of days that usually elapsed between her monthly courses, the fact that she was currently looking at her desk calendar and counting to forty-three was cause for some concern.

"It can't be possible," she said to the calendar, half expecting it to reply. She sat down slowly, trying to recall the events of the past six weeks. Maybe she'd counted wrong. She'd bled while she was visiting her mother, and that had been on March twenty-fifth and twenty-sixth, which meant that . . . She counted again, physically this time, poking each square on the calendar with her index finger.

Forty-three days.

She was pregnant.

"Good God."

Once again, the calendar had little to say on the matter.

No. No, it couldn't be. She was forty-one years old. Which wasn't to say that no woman in the history of the world had given birth at forty-two, but it had been seventeen years since she'd last conceived. Seventeen years of rather delightful relations with her husband during which time they had done nothing—absolutely nothing—to block conception.

Daphne had assumed she was simply done being fertile. She'd had her four children in rapid succession, one a year for the first four years of her marriage. Then . . . nothing.

She had been surprised when she realized that her youngest had reached his first birthday, and she was not pregnant again. And then he was two, then three, and her belly remained flat, and Daphne looked at her brood—Amelia, Belinda, Caroline, and David—and decided she had been blessed beyond measure. Four children, healthy and strong, with a strapping little boy who would one day take his father's place as the Duke of Hastings.

Besides, Daphne did not particularly enjoy being pregnant. Her ankles swelled and her cheeks got puffy, and her digestive tract did things that she absolutely did not wish to experience again. She thought of her sister-in-law Lucy, who positively glowed throughout pregnancy—which was a good thing, as Lucy was currently fourteen months pregnant with her fifth child.

Or nine months, as the case might be. But Daphne had seen her just a few days earlier, and she *looked* as if she were fourteen months along.

Huge. Staggeringly huge. But still glowing, and with astonishingly dainty ankles.

"I can't be pregnant," Daphne said, placing a hand on her flat belly. Maybe she was going through the change. Forty-one did seem a bit young, but then again, it wasn't one of those things anyone ever talked about. Maybe lots of women stopped their monthly courses at forty-one.

She should be happy. Grateful. Really, bleeding was such a bother.

She heard footsteps coming toward her in the hallway, and she quickly slid a book on top of the calendar, although what she thought she might be hiding she had no idea. It was just a calendar. There was no big red X, followed by the notation, "Bled this day."

Her husband strode into the room. "Oh good, there you are. Amelia has been looking for you."

"For me?"

"If there is a merciful God, she is not looking for *me*," Simon returned.

"Oh, dear," Daphne murmured. Normally she'd have a more quick-witted response, but her mind was still in the possibly-pregnant-possibly-growing-very-old fog.

"Something about a dress."

"The pink one or the green one?"

Simon stared at her. "Really?"

"No, of course you wouldn't know," she said distractedly.

He pressed his fingers to his temples and sank into a nearby chair. "When will she be married?"

"Not until she's engaged."

"And when will that be?"

Daphne smiled. "She had five proposals last year. You were the one who insisted that she hold out for a love match."

"I did not hear you disagreeing."

"I did not disagree."

He sighed. "How is it we have managed to have three girls out in society at the same time?"

"Procreative industriousness at the outset of our marriage," Daphne answered pertly, then remembered the calendar on her desk. The one with the red X that no one could see but her.

"Industriousness, hmmm?" He glanced over at the open door. "An interesting choice of words."

She took one look at his expression and felt herself turn pink. "Simon, it's the middle of the day!"

His lips slid into a slow grin. "I don't recall that stopping us when we were at the height of our industriousness."

"If the girls come upstairs . . ."

He bound to his feet. "I'll lock the door."

"Oh, good heavens, they'll *know*."

He gave the lock a decisive click and turned back to her with an arched brow. "And whose fault is that?"

Daphne drew back. Just a tiny bit. "There is no way I am sending any of my daughters into marriage as hopelessly ignorant as I was."

"Charmingly ignorant," he murmured, crossing the room to take her hand.

She allowed him to tug her to her feet. "You didn't think it was so charming when I assumed you were impotent."

He winced. "Many things in life are more charming in retrospect."

"Simon . . ."

He nuzzled her ear. "Daphne . . ."

His mouth moved along the line of her throat, and she felt herself melting. Twenty-one years of marriage and still . . .

"At least draw the curtains," she murmured. Not that anyone could possibly see in with the sun shining so brightly, but she would feel more comfortable. They were in the middle of Mayfair, after all, with her entire circle of acquaintances quite possibly strolling outside the window.

He positively dashed over to the window but pulled shut only the sheer scrim. "I like to see you," he said with a boyish smile.

And then, with remarkable speed and agility, he adjusted the situation so that he was seeing *all* of her, and she was on the bed, moaning softly as he kissed the inside of her knee.

"Oh, Simon," she sighed. She knew exactly what he was going to do next. He'd move up, kissing and licking his way along her thigh.

And he did it *so* well.

"What are you thinking about?" he murmured.

"Right now?" she asked, trying to blink her way out of her daze. He had his tongue at the crease between her leg and her abdomen and he thought she could *think*?

"Do you know what I'm thinking?" he asked.

"If it's not about me, I'm going to be terribly disappointed."

He chuckled, moved his head so that he could drop a

light kiss on her belly button, then scooted up to brush his lips softly against hers. "I was thinking how marvelous it is to know another person so completely."

She reached out and hugged him. She couldn't help it. She buried her face in the warm crook of his neck, inhaled the familiar scent of him, and said, "I love you."

"I adore you."

Oh, so he was going to make a competition of it, was he? She pulled away, just far enough to say, "I fancy you."

He quirked a brow. "You *fancy* me?"

"It was the best I could summon on such short notice." She gave a tiny shrug. "And besides, I do."

"Very well." His eyes darkened. "I *worship* you."

Daphne's lips parted. Her heart thumped, then flipped, and any facility she might have possessed for synonym retrieval flew right out of her. "I think you've won," she said, her voice so husky she barely recognized it.

He kissed her again, long, hot, and achingly sweet. "Oh, I know I have."

Her head fell back as he made his way back down to her belly. "You still have to worship me," she said.

He moved lower. "In that, Your Grace, I am ever your servant."

And that was the last thing either of them said for quite some time.

Several days later Daphne found herself staring at her calendar once more. It had been forty-six days now since she'd last bled, and she still had not said anything to Simon. She knew that she should, but it felt somewhat premature. There could be another explanation for the lack of her courses—one had only to recall her last visit with her mother. Violet Bridgerton had been constantly fanning herself, insisting that the air was stifling even though Daphne had found it to be perfectly pleasant.

The one time Daphne had asked someone to light a fire, Violet had countermanded her with such ferocity that Daphne had half expected her to guard the grate with a poker.

"Do not so much as strike a match," Violet had growled.

To which Daphne had wisely replied, "I do believe I shall fetch a shawl." She looked at her mother's housemaid, shivering next to the fireplace. "Er, and perhaps you should, too."

But she did not feel hot *now*. She felt . . .

She did not know what she felt. Perfectly normal, really. Which was suspicious, as she had never felt the least bit normal while pregnant before.

"Mama!"

Daphne flipped over her calendar and looked up from her writing desk just in time to see her second daughter, Belinda, pause at the entrance of the room.

"Come in," Daphne said, welcoming the distraction. "Please."

Belinda sat down in a nearby comfortable chair, her bright blue eyes meeting her mother's with her usual directness. "You must do something about Caroline."

"*I* must?" Daphne queried, her voice lingering ever-so-slightly longer on the "I."

Belinda ignored the sarcasm. "If she does not stop talking about Frederick Snowe-Mann-Formsby, I shall go mad."

"Can't you simply ignore her?"

"His *name* is Frederick Snowe . . . Mann . . . *Formsby*!"

Daphne blinked.

"Snowman, Mama! Snowman!"

"It *is* unfortunate," Daphne allowed. "But, Lady Belinda Basset, do not forget that you could be likened to a rather droopy hound."

Belinda's gaze grew very jaded, and it became instantly clear that someone had indeed likened her to a basset hound.

"Oh," Daphne said, somewhat surprised that Belinda had never told her about it. "I'm so sorry."

"It was long ago," Belinda said with a sniff. "And I assure you, it was not said more than once."

Daphne pressed her lips together, trying not to smile. It was definitely not good form to encourage fisticuffs, but as she had fought her way to adulthood with seven siblings, four of them brothers, she could not help but utter a quiet "Well-done."

Belinda gave her a regal nod, then said, "Will you have a talk with Caroline?"

"What is it you wish for me to say?"

"I don't know. Whatever it is you usually say. It always seems to work."

There was a compliment in there somewhere, Daphne was fairly certain, but before she could dissect the sentence, her stomach did a nasty flip, followed by the oddest sort of squeeze, and then—

"Excuse me!" she yelped, and she made it to the washroom just in time to reach the chamber pot.

Oh dear God. This wasn't the change. She was pregnant.

"Mama?"

Daphne flicked her hand back at Belinda, trying to dismiss her.

"Mama? Are you all right?"

Daphne retched again.

"I'm getting Father," Belinda announced.

"No!" Daphne fairly howled.

"Was it the fish? Because I thought the fish tasted a bit dodgy."

Daphne nodded, hoping that would be the end of it.

"Oh, wait a moment, you didn't have the fish. I remember it quite distinctly."

Oh, bugger Belinda and her bloody attention to detail.

It was not the most maternal of sentiments, Daphne thought as she once again heaved her innards, but she was not feeling particularly charitable at the moment.

"You had the squab. I had the fish, and so did David, but you and Caroline ate only squab, and I think Father and Amelia had both, and we all had the soup, although—"

"Stop!" Daphne begged. She didn't want to talk about food. Even the mere mention . . .

"I think I had better get Father," Belinda said again.

"No, I'm fine," Daphne gasped, still jerking her hand behind her in a shushing motion. She didn't want Simon to see her like this. He would know instantly what was about.

Or perhaps more to the point, what was about to happen. In seven and a half months, give or take a few weeks.

"Very well," Belinda conceded, "but at least let me fetch your maid. You should be in bed."

Daphne threw up again.

"After you're through," Belinda corrected. "You should be in bed once you're through with . . . ah . . . *that*."

"My maid," Daphne finally agreed. Maria would deduce the truth instantly, but she would not say a word to anyone, servants or family. And perhaps more pressing, Maria would know exactly what to bring as a remedy. It would taste vile and smell worse, but it would settle her stomach.

Belinda dashed off, and Daphne—once she was convinced there could be nothing left in her stomach—staggered to her bed. She held herself extremely still; even the slightest rocking motion made her feel as if she were at sea. "I'm too old for this," she moaned, because she was. Surely, she was. If she remained true to form—and really, why should this confinement be any different from the previous four—she would be gripped by nausea for at least two more months. The lack of food would keep her slender, but that would last only until mid-summer, when she would double in size, practically overnight. Her fingers would swell to the point that she could not wear her rings, she would not fit into any of her shoes, and even a single flight of stairs would leave her gasping for breath.

She would be an elephant. A two-legged, chestnut-haired elephant.

"Your Grace!"

Daphne could not lift her head, so she lifted her hand instead, a pathetic silent greeting to Maria, who was by now standing by the bed, staring down at her with an expression of horror . . .

. . . that was quickly sliding into one of suspicion.

"Your Grace," Maria said again, this time with unmistakable inflection. She smiled.

"I know," Daphne said. "I know."

"Does the duke know?"

"Not yet."

"Well, you won't be able to hide it for long."

"He leaves this afternoon for a few nights at Clyvedon," Daphne said. "I will tell him when he returns."

"You should tell him now," Maria said. Twenty years of employment did give a maid some license to speak freely.

Daphne carefully edged herself up into a reclining position, stopping once to calm a wave of nausea. "It might not take," she said. "At my age, they very often don't."

"Oh, I think it's taken," Maria said. "Have you looked in the mirror yet?"

Daphne shook her head.

"You're green."

"It might not—"

"You're not going to throw the baby up."

"Maria!"

Maria crossed her arms and speared Daphne with a stare. "You know the truth, Your Grace. You just don't want to admit it."

Daphne opened her mouth to speak, but she had nothing to say. She knew Maria was right.

"If the baby hadn't taken," Maria said, a bit more

gently, "you wouldn't be feeling so sickly. My mum had eight babies after me, and four losses early on. She never was sick, not even once, with the ones that didn't take."

Daphne sighed and then nodded, conceding the point. "I'm still going to wait, though," she said. "Just a bit longer." She wasn't sure why she wanted to keep this to herself for a few more days, but she did. And as she was the one whose body was currently trying to turn itself inside out, she rather thought it was her decision to make.

"Oh, I almost forgot," Maria said. "We received word from your brother. He's coming to town next week."

"Colin?" Daphne asked.

Maria nodded. "With his family."

"They must stay with us," Daphne said. Colin and Penelope did not own a home in town, and to economize they tended to stay with either Daphne or their oldest brother, Anthony, who had inherited the title and all that went with it. "Please ask Belinda to pen a letter on my behalf, insisting that they come to Hastings House."

Maria gave a nod and departed.

Daphne moaned and went to sleep.

By the time Colin and Penelope arrived, with their four darling children in tow, Daphne was throwing up several times a day. Simon still didn't know about her condition;

he'd been delayed in the country—something about a flooded field—and now he wasn't due back until the end of the week.

But Daphne wasn't going to let a queasy belly get in the way of greeting her favorite brother. "Colin!" she exclaimed, her smile growing positively giddy at the familiar sight of his sparkling green eyes. "It has been much too long."

"I fully agree," he said, giving her a quick hug while Penelope attempted to shoo their children into the house.

"No, you may not chase that pigeon!" she said sternly. "So sorry, Daphne, but—" She dashed back out onto the front steps, neatly nabbing seven-year-old Thomas by the collar.

"Be grateful your urchins are grown," Colin said with a chuckle as he took a step back. "We can't keep— Good God, Daff, what's wrong with you?"

Trust a brother to dispense with tact.

"You look awful," he said, as if he hadn't made that clear with his first statement.

"Just a bit under the weather," she mumbled. "I think it was the fish."

"Uncle Colin!"

Colin's attention was thankfully distracted by Belinda and Caroline, who were racing down the stairs with a decided lack of ladylike grace.

"You!" he said with a grin, pulling one into a hug. "And you!" He looked up. "Where's the other you?"

"Amelia's off shopping," Belinda said, before turning her attention to her little cousins. Agatha had just turned nine, Thomas was seven, and Jane was six. Little Georgie would be three the following month.

"You're getting so big!" Belinda said to Jane, beaming down at her.

"I grew two inches in the last month!" she announced.

"In the last year," Penelope corrected gently. She couldn't quite reach Daphne for a hug, so she leaned over and squeezed her hand. "I know your girls were quite grown up last time I saw them, but I swear, I am still surprised by it every time."

"So am I," Daphne admitted. She still woke some mornings half expecting her girls to be in pinafores. The fact that they were ladies, fully grown . . .

It was baffling.

"Well, you know what they say about motherhood," Penelope said.

" 'They'?" Daphne murmured.

Penelope paused just long enough to shoot her a wry grin. "The years fly by, and the days are endless."

"That's impossible," Thomas announced.

Agatha let out an aggrieved sigh. "He's so literal."

Daphne reached out to ruffle Agatha's light brown hair.

"Are you really only nine?" She adored Agatha, always had. There was something about that little girl, so serious and determined, that had always touched her heart.

Agatha, being Agatha, immediately recognized the question as rhetorical and popped up to her tiptoes to give her aunt a kiss.

Daphne returned the gesture with a peck on the cheek, then turned to the young family's nurse, standing near the doorway holding little Georgie. "And how are you, you darling thing?" she cooed, reaching out to take the boy into her arms. He was plump and blond with pink cheeks and a heavenly baby smell despite the fact that he wasn't really a baby any longer. "You look scrumptious," she said, pretending to take a nibble of his neck. She tested the weight of him, rocking slightly back and forth in that instinctive motherly way.

"You don't need to be rocked anymore, do you?" she murmured, kissing him again. His skin was so soft, and it took her back to her days as a young mother. She'd had nurses and nannies, of course, but she couldn't even count the number of times she'd crept into the children's rooms to sneak a kiss on the cheek and watch them sleep.

Ah well. She was sentimental. This was nothing new.

"How old are you now, Georgie?" she asked, thinking that maybe she *could* do this again. Not that she had much choice, but still, she felt reassured, standing here with this little boy in her arms.

Agatha tugged on her sleeve and whispered, "He doesn't talk."

Daphne blinked. "I beg your pardon?"

Agatha glanced over at her parents, as if she wasn't sure she should be saying anything. They were busy chatting with Belinda and Caroline and took no notice. "He doesn't talk," she said again. "Not a word."

Daphne pulled back slightly so that she could look at Georgie's face again. He smiled at her, his eyes crinkling at the corners exactly the same way Colin's did.

Daphne looked back at Agatha. "Does he understand what people say?"

Agatha nodded. "Every word. I'm sure of it." Her voice dropped to a whisper. "I think my mother and father are concerned."

A child nearing his third birthday without a word? Daphne was *sure* they were concerned. Suddenly the reason for Colin and Penelope's unexpected trip to town became clear. They were looking for guidance. Simon had been just the same way as child. He hadn't spoken a word until he was four. And then he'd suffered a debilitating stutter for years. Even now, when he was particularly upset about something, it would creep back over him, and she'd hear it in his voice. A strange pause, a repeated sound, a halting catch. He was still self-conscious about it, although not nearly so much as he had been when they'd first met.

But she could see it in his eyes. A flash of pain. Or maybe anger. At himself, at his own weakness. Daphne supposed that there were some things people never got past, not completely.

Reluctantly, Daphne handed Georgie back to his nurse and urged Agatha toward the stairs. "Come along, darling," she said. "The nursery is waiting. We took out all of the girls' old toys."

She watched with pride as Belinda took Agatha by the hand. "You may play with my favorite doll," Belinda said with great gravity.

Agatha looked up at her cousin with an expression that could only be described as reverence and then followed her up the stairs.

Daphne waited until all the children were gone and then turned back to her brother and his wife. "Tea?" she asked. "Or do you wish to change out of your traveling clothes?"

"Tea," Penelope said with the sigh of an exhausted mother. "Please."

Colin nodded his agreement, and together they went

into the drawing room. Once they were seated Daphne decided there was no point in being anything but direct. This was her brother, after all, and he knew he could talk to her about anything.

"You're worried about Georgie," she said. It was a statement, not a question.

"He hasn't said a word," Penelope said quietly. Her voice was even, but her throat caught in an uncomfortable swallow.

"He understands us," Colin said. "I'm sure of it. Just the other day I asked him to pick up his toys, and he did so. Immediately."

"Simon was the same way," Daphne said. She looked from Colin to Penelope and back. "I assume that is why you came? To speak with Simon?"

"We hoped he might offer some insight," Penelope said.

Daphne nodded slowly. "I'm sure he will. He was detained in the country, I'm afraid, but he is expected back before the week's end."

"There is no rush," Colin said.

Out of the corner of her eye, Daphne saw Penelope's shoulders slump. It was a tiny motion but one any mother would recognize. Penelope knew there was no rush. They had waited nearly three years for Georgie to talk; a few more days wouldn't make a difference. And yet she wanted so desperately to do *some*thing. To take an action, to make her child whole.

To have come this far only to find that Simon was gone . . . It had to be discouraging.

"I think it is a very good sign that he understands you," Daphne said. "I would be much more concerned if he did not."

"Everything else about him is completely normal," Penelope said passionately. "He runs, he jumps, he eats. He even reads, I think."

Colin turned to her in surprise. "He does?"

"I believe so," Penelope said. "I saw him with William's primer last week."

"He was probably just looking at the illustrations," Colin said gently.

"That's what I thought, but then I watched his eyes! They were moving back and forth, following the words."

They both turned to Daphne, as if she might have all the answers.

"I suppose he might be reading," Daphne said, feeling rather inadequate. She wanted to have all the answers. She wanted to say something to them other than *I suppose* or *Perhaps*. "He's rather young, but there's no reason he couldn't be reading."

"He's very bright," Penelope said.

Colin gave a look that was mostly indulgent. "Darling . . ."

"He is! And William read when he was four. Agatha, too."

"Actually," Colin admitted thoughtfully, "Agatha did start to read at three. Nothing terribly involved, but I know she was reading short words. I remember it quite well."

"Georgie is reading," Penelope said firmly. "I am sure of it."

"Well, then, that means we have even less to be concerned about," Daphne said with determined good cheer. "Any child who is reading before his third birthday will have no trouble speaking when he is ready to do so."

She had no idea if this was actually the case. But she rather thought it ought to be. And it *seemed* reasonable. And if Georgie turned out to have a stutter, just like Simon, his family would still love him and adore him and give him all the support he needed to grow into the wonderful person she knew he would be.

He'd have everything Simon hadn't had as a child.

"It will be all right," Daphne said, leaning forward to take Penelope's hand in hers. "You'll see."

Penelope's lips pressed together, and Daphne saw her throat tighten. She turned away, wanting to give her sister-in-law a moment to compose herself. Colin was munching on his third biscuit and reaching for a cup of tea, so Daphne decided to direct her next question to him.

"Is everything well with the rest of the children?" she asked.

He swallowed his tea. "Quite well. And yours?"

"David has got into a bit of mischief at school, but he seems to be settling down."

He picked up another biscuit. "And the girls aren't giving you fits?"

Daphne blinked with surprise. "No, of course not. Why do you ask?"

"You look terrible," he said.

"Colin!" Penelope interjected.

He shrugged. "She does. I asked about it when we first arrived."

"But still," his wife admonished, "you shouldn't—"

"If I can't say something to her, who can?" he said plainly. "Or more to the point, who *will*?"

Penelope dropped her voice to an urgent whisper. "It's not the sort of thing one talks about."

He stared at her for a moment. Then he looked at Daphne. Then he turned back to his wife. "I have no idea what you're talking about," he said.

Penelope's lips parted, and her cheeks went a bit pink. She looked over at Daphne, as if to say, *Well?*

Daphne just sighed. Was her condition *that* obvious?

Penelope gave Colin an impatient look. "She's—" She turned back to Daphne. "You are, aren't you?"

Daphne gave a tiny nod of confirmation.

Penelope looked at her husband with a certain degree of smugness. "She's pregnant."

Colin froze for about one half a second before continuing on in his usual unflappable manner. "No, she's not."

"She is," Penelope replied.

Daphne decided not to speak. She was feeling queasy, anyway.

"Her youngest is seventeen," Colin pointed out. He glanced over at Daphne. "He is, isn't he?"

"Sixteen," Daphne murmured.

"Sixteen," he repeated, directing this at Penelope. "Still."

"Still?"

"Still."

Daphne yawned. She couldn't help it. She was just *exhausted* these days.

"Colin," Penelope said, in that patient yet vaguely condescending tone that Daphne *loved* to hear directed at her brother, "David's age hardly has anything to do with—"

"I realize that," he cut in, giving her a vaguely annoyed look. "But don't you think, if she were going to . . ." He waved a hand in Daphne's general direction, leaving her to wonder if he could not bring himself to utter the word *pregnant* in relation to his own sister.

He cleared his throat. "Well, there wouldn't have been a sixteen-year gap."

Daphne closed her eyes for a moment, then let her head settle against the back of the sofa. She really *should* feel embarrassed. This was her brother. And even if he was using rather vague terms, he was talking about the most intimate aspects of her marriage.

She let out a tired little noise, something between a sigh and a hum. She was too sleepy to be embarrassed. And maybe too old, too. Women ought to be able to dispense with maidenly fits of modesty when they passed forty.

Besides, Colin and Penelope were bickering, and that was a good thing. It took their minds off Georgie.

Daphne found it rather entertaining, really. It was lovely to watch any of her brothers stuck in a stalemate with his wife.

Forty-one definitely wasn't too old to feel just a little bit of pleasure at the discomfort of one's brothers. Although—she yawned again—it would be more entertaining if she were a bit more alert to enjoy it. Still . . .

"Did she fall asleep?"

Colin stared at his sister in disbelief.

"I think she did," Penelope replied.

He stretched toward her, craning his neck for a better view. "There are so many things I could do to her right now," he mused. "Frogs, locusts, rivers turning to blood."

"Colin!"

"It's so tempting."

"It's also proof," Penelope said with a hint of a smirk.

"Proof?"

"She's pregnant! Just like I said." When he did not agree with her quickly enough, she added, "Have you ever known her to fall asleep in the middle of a conversation?"

"Not since—" He cut himself off.

Penelope's smirk grew significantly less subtle. "Exactly."

"I hate when you're right," he grumbled.

"I know. Pity for you I so often am."

He glanced back over at Daphne, who was starting to snore. "I suppose we should stay with her," he said, somewhat reluctantly.

"I'll ring for her maid," Penelope said.

"Do you think Simon knows?"

Penelope glanced over her shoulder once she reached the bellpull. "I have no idea."

Colin just shook his head. "Poor bloke is in for the surprise of his life."

When Simon finally returned to London, fully one week delayed, he was exhausted. He had always been a more involved landowner than most of his peers—even as he found himself approaching the age of fifty. And so when several of his fields flooded, including one that provided the sole income for a tenant family, he rolled up his sleeves and got to work alongside his men.

Figuratively, of course. All sleeves had most definitely been down. It had been bloody cold in Sussex. Worse when one was wet. Which of course they all had been, what with the flood and all.

So he was tired, and he was still cold—he wasn't sure his fingers would ever regain their previous temperature—and he missed his family. He would have asked them to join him in the country, but the girls were preparing for the season, and Daphne had looked a bit peaked when he left.

He hoped she wasn't coming down with a cold. When she got sick, the entire household felt it.

She thought she was a stoic. He had once tried to point out that a true stoic wouldn't go about the house repeatedly saying, "No, no, I'm fine," as she sagged into a chair.

Actually, he had tried to point this out twice. The first time he said something she had not responded. At the time, he'd thought she hadn't heard him. In retrospect, however, it was far more likely that she had *chosen* not to hear him, because the second time he said something about the true nature of a stoic, her response had been such that . . .

Well, let it be said that when it came to his wife and

the common cold, his lips would never again form words other than "You poor, poor dear" and "May I fetch you some tea?"

There were some things a man learned after two decades of marriage.

When he stepped into the front hall, the butler was waiting, his face in its usual mode—that is to say, completely devoid of expression.

"Thank you, Jeffries," Simon murmured, handing him his hat.

"Your brother-in-law is here," Jeffries told him.

Simon paused. "Which one?" He had seven.

"Mr. Colin Bridgerton, Your Grace. With his family."

Simon cocked his head. "Really?" He didn't hear chaos and commotion.

"They are out, Your Grace."

"And the duchess?"

"She is resting."

Simon could not suppress a groan. "She's not ill, is she?"

Jeffries, in a most un-Jeffries-like manner, blushed. "I could not say, Your Grace."

Simon regarded Jeffries with a curious eye. "Is she ill, or isn't she?"

Jeffries swallowed, cleared his throat, and then said, "I believe she is tired, Your Grace."

"Tired," Simon repeated, mostly to himself since it was clear that Jeffries would expire of inexplicable embarrassment if he pursued the conversation further. Shaking his head, he headed upstairs, adding, "Of course, she's tired. Colin's got four children under the age of ten, and she probably thinks she's got to mother the lot while they're here."

Maybe he'd have a lie-down next to her. He was exhausted, too, and he always slept better when she was near.

The door to their room was shut when he got to it, and he almost knocked—it was a habit to do so at a closed door, even if it did lead to his own bedchamber—but at the last moment he instead gripped the doorknob and gave a soft push. She could be sleeping. If she truly was tired, he ought to let her rest.

Stepping lightly, he entered the room. The curtains were partway drawn, and he could see Daphne lying in bed, still as a bone. He tiptoed closer. She *did* look pale, although it was hard to tell in the dim light.

He yawned and sat on the opposite side of the bed, leaning forward to pull off his boots. He loosened his cravat and then slid it off entirely, scooting himself toward her. He wasn't going to wake her, just snuggle up for a bit of warmth.

He'd missed her.

Settling in with a contented sigh, he put his arm around her, resting its weight just below her rib cage, and—

"Grughargh!"

Daphne shot up like a bullet and practically hurled herself from the bed.

"Daphne?" Simon sat up, too, just in time to see her race for the chamber pot.

The chamber pot????

"Oh dear," he said, wincing as she retched. "Fish?"

"Don't say that word," she gasped.

Must have been fish. They really needed to find a new fishmonger here in town.

He crawled out of bed to find a towel. "Can I get you anything?"

She didn't answer. He hadn't really expected her to. Still, he held out the towel, trying not to flinch when she threw up for what had to be the fourth time.

"You poor, poor dear," he murmured. "I'm so sorry this happened to you. You haven't been like this since—"

Since . . .

Oh, dear God.

"*Daphne?*" His voice shook. Hell, his whole body shook.

She nodded.

"But . . . how . . . ?"

"The usual way, I imagine," she said, gratefully taking the towel.

"But it's been— It's been—" He tried to think. He couldn't think. His brain had completely ceased working.

"I think I'm done," she said. She sounded exhausted. "Could you get me a bit of water?"

"Are you certain?" If he recalled correctly, the water would pop right back up and into the chamber pot.

"It's over there," she said, motioning weakly to a pitcher on a table. "I'm not going to swallow it."

He poured her a glass and waited while she swished out her mouth.

"Well," he said, clearing his throat several times, "I . . . ah . . ." He coughed again. He could not get a word out to save his life. And he couldn't blame his stutter this time.

"Everyone knows," Daphne said, placing her hand on his arm for support as she moved back to bed.

"Everyone?" he echoed.

"I hadn't planned to say anything until you returned, but they guessed."

He nodded slowly, still trying to absorb it all. A baby. At his age. At *her* age.

It was . . .

It was . . .

It was *amazing*.

Strange how it came over him so suddenly. But now, after the initial shock wore off, all he could feel was pure joy.

"This is wonderful news!" he exclaimed. He reached out to hug her, then thought better of it when he saw her pasty complexion. "You never cease to delight me," he said, instead giving her an awkward pat on the shoulder.

She winced and closed her eyes. "Don't rock the bed," she moaned. "You're making me seasick."

"You don't get seasick," he reminded her.

"I do when I'm expecting."

"You're an odd duck, Daphne Basset," he murmured, and then stepped back to A) stop rocking the bed and B) remove himself from her immediate vicinity should she take exception to the duck comparison.

(There was a certain history to this. While heavily pregnant with Amelia, she had asked him if she was radiant or if she just looked like a waddling duck. He told her she'd looked like a radiant duck. This had not been the correct answer.)

He cleared his throat and said, "You poor, poor dear." Then he fled.

Several hours later Simon was seated at his massive oak desk, his elbows resting atop the smooth wood, his right index finger ringing the top of the brandy snifter that he had already refilled twice.

It had been a momentous day.

An hour or so after he'd left Daphne to her nap, Colin and Penelope had returned with their progeny, and they'd all had tea and biscuits in the breakfast room. Simon had started for the drawing room, but Penelope had requested an alternative, someplace without "expensive fabrics and upholstery."

Little Georgie had grinned up at him at that, his face

still smeared with a substance Simon hoped was choco-
late.

As Simon regarded the blanket of crumbs spilling from
the table to the floor, along with the wet napkin they'd
used to sop up Agatha's overturned tea, he remembered
that he and Daphne had always taken their tea here when
the children were small.

Funny how one forgot such details.

Once the tea party had dispersed, however, Colin had
asked for a private word. They had repaired to Simon's
study, and it was there that Colin confided in him about
Georgie.

He wasn't talking.

His eyes were sharp. Colin thought he was reading.

But he wasn't talking.

Colin had asked for his advice, and Simon realized
he had none. He'd thought about this, of course. It had
haunted him every time Daphne had been pregnant,
straight through until each of his children had begun to
form sentences.

He supposed it would haunt him now. There would be
another baby, another soul to love desperately . . . and
worry over.

All he'd known to tell Colin was to love the boy. To
talk to him, and praise him, and take him riding and fish-
ing and all those things a father ought to do with a son.

All those things his father had never done with him.

He didn't think about him often these days, his father. He had Daphne to thank for that. Before they'd met, Simon had been obsessed with revenge. He'd wanted so badly to hurt his father, to make him suffer the way he had suffered as a boy, with all the pain and anguish of knowing he had been rejected and found wanting.

It hadn't mattered that his father was dead. Simon had thirsted for vengeance all the same, and it had taken love, first with Daphne and then with his children, to banish that ghost. He'd finally realized that he was free when Daphne had given him a bundle of letters from his father that had been entrusted into her care. He hadn't wanted to burn them; he hadn't wanted to rip them to shreds.

He hadn't particularly wanted to read them, either.

He'd looked down at the stack of envelopes, tied neatly with a red and gold ribbon, and realized that he felt nothing. Not anger, not sorrow, not even regret. It had been the greatest victory he could have imagined.

He wasn't sure how long the letters had sat in Daphne's desk. He knew she'd put them in her bottom drawer, and every now and then he'd taken a peek to see if they were still there.

But eventually even that had tapered off. He hadn't forgotten about the letters—every now and then something would happen that would spring them to mind—

but he'd forgotten about them with such constancy. And they had probably been absent from his mind for months when he opened his bottom desk drawer and saw that Daphne had moved them there.

That had been twenty years ago.

And although he still lacked the urge to burn or shred, he'd also never felt the need to open them.

Until now.

Well, no.

Maybe?

He looked at them again, still tied in that bow. *Did* he want to open them? Could there be anything in his father's letters that might be of help to Colin and Penelope as they guided Georgie through what might be a difficult childhood?

No. It was impossible. His father had been a hard man, unfeeling and unforgiving. He'd been so obsessed with his heritage and title that he'd turned his back on his only child. There could be nothing—nothing—that he might have written that could help Georgie.

Simon picked up the letters. The papers were dry. They smelled old.

The fire in the grate felt new. Hot, and bright, and redemptive. He stared at the flames until his vision blurred, just sat there for endless minutes, clutching his father's final words to him. They had not spoken for over five years when his father died. If there was anything the old duke had wanted to say to him, it would be here.

"Simon?"

He looked up slowly, barely able to pull himself from his daze. Daphne was standing in the doorway, her hand resting lightly on the edge of the door. She was dressed in her favorite pale blue dressing gown. She'd had it for years; every time he asked if she wanted to replace it, she refused. Some things were best soft and comfortable.

"Are you coming to bed?" she asked.

He nodded, coming to his feet. "Soon. I was just—" He cleared his throat, because the truth was—he wasn't sure what he'd been doing. He wasn't even sure what he'd been thinking. "How are you feeling?" he asked her.

"Better. It's always better in the evening." She took a few steps forward. "I had a bit of toast, and even some jam, and I—" She stopped, the only movement in her face the quick blink of her eyes. She was staring at the letters. He hadn't realized he was still holding them when he stood.

"Are you going to read them?" she asked quietly.

"I thought . . . perhaps . . ." He swallowed. "I don't know."

"But why now?"

"Colin told me about Georgie. I thought there might

be something in here." He moved his hand slightly, holding the stack of letters just a little bit higher. "Something that might help him."

Daphne's lips parted, but several seconds passed before she was able to speak. "I think you might be one of the kindest, most generous men I have ever known."

He looked at her in confusion.

"I know you don't want to read those," she said.

"I really don't care—"

"No, you do," she interrupted gently. "Not enough to destroy them, but they still mean something to you."

"I hardly ever think about them," he said. It was the truth.

"I know." She reached out and took his hand, her thumb moving lightly over his knuckles. "But just because you let go of your father, it doesn't mean he never mattered."

He didn't speak. He didn't know what to say.

"I'm not surprised that if you do finally decide to read them, it will be to help someone else."

He swallowed, then grasped her hand like a lifeline.

"Do you want me to open them?"

He nodded, wordlessly handing her the stack.

Daphne moved to a nearby chair and sat, tugging at the ribbon until the bow fell loose. "Are these in order?" she asked.

"I don't know," he admitted. He sat back down behind his desk. It was far enough away that he couldn't see the pages.

She gave an acknowledging nod, then carefully broke the seal on the first envelope. Her eyes moved along the lines—or at least he thought they did. The light was too dim to see her expression clearly, but he had seen her reading letters enough times to know exactly what she must look like.

"He had terrible penmanship," Daphne murmured.

"Did he?" Now that he thought about it, Simon wasn't sure he'd ever seen his father's handwriting. He must have done, at some point. But it wasn't anything he recalled.

He waited a bit longer, trying not to hold his breath as she turned the page.

"He didn't write on the back," she said with some surprise.

"He wouldn't," Simon said. "He would never do anything that smacked of economization."

She looked up, her brows arched.

"The Duke of Hastings does not need to economize," Simon said dryly.

"Really?" She turned to the next page, murmuring, "I shall have to remember that the next time I go to the dressmaker."

He smiled. He loved that she could make him smile at such a moment.

After another few moments, she refolded the papers and looked up. She paused briefly, perhaps in case he wanted to say anything, and then when he did not, said, "It's rather dull, actually."

"Dull?" He wasn't sure what he had been expecting, but not this.

Daphne gave a little shrug. "It's about the harvest, and an improvement to the east wing of the house, and several tenants he suspects of cheating him." She pressed her lips together disapprovingly. "They weren't, of course. It is Mr. Miller and Mr. Bethum. They would never cheat anyone."

Simon blinked. He'd thought his father's letters might include an apology. Or if not that, then more accusations of inadequacy. It had never occurred to him that his father might have simply sent him an accounting of the estate.

"Your father was a very suspicious man," Daphne muttered.

"Oh, yes."

"Shall I read the next?"

"Please do."

She did, and it was much the same, except this time it was about a bridge that needed repairing and a window that had not been made to his specifications.

And on it went. Rents, accounts, repairs, complaints . . . There was the occasional overture, but nothing more personal than *I am considering hosting a shooting party next month, do let me know if you are interested in attending.* It was astounding. His father had not only denied his existence when he'd thought him a stuttering idiot, he'd managed to deny his own denial once Simon was speaking clearly and up to snuff. He acted as if it had never happened, as if he had never wished his own son were dead.

"Good God," Simon said, because *some*thing had to be said.

Daphne looked up. "Hmmm?"

"Nothing," he muttered.

"It's the last one," she said, holding the letter up.

He sighed.

"Do you want me to read it?"

"Of course," he said sarcastically. "It might be about rents. Or accounts."

"Or a bad harvest," Daphne quipped, obviously trying not to smile.

"Or that," he replied.

"Rents," she said once she'd finished reading. "And accounts."

"The harvest?"

She smiled slightly. "It was good that season."

Simon closed his eyes for a moment, as a strange tension eased from his body.

"It's odd," Daphne said. "I wonder why he never mailed these to you."

"What do you mean?"

"Well, he didn't. Don't you recall? He held on to all of them, then gave them to Lord Middlethorpe before he died."

"I suppose it was because I was out of the country. He wouldn't have known where to send them."

"Oh yes, of course." She frowned. "Still, I find it interesting that he would take the time to write you letters with no hope of sending them to you. If I were going to write letters to someone I couldn't send them to, it would be because I had something to say, something meaningful that I would want them to know, even after I was gone."

"One of the many ways in which you are unlike my father," Simon said.

She smiled ruefully. "Well, yes. I suppose." She stood, setting the letters down on a small table. "Shall we go to bed?"

He nodded and walked to her side. But before he took her arm, he reached down, scooped up the letters, and tossed them into the fire. Daphne let out a little gasp as she turned in time to see them blacken and shrivel.

"There's nothing worth saving," he said. He leaned down and kissed her, once on the nose and then once on the mouth. "Let's go to bed."

"What are you going to tell Colin and Penelope?" she asked as they walked arm in arm toward the stairs.

"About Georgie? The same thing I told them this afternoon." He kissed her again, this time on her brow. "Just love him. That's all they can do. If he talks, he talks. If he doesn't, he doesn't. But either way, it will all be fine, as long as they just love him."

"You, Simon Arthur Fitzranulph Basset, are a very good father."

He tried not to puff with pride. "You forgot the Henry."

"What?"

"Simon Arthur *Henry* Fitzranulph Basset."

She pfffted that. "You have too many names."

"But not too many children." He stopped walking and tugged her toward him until they were face to face. He rested one hand lightly on her abdomen. "Do you think we can do it all once more?"

She nodded. "As long as I have you."

"No," he said softly. "As long as I have *you*."

The Viscount Who Loved Me

Without a doubt, readers' favorite scene in *The Viscount Who Loved Me* (and perhaps in all of my books) is when the Bridgertons get together to play Pall Mall, the nineteenth-century version of croquet. They are viciously competitive and completely dismissive of the rules, having long since decided that the only thing better than winning is making sure your siblings lose. When it came time to revisit the characters from this book, I knew it had to be at a Pall Mall rematch.

The Viscount Who Loved Me:
The 2nd Epilogue

Two days prior . . .

Kate stomped across the lawn, glancing over her shoulder to make sure that her husband was not following her. Fifteen years of marriage had taught her a thing or two, and she knew that he would be watching her every move.

But she was clever. And she was determined. And she knew that for a pound, Anthony's valet could feign the most marvelous sartorial disaster. Something involving jam on the iron, or perhaps an infestation in the wardrobe—spiders, mice, it really didn't matter which—Kate was more than happy to leave the details up to the valet as long as Anthony was suitably distracted long enough for her to make her escape.

"It is mine, all mine," she chortled, in much the same tones she'd used during the previous month's Bridgerton family production of *Macbeth*. Her eldest son had casted the roles; she had been named First Witch.

Kate had pretended not to notice when Anthony had rewarded him with a new horse.

He'd pay now. His shirts would be stained pink with raspberry jam, and she—

She was smiling so hard she was laughing.

"Mine mine mine *miiiiiiiiiiine*," she sang, wrenching open the door to the shed on the last syllable, which just so happened to be the deep, serious note of Beethoven's Fifth.

"Mine mine mine *miiiiiiiiiine*."

She would have it. It was hers. She could practically taste it. She would have tasted it, even, if this would somehow have bonded it to her side. She had no taste for wood, of course, but this was no ordinary implement of destruction. This was . . .

The mallet of death.

"Mine mine mine *mine* mine mine mine *mine* mine mine mine *miiiiiiiiiine*," she continued, moving into the hoppy little section that followed the familiar refrain.

She could barely contain herself as she tossed a blanket aside. The Pall Mall set would be resting in the corner, as it always was, and in just a moment—

"Looking for this?"

Kate whirled around. There was Anthony, standing in the doorway, smiling diabolically as he spun the black Pall Mall mallet in his hands.

His shirt was blindingly white.

"You . . . You . . ."

One of his brows lifted dangerously. "You never were terribly skilled at vocabulary retrieval when crossed."

"How did you . . . How did you . . ."

He leaned forward, his eyes narrowing. "I paid him *five* pounds."

"You gave Milton five pounds?" Good Lord, that was practically his annual salary.

"It's a deuced sight cheaper than replacing all of my shirts," he said with a scowl. "Raspberry jam. Really. Have you no thought toward economies?"

Kate stared longingly at the mallet.

"Game's in three days," Anthony said with a pleased sigh, "and I have already won."

Kate didn't contradict him. The other Bridgertons might think the annual Pall Mall rematch began and ended in a day, but she and Anthony knew better.

She'd beaten him to the mallet for three years running.

She was damned if he was going to get the better of her this time.

"Give up now, dear wife," Anthony taunted. "Admit defeat, and we shall all be happier."

Kate sighed softly, almost as if she acquiesced.

Anthony's eyes narrowed.

Kate idly touched her fingers to the neckline of her frock.

Anthony's eyes widened.

"It's hot in here, don't you think?" she asked, her voice soft, and sweet, and terribly breathless.

"You little minx," he murmured.

She slid the fabric from her shoulders. She wasn't wearing anything underneath.

"No buttons?" he whispered.

She shook her head. She wasn't stupid. Even the best laid plans could find their way awry. One always had to dress for the occasion. There was still a slight chill in the air, and she felt her nipples tighten into insulted little buds.

Kate shivered, then tried to hide it with a breathy pant, as if she were desperately aroused.

Which she might have been, had she not been single-mindedly focused on trying *not* to focus on the mallet in her husband's hand.

Not to mention the chill.

"Lovely," Anthony murmured, reaching out and stroking the side of her breast.

Kate made a mewling sound. He could never resist that.

Anthony smiled slowly, then moved his hand forward, until he could roll her nipple between his fingers.

Kate let out a gasp, and her eyes flew to his. He looked—not calculating exactly, but still, very much in control. And it occurred to her—he knew precisely what *she* could never resist.

"Ah, wife," he murmured, cupping her breast from the bottom, and lifting it higher until it sat plump in his hand.

He smiled.

Kate stopped breathing.

He bent forward and took the bud in his mouth.

"*Oh!*" She wasn't faking anything now.

He repeated his torture on the other side.

Then he stepped back.

Back.

Kate stood still, panting.

"Ah, to have a painting of this," he said. "I would hang it in my office."

Kate's mouth fell open.

He held up the mallet in triumph. "Goodbye, dear wife." He exited the shed, then poked his head back 'round the corner. "Try not to catch a chill. You'd hate to miss the rematch, wouldn't you?"

He was lucky, Kate later reflected, that she hadn't thought to grab one of the Pall Mall balls when she'd been rummaging for the set. Although on second thought, his head was probably far too hard for her to have made a dent.

One day prior

There were few moments, Anthony decided, quite so delicious as the utter and complete besting of one's wife. It depended upon the wife, of course, but as he had chosen to wed a woman of superb intellect and wit, his moments, he was sure, were more delicious than most.

He savored this over tea in his office, sighing with pleasure as he gazed upon the black mallet, which lay across his desk like a prized trophy. It looked gorgeous, gleaming in the morning light—or at least gleaming where it wasn't scuffed and battered from decades of rough play.

No matter. Anthony loved every last dent and scratch. Perhaps it was childish, infantile even, but he *adored* it.

Mostly he adored that he had it in his possession, but he was still rather fond of it. When he was able to forget that he had brilliantly snatched it from under Kate's nose, he actually recalled that it marked something else—

The day he'd fallen in love.

Not that he'd realized it at the time. Nor had Kate, he imagined, but he was certain that that was the day they had been fated to be together—the day of the infamous Pall Mall match.

She left him with the pink mallet. She had sent his ball into the lake.

God, what a woman.

It had been a most excellent fifteen years.

He smiled contentedly, then let his gaze drop to the black mallet again. Every year they replayed the match. All of the original players—Anthony, Kate, his brother Colin, his sister Daphne and her husband Simon, and Kate's sister Edwina—they all trooped dutifully to Aubrey Hall each spring and took up their places on the ever-shifting course. Some agreed to attend with zeal and some with mere amusement, but they were all there, every year.

And this year—

Anthony chortled with glee. He had the mallet and Kate did not.

Life was good. Life was very very good.

"Kaaaaaaaaaaate!"

Kate looked up from her book.

"Kaaaaaaaaaaate!"

She tried to gauge his distance. After fifteen years of hearing her name bellowed in much the same fashion, she'd become quite proficient at calculating the time between the first roar and her husband's appearance.

It was not as straightforward a calculation as it might seem. There was her location to consider—was she upstairs or down, visible from the doorway, et cetera, et cetera.

Then one had to add in the children. Were they at home? Possibly in his way? They would slow him down, certainly, perhaps even by a full minute, and—

"*You!*"

Kate blinked with surprise. Anthony was in the doorway, panting with exertion and glaring at her with a surprising degree of venom.

"Where is it?" he demanded.

Well, perhaps not so surprising.

She blinked impassively. "Would you like to sit down?" she inquired. "You look somewhat overexerted."

"Kate . . ."

"You're not as young as you used to be," she said with a sigh.

"Kate . . ." The volume was rising.

"I can ring for tea," she said sweetly.

"It was locked," he growled. "My office was locked."

"Was it?" she murmured.

"I have the only key."

"Do you?"

His eyes widened. "What have you done?"

She flipped a page, even though she wasn't looking at the print. "When?"

"What do you mean, when?"

"I mean . . ." She paused, because this was not a moment to let pass without proper internal celebration. "When. This morning? Or last month?"

It took him a moment. No more than a second or two, but it was just long enough for Kate to watch his expression slide from confusion to suspicion to outrage.

It was glorious. Enchanting. Delicious. She'd have cackled with it, but that would only encourage another month of double-double-toil-and-trouble jokes, and she'd only just got him to cease.

"You made a key to my office?"

"I am your wife," she said, glancing at her fingernails. "There should be no secrets between us, don't you think?"

"You made a key?"

"You wouldn't wish for me to keep secrets, would you?"

His fingers gripped the door frame until his knuckles turned white. "Stop looking like you're enjoying this," he ground out.

"Ah, but that would be a lie, and it's a sin to lie to one's husband."

Strange choking sounds began to emanate from his throat.

Kate smiled. "Didn't I pledge honesty at some point?"

"That was *obedience*," he growled.

"Obedience? Surely not."

"Where is it?"

She shrugged. "Not telling."

"Kate!"

She slid into a singsong. "Not *tellllllllling*."

"Woman . . ." He moved forward. Dangerously.

Kate swallowed. There was a small, rather tiny actually but nonetheless very real chance that she might have gone just a wee bit too far.

"I will tie you to the bed," he warned.

"Yeeeessss," she said, acknowledging his point as she gauged the distance to the door. "But I might not *mind* it precisely."

His eyes flared, not quite with desire—he was still too focused on the Pall Mall mallet for that—but she rather thought she saw a flash of . . . *interest* there.

"Tie you up, you say," he murmured, moving forward, "and you'd like it, eh?"

Kate caught his meaning and gasped. "You wouldn't!"

"Oh, I would."

He was aiming for a repeat performance. He was going

to tie her up and *leave* her there while he searched for the mallet.

Not if she had anything to say about it.

Kate scrambled over the arm of her chair and then scooted behind it. Always good to have a physical barrier in situations like these.

"Oh, Kaaaaate," he taunted, moving toward her.

"It's mine," she declared. "It was mine fifteen years ago, and it's still mine."

"It was mine before it was yours."

"But you married me!"

"And this makes it yours?"

She said nothing, just locked her eyes with his. She was breathless, panting, caught up in the rush of the moment.

And then, fast as lightning, he jumped forward, reaching over the chair, catching hold of her shoulder for a brief moment before she squirmed away.

"You will never find it," she practically shrieked, scooting behind the sofa.

"Don't think you'll escape now," he warned, doing a sideways sort of maneuver that put him between her and the door.

She eyed the window.

"The fall would kill you," he said.

"Oh, for the love of God," came a voice from the doorway.

Kate and Anthony turned. Anthony's brother Colin was standing there, regarding them both with an air of disgust.

"Colin," Anthony said tightly. "How nice to see you."

Colin merely quirked a brow. "I suppose you're looking for *this*."

Kate gasped. He was holding the black mallet. "How did you—"

Colin stroked the blunt, cylindrical end almost lovingly. "I can only speak for myself, of course," he said with a happy sigh, "but as far as I'm concerned, I've already won."

Game day

"I fail to comprehend," Anthony's sister Daphne remarked, "why you get to set up the course."

"Because I bloody well own the lawn," he bit off. He held his hand up to shield his eyes from the sun as he inspected his work. He'd done a brilliant job this time, if he did say so himself. It was diabolical.

Pure genius.

"Any chance you might be capable of refraining from profanity in the company of ladies?" This, from Daphne's husband, Simon, the Duke of Hastings.

"She's no lady," Anthony grumbled. "She's my sister."

"She's *my* wife."

Anthony smirked. "She was my sister first."

Simon turned to Kate, who was tapping her mallet—green, which she'd declared herself happy with, but Anthony knew better—against the grass.

"How," he asked, "do you tolerate him?"

She shrugged. "It's a talent few possess."

Colin stepped up, clutching the black mallet like the Holy Grail. "Shall we begin?" he asked grandly.

Simon's lips parted with surprise. "The mallet of death?"

"I'm very clever," Colin confirmed.

"He bribed the housemaid," Kate grumbled.

"You bribed my valet," Anthony pointed out.

"So did you!"

"I bribed no one," Simon said, to no one in particular.

Daphne patted his arm condescendingly. "You were not born to this family."

"Neither was she," he returned, motioning to Kate.

Daphne pondered that. "She is an aberration," she finally concluded.

"An aberration?" Kate demanded.

"It's the highest of compliments," Daphne informed her. She paused, then added, "In this context." She then turned to Colin. "How much?"

"How much what?"

"How much did you give the housemaid?"

He shrugged. "Ten pounds."

"Ten *pounds*?" Daphne nearly shrieked.

"Are you mad?" Anthony demanded.

"You gave the valet five," Kate reminded him.

"I hope it wasn't one of the *good* housemaids," Anthony grumbled, "for she'll surely quit by the day's end with that sort of money in her pocket."

"All of the housemaids are good," Kate said, with some irritation.

"Ten pounds," Daphne repeated, shaking her head. "I'm going to tell your wife."

"Go ahead," Colin said indifferently as he nodded toward the hill sloping down to the Pall Mall course. "She's right there."

Daphne looked up. "Penelope's here?"

"Penelope's here?" Anthony barked. "Why?"

"She's my wife," Colin returned.

"She's never attended before."

"She wanted to see me win," Colin shot back, rewarding his brother with a sickly stretch of a smile.

Anthony resisted the urge to throttle him. Barely. "And how do you know you're going to win?"

Colin waved the black mallet before him. "I already have."

"Good day, all," Penelope said, ambling down to the gathering.

"No cheering," Anthony warned her.

Penelope blinked in confusion. "I beg your pardon?"

"And under no circumstances," he continued, because really, someone had to make sure the game retained some integrity, "may you come within ten paces of your husband."

Penelope looked at Colin, bobbed her head nine times as she estimated the steps between them, and took a step back.

"There will be no cheating," Anthony warned.

"At least no *new* types of cheating," Simon added. "Previously established cheating techniques are permissible."

"May I speak with my husband during the course of play?" Penelope inquired mildly.

"No!" A resounding chorus, three voices strong.

"You'll notice," Simon said to her, "that I made no objection."

"As I said," Daphne said, brushing by him on her way to inspect a wicket, "you were not born of this family."

"Where is Edwina?" Colin asked briskly, squinting up toward the house.

"She'll be down shortly," Kate replied. "She was finishing breakfast."

"She is delaying the play."

Kate turned to Daphne. "My sister does not share our devotion to the game."

"She thinks we're all mad?" Daphne asked.

"Quite."

"Well, she is sweet to come down every year," Daphne said.

"It's tradition," Anthony barked. He'd managed to get hold of the orange mallet and was swinging it against an imaginary ball, narrowing his eyes as he rehearsed his aim.

"He hasn't been practicing the course, has he?" Colin demanded.

"How could he?" Simon asked. "He only just set it up this morning. We all watched him."

Colin ignored him and turned to Kate. "Has he made any strange nocturnal disappearances recently?"

She gaped at him. "You think he's been sneaking out to play Pall Mall by the light of the moon?"

"I wouldn't put it past him," Colin grumbled.

"Neither would I," Kate replied, "but I assure you, he has been sleeping in his own bed."

"It's not a matter of *beds*," Colin informed her. "It's a matter of competition."

"This can't be an appropriate conversation in front of a lady," Simon said, but it was clear he was enjoying himself.

Anthony shot Colin an irritated look, then sent one

in Simon's direction for good measure. The conversation was growing ludicrous, and it was well past time they began the match. "Where *is* Edwina?" he demanded.

"I see her coming down the hill," Kate replied.

He looked up to see Edwina Bagwell, Kate's younger sister, trudging down the slope. She'd never been much for outdoor pursuits, and he could well imagine her sighing and rolling her eyes.

"Pink for me this year," Daphne declared, plucking one of the remaining mallets from the stack. "I am feeling feminine and delicate." She gave her brothers an arch look. "Deceptively so."

Simon reached behind her and selected the yellow mallet. "Blue for Edwina, of course."

"Edwina always gets blue," Kate said to Penelope.

"Why?"

Kate paused. "I don't know."

"What about purple?" Penelope asked.

"Oh, we never use *that*."

"Why?"

Kate paused again. "I don't know."

"Tradition," Anthony put in.

"Then why do the rest of you switch colors every year?" Penelope persisted.

Anthony turned to his brother. "Does she always ask so many questions?"

"Always."

He turned back to Penelope and said, "We like it this way."

"I'm here!" Edwina called out cheerfully as she approached the rest of the players. "Oh, blue again. How thoughtful." She picked up her equipment, then turned to Anthony. "Shall we play?"

He gave a nod, then turned to Simon. "You're first, Hastings."

"As always," he murmured, and he dropped his ball into the starting position. "Stand back," he warned, even though no one was within swinging distance. He drew his mallet back and then brought it forward with a magnificent crack. The ball went sailing across the lawn, straight and true, landing mere yards from the next wicket.

"Oh, well-done!" Penelope cheered, clapping her hands.

"I said no cheering," Anthony grumbled. Couldn't anyone follow instructions these days?

"Even for Simon?" Penelope returned. "I thought it was just Colin."

Anthony set his ball down carefully. "It's distracting."

"As if the rest of us aren't distracting," Colin commented. "Cheer away, darling."

But she held silent as Anthony took aim. His swing was even more powerful than the duke's, and his ball rolled even farther.

"Hmmm, bad luck there," Kate said.

Anthony turned on her suspiciously. "What do you mean? It was a brilliant swing."

"Well, yes, but—"

"Out of my way," Colin ordered, marching to the starting position.

Anthony locked eyes with his wife. "What do you *mean*?"

"Nothing," she said offhandedly, "just that it's a trifle muddy right there."

"Muddy?" Anthony looked toward his ball, then back to his wife, then back to the ball. "It hasn't rained for days."

"Hmmm, no."

He looked back to his wife. His maddening, diabolical, and soon-to-be-locked-in-a-dungeon wife. "How did it get muddy?"

"Well, perhaps not *muddy* . . ."

"Not muddy," he repeated, with far more patience than she deserved.

"Puddle-ish might be more appropriate."

Words failed him.

"Puddly?" She scrunched her face a touch. "How does one make an adjective out of a puddle?"

He took a step in her direction. She darted behind Daphne.

"What is happening?" Daphne asked, twisting about.

Kate poked her head out and smiled triumphantly. "I do believe he's going to kill me."

"With so many witnesses?" Simon asked.

"How," Anthony demanded, "did a puddle form in the midst of the driest spring of my recollection?"

Kate shot him another one of her annoying grins. "I spilled my tea."

"An entire puddle's worth?"

She shrugged. "I was cold."

"Cold."

"And thirsty."

"And apparently clumsy, as well," Simon put in.

Anthony glared at him.

"Well, if you are going to kill her," Simon said, "would you mind waiting until my wife is out from between you?" He turned to Kate. "How did you know where to put the puddle?"

"He's very predictable," she replied.

Anthony stretched out his fingers and measured her throat.

"Every year," she said, smiling straight at him. "You always put the first wicket in the same place, and you always hit the ball precisely the same way."

Colin chose that moment to return. "Your play, Kate."

She darted out from behind Daphne and scooted

toward the starting pole. "All's fair, dear husband," she called out gaily. And then she bent forward, aimed, and sent the green ball flying.

Straight into the puddle.

Anthony sighed happily. There was justice in this world, after all.

Thirty minutes later Kate was waiting by her ball near the third wicket.

"Pity about the mud," Colin said, strolling past.

She glared at him.

Daphne passed by a moment later. "You've a bit in . . ." She motioned to her hair. "Yes, there," she added, when Kate brushed furiously against her temple. "Although there is a bit more, well . . ." She cleared her throat. "Er, everywhere."

Kate glared at her.

Simon stepped up to join them. Good God, did everyone need to pass by the third wicket on their way to the sixth?

"You've a bit of mud," he said helpfully.

Kate's fingers wrapped more tightly around her mallet. His head was so very, very close.

"But at least it's mixed with tea," he added.

"What has that to do with anything?" Daphne asked.

"I'm not certain," Kate heard him say as he and Daphne took their leave toward wicket number five, "but it seemed as if I ought to say *some*thing."

Kate counted to ten in her head, and then sure enough, Edwina happened across her, Penelope trailing three steps behind. The pair had become something of a team, with Edwina doing all the swinging and Penelope consulting on strategy.

"Oh, Kate," Edwina said with a pitying sigh.

"Don't say it," Kate growled.

"You did make the puddle," Edwina pointed out.

"Whose sister *are* you?" Kate demanded.

Edwina gave her an arch smile. "Sisterly devotion does not obscure my sense of fair play."

"This is Pall Mall. There *is* no fair play."

"Apparently not," Penelope remarked.

"Ten paces," Kate warned.

"From Colin, not from you," Penelope returned. "Although I do believe I shall remain at least a mallet's length away at all times."

"Shall we go?" Edwina inquired. She turned to Kate. "We just finished with the fourth wicket."

"And you needed to take the long way 'round?" Kate muttered.

"It seemed only sporting to pay you a visit," Edwina demurred.

She and Penelope turned to walk away, and then Kate blurted it out. She couldn't help herself:

"Where is Anthony?"

Edwina and Penelope turned. "Do you really want to know?" Penelope asked.

Kate forced herself to nod.

"On the last wicket, I'm afraid," Penelope replied.

"Before or after?" Kate ground out.

"I beg your pardon?"

"Is he before the wicket or after it?" she repeated impatiently. And then, when Penelope did not answer instantly she added, "Has he gone through the bloody thing yet?"

Penelope blinked with surprise. "Er, no. He has about two more strokes, I should think. Perhaps three."

Kate watched them depart through narrowed eyes. She wasn't going to win—there was no chance of that now. But if she couldn't win, then by God, neither would Anthony. He deserved no glory this day, not after tripping her and sending her tumbling into the mud puddle.

Oh, he'd claimed it was an accident, but Kate found it highly suspicious that his ball had gone spluttering out of the puddle at the exact moment she'd stepped forward to reach her own ball. She'd had to do a little hop to avoid it and was congratulating herself on her near miss when Anthony had swung around with a patently false "I say, are you all right?"

His mallet had swung with him, conveniently at ankle level. Kate had not been able to outhop that one, and she'd gone flying into the mud.

Face down.

And then Anthony had had the gall to offer her a hand-kerchief.

She was going to kill him.

Kill.

Kill kill kill.

But first she was going to make sure he didn't win.

Anthony was smiling broadly—whistling, even—as he waited his turn. It was taking a ridiculously long amount of time to get back 'round to him, what with Kate so far behind that someone had to dash back to let her know when it was her turn, not to mention Edwina, who never seemed to understand the virtue of speedy play. It had been bad enough the last fourteen years, with her ambling along as if she had all day, but now she had Penelope, who would not allow her to hit the ball without her analysis and advice.

But for once, Anthony didn't mind. He was in the lead, so far so that no one could possibly catch up. And just to make his victory all the sweeter, Kate was in last place.

So far so that she could not hope to overtake anyone.

It almost made up for the fact that Colin had snatched the mallet of death.

He turned toward the last wicket. He needed one stroke to get his ball at the ready, and one more to push it through. After that, he needed only to steer it to the final pole and end the game with a tap.

Child's play.

He glanced back over his shoulder. He could see Daphne standing by the old oak tree. She was at the crest of a hill, and thus could see down where he could not.

"Whose turn is it?" he called out.

She craned her neck as she watched the others playing down the hill. "Colin's, I believe," she said, twisting back around, "which means Kate is next."

He smiled at that.

He'd set the course up a little differently this year, in something of a circular fashion. The players had to follow a twisting pattern, which meant that as the crow flew, he was actually closer to Kate than he was to the others. In fact, he need only move about ten yards to the south, and he'd be able to watch her as she pushed on toward the fourth wicket.

Or was it merely the third?

Either way, he wasn't going to miss it.

So, with a grin on his face, he jogged over. Should he call out? It would irritate her more if he called out.

But that would be cruel. And on the other hand—

CRACK!

Anthony looked up from his ponderings just in time to see the green ball hurtling in his direction.

What the devil?

Kate let out a triumphant cackle, picked up her skirts, and began running over.

"What in God's name are you doing?" Anthony demanded. "The fourth wicket is *that* way." He jabbed his finger in the appropriate direction even though he knew she knew where it was.

"I'm only on the third wicket," she said archly, "and anyway, I've given up on winning. It's hopeless at this point, don't you think?"

Anthony looked at her, then he looked at his ball, resting peacefully near the last wicket.

Then he looked at her again.

"Oh no you don't," he growled.

She smiled slowly.

Deviously.

Like a witch.

"Watch me," she said.

Just then Colin came dashing over the rise. "Your turn, Anthony!"

"How is that possible?" he demanded. "Kate just went, so there is Daphne, Edwina, and Simon between."

"We went very quickly," Simon said, striding forward. "We certainly don't want to miss *this*."

"Oh, for God's sake," he muttered, watching as the rest of them hurried near. He stalked over to his ball, narrowing his eyes as he prepared his aim.

"Be careful of the tree root!" Penelope called out.

Anthony grit his teeth.

"It wasn't cheering," she said, her face magnificently bland. "Surely a warning doesn't qualify as cheer—"

"Shut *up*," Anthony ground out.

"We all have our place in this game," she said, lips twitching.

Anthony turned around. "Colin!" he barked. "If you don't wish to find yourself a widower, kindly muzzle your wife."

Colin walked over to Penelope. "I love you," he said, kissing her on the cheek.

"And I—"

"Stop it!" Anthony exploded. When all eyes turned to him, he added, rather in a grunt, "I'm trying to concentrate."

Kate danced in a little closer.

"Get away from me, woman."

"I just want to *see*," she said. "I've hardly had the chance to *see* anything this game, being so far behind the entire time."

He narrowed his eyes. "I *might* be responsible for the mud, and please note my emphasis on the word *might*, which does not imply any sort of confirmation on my part."

He paused, quite pointedly ignoring the rest of the gathering, all of whom were gaping at him.

"However," he continued, "I fail to see how your position in last place is *my* responsibility."

"The mud made my hands slippery," she ground out. "I could not properly grip the mallet."

Off to the side, Colin winced. "Weak, I'm afraid, Kate. I'll have to grant this point to Anthony, much as it pains me."

"Fine," she said, after tossing Colin a withering glare. "It's no one's fault but my own. However."

And then she said nothing.

"Er, however what?" Edwina finally inquired.

Kate could have been a queen with her scepter as she stood there, all covered with mud. "However," she continued regally, "I don't have to like it. And this being Pall Mall, and we being Bridgertons, I don't have to play fair."

Anthony shook his head and bent back down to make his aim.

"She has a point this time," Colin said, irritating sod that he was. "Good sportsmanship has never been valued highly in this game."

"Be quiet," Anthony grunted.

"In fact," Colin continued, "one could make the argument that—"

"I said be quiet."

"—the opposite is true, and that *bad* sportsmanship—"

"Shut *up*, Colin."

"—is in fact to be lauded, and—"

Anthony decided to give up and take a swing. At this rate they'd be standing there until Michaelmas. Colin was never to going stop talking, not when he thought he had a chance of irritating his brother.

Anthony forced himself to hear nothing but the wind. Or at least he tried.

He aimed.

He drew back.

Crack!

Not too hard, not too hard.

The ball rolled forward, unfortunately not quite far enough. He was not going to make it through the last wicket on his next try. At least not without intervention divine enough to send his ball around a fist-sized stone.

"Colin, you're next," Daphne said, but he was already dashing back to his ball. He gave it a haphazard tap, then yelled out, "Kate!"

She stepped forward, blinking as she assessed the lay of the land. Her ball was about a foot away from his. The stone, however, was on the other side, meaning that if she attempted to sabotage him, she couldn't send him very far—surely the stone would stop the ball.

"An interesting dilemma," Anthony murmured.

Kate circled around the balls. "It would be a romantic gesture," she mused, "if I allowed you to win."

"Oh, it's not a question of your *allowing*," he taunted.

"Wrong answer," she said, and she aimed.

Anthony narrowed his eyes. What was she doing?

Kate hit the ball with a fair bit of force, aiming not squarely at his ball but at the left side. Her ball slammed into his, sending it spiraling off to the right. Because of the angle, she couldn't send it as far as she might have with a direct shot, but she did manage to get it right to the top of the hill.

Right to the top.

Right to the top.

And then down it.

Kate let out a whoop of delight that would not have been out of place on a battlefield.

"You'll pay," Anthony said.

She was too busy jumping up and down to pay him any attention.

"Who do you suppose will win now?" Penelope asked.

"Do you know," Anthony said quietly, "I don't care." And then he walked over to the green ball and took aim.

"Hold up, it's not your turn!" Edwina called out.

"And it's not your ball," Penelope added.

"Is that so?" he murmured, and then let fly, smashing

his mallet into Kate's ball and sending it hurtling across the lawn, down the shallower slope, and into the lake.

Kate let out a huff of outrage. "That wasn't very sporting of you!"

He gave her a maddening grin. "All's fair and all that, wife."

"You will fish it out," she retorted.

"You're the one who needs a bath."

Daphne let out a chuckle, and then said, "I think it must be my turn. Shall we continue?"

She departed, Simon, Edwina, and Penelope in her wake.

"Colin!" Daphne barked.

"Oh, very well," he grumbled, and he trailed along after.

Kate looked up at her husband, her lips beginning to twitch. "Well," she said, scratching at a spot on her ear that was particularly caked with mud, "I suppose that's the end of the match for us."

"I'd say."

"Brilliant job this year."

"You as well," he added, smiling down at her. "The puddle was inspired."

"I thought so," she said, with no modesty whatsoever. "And, well, about the mud . . ."

"It was not *quite* on purpose," he murmured.

"I should have done the same," she allowed.

"Yes, I know."

"I am filthy," she said, looking down at herself.

"The lake's right there," he said.

"It's so cold."

"A bath, then?"

She smiled seductively. "You'll join me?"

"But of course."

He held out his arm and together they began to stroll back toward the house.

"Should we have told them we forfeit?" Kate asked.

"No."

"Colin's going to try to steal the black mallet, you know."

He looked at her with interest. "You think he'll attempt to remove it from Aubrey Hall?"

"Wouldn't you?"

"Absolutely," he replied, with great emphasis. "We shall have to join forces."

"Oh, indeed."

They walked on a few more yards, and then Kate said, "But once we have it back . . ."

He looked at her in horror. "Oh, then it's every man for himself. You didn't think—"

"No," she said hastily. "Absolutely not."

"Then we are agreed," Anthony said, with some relief. Really, where would the fun be if he couldn't trounce Kate?

They walked on a few seconds more, and then Kate said, "I'm going to win next year."

"I know you think you will."

"No, I will. I have ideas. Strategies."

Anthony laughed, then leaned down to kiss her, mud and all. "I have ideas, too," he said with a smile. "And many, many strategies."

She licked her lips. "We're not talking about Pall Mall any longer, are we?"

He shook his head.

She wrapped her arms around him, her hands pulling his head back down to hers. And then, in the moment before his lips took hers, he heard her sigh—

"Good."

An Offer From a Gentleman

An Offer From a Gentleman is my homage to Cinderella, but it soon became apparent that the story had one too many wicked stepsisters. Where Rosamund was malicious and unkind, Posy had a heart of gold, and when the story reached its climax, she was the one who risked everything to save the day. It seems only fair that she, too, would get her happy ending . . .

An Offer From a Gentleman:
The 2nd Epilogue

At five and twenty, Miss Posy Reiling was considered *nearly* a spinster. There were those who might have considered her past the cutoff from young miss to hopeless ape leader; three and twenty was often cited as the unkind chronological border. But Posy was, as Lady Bridgerton (her unofficial guardian) often remarked, a unique case.

In debutante years, Lady Bridgerton insisted, Posy was only twenty, *maybe* twenty-one.

Eloise Bridgerton, the eldest unmarried daughter of the house, put it a little more bluntly: Posy's first few years out in society had been worthless and should not be counted against her.

Eloise's youngest sister, Hyacinth, never one to be

verbally outdone, simply stated that Posy's years between the ages of seventeen and twenty-two had been "utter rot."

It was at this point that Lady Bridgerton had sighed, poured herself a stiff drink, and sunk into a chair. Eloise, whose mouth was as sharp as Hyacinth's (though thankfully tempered by some discretion), had remarked that they had best get Hyacinth married off quickly or their mother was going to become an alcoholic. Lady Bridgerton had not appreciated the comment, although she privately thought it might be true.

Hyacinth was like that.

But this is a story about Posy. And as Hyacinth has a tendency to take over anything in which she is involved . . . please do forget about her for the remainder of the tale.

The truth was, Posy's first few years on the Marriage Mart *had* been utter rot. It was true that she'd made her debut at a proper age of seventeen. And, indeed, she was the stepdaughter of the late Earl of Penwood, who had so prudently made arrangements for her dowry before his untimely death several years prior.

She was perfectly pleasant to look at, if perhaps a little plump, she had all of her teeth, and it had been remarked upon more than once that she had uncommonly kind eyes.

Anyone assessing her on paper would not understand why she'd gone so long without even a single proposal.

But anyone assessing her on paper might not have known about Posy's mother, Araminta Gunningworth, the dowager Countess of Penwood.

Araminta was splendidly beautiful, even more so than Posy's elder sister, Rosamund, who had been blessed with fair hair, a rosebud mouth, and eyes of cerulean blue.

Araminta was ambitious, too, and enormously proud of her ascension from the gentry to the aristocracy. She'd gone from Miss Wincheslea to Mrs. Reiling to Lady Penwood, although to hear her speak of it, her mouth had been dripping silver spoons since the day of her birth.

But Araminta had failed in one regard; she had not been able to provide the earl with an heir. Which meant that despite the *Lady* before her name, she did not wield a terribly large amount of power. Nor did she have access to the type of fortune she felt was her due.

And so she pinned her hopes on Rosamund. Rosamund, she was sure, would make a splendid match. Rosamund was achingly beautiful. Rosamund could sing and play the pianoforte, and if she wasn't talented with a needle, then she knew exactly how to poke Posy, who was. And since Posy did not enjoy repeated needle-sized skin punctures, it was Rosamund's embroidery that always looked exquisite.

Posy's, on the other hand, generally went unfinished.

And since money was not as plentiful as Araminta would have her peers believe, she lavished what they had on Rosamund's wardrobe, and Rosamund's lessons, and Rosamund's *everything*.

She wasn't about to let Posy look embarrassingly shabby, but really, there was no point in spending more than she had to on her. You couldn't turn a sow's ear into a silk purse, and you certainly couldn't turn a Posy into a Rosamund.

But.

(And this is a rather large but.)

Things didn't turn out so well for Araminta. It's a terribly long story, and one probably deserving of a book of its own, but suffice it to say that Araminta cheated another young girl of her inheritance, one Sophia Beckett, who happened to be the earl's illegitimate daughter. She would have got away with it completely, because who cares about a bastard, except that Sophie had had the temerity to fall in love with Benedict Bridgerton, second son in the aforementioned (and extremely well-connected) Bridgerton family.

This would not have been enough to seal Araminta's fate, except that Benedict decided he loved Sophie back. Quite madly. And while he might have overlooked embezzlement, he certainly could not do the same for having

Sophie hauled off to jail (on mostly fraudulent charges).

Things were looking grim for dear Sophie, even with intervention on the part of Benedict and his mother, the also aforementioned Lady Bridgerton. But then who should show up to save the day but Posy?

Posy, who had been ignored for most of her life.

Posy, who had spent years feeling guilty for not standing up to her mother.

Posy, who was still a little bit plump and never would be as beautiful as her sister, but who would always have the *kindest* eyes.

Araminta had disowned her on the spot, but before Posy had even a moment to wonder if this constituted good or bad fortune, Lady Bridgerton had invited her to live in her home, for as long as she wished.

Posy might have spent twenty-two years being poked and pricked by her sister, but she was no fool. She accepted gladly, and did not even bother to return home to collect her belongings.

As for Araminta, well, she'd quickly ascertained that it was in her best interest not to make any public comment about the soon-to-be Sophia Bridgerton unless it was to declare her an absolute joy and delight.

Which she didn't do. But she didn't go around calling her a bastard, either, which was all anyone could have expected.

All of this explains (in an admittedly roundabout way) why Lady Bridgerton was Posy's unofficial guardian, and why she considered her a unique case. To her mind, Posy had not truly debuted until she came to live with her. Penwood dowry or no, who on earth would have looked twice at a girl in ill-fitting clothes, always stuck off in the corner, trying her best not to be noticed by her own mother?

And if she was still unmarried at twenty-five, why, that was certainly equal to a mere twenty for anyone else. Or so Lady Bridgerton said.

And no one really wanted to contradict her.

As for *Posy*, she often said that her life had not really begun until she went to jail.

This tended to require some explaining, but most of Posy's statements did.

Posy didn't mind. The Bridgertons actually *liked* her explanations. They liked *her*.

Even better, she rather liked herself.

Which was more important than she'd ever realized.

Sophie Bridgerton considered her life to be almost perfect. She adored her husband, loved her cozy home, and was quite certain that her two little boys were the most handsome, brilliant creatures ever to be born anywhere, anytime, any . . . well, any *any* one could come up with.

It was true that they *had* to live in the country because even with the sizable influence of the Bridgerton family, Sophie was, on account of her birth, not likely to be accepted by some of the more particular London hostesses.

(Sophie called them particular. Benedict called them something else entirely.)

But that didn't matter. Not really. She and Benedict preferred life in the country, so it was no great loss. And even though it would always be whispered that Sophie's birth was not what it should be, the official story was that she was a distant—and completely legitimate—relative of the late Earl of Penwood. And even though no one *really* believed Araminta when she'd confirmed the story, confirmed it she had.

Sophie knew that by the time her children were grown, the rumors would be old enough so that no doors would be closed to them, should they wish to take their spots in London society.

All was well. All was perfect.

Almost. Really, all she needed to do was find a husband for Posy. Not just any husband, of course. Posy deserved the best.

"She is not for everyone," Sophie had admitted to Benedict the previous day, "but that does not mean she is not a brilliant catch."

"Of course not," he murmured. He was trying to read

the newspaper. It was three days old, but to his mind it was all still news to him.

She looked at him sharply.

"I mean, of course," he said quickly. And then, when she did not immediately carry on, he amended, "I mean whichever one means that she will make someone a splendid wife."

Sophie let out a sigh. "The problem is that most people don't seem to realize how lovely she is."

Benedict gave a dutiful nod. He understood his role in this particular tableau. It was the sort of conversation that wasn't really a conversation. Sophie was thinking aloud, and he was there to provide the occasional verbal prompt or gesture.

"Or at least that's what your mother reports," Sophie continued.

"Mmm-hmm."

"She doesn't get asked to dance nearly as often as she ought."

"Men are beasts," Benedict agreed, flipping to the next page.

"It's true," Sophie said with some emotion. "Present company excluded, of course."

"Oh, of course."

"Most of the time," she added, a little waspishly.

He gave her a wave. "Think nothing of it."

"Are you listening to me?" she asked, her eyes narrowing.

"Every word," he assured her, actually lowering the paper enough to see her above the top edge. He hadn't actually *seen* her eyes narrow, but he knew her well enough to hear it in her voice.

"We need to find a husband for Posy."

He considered that. "Perhaps she doesn't want one."

"Of course she wants one!"

"I have been told," Benedict opined, "that every woman wants a husband, but in my experience, this is not precisely true."

Sophie just stared at him, which he did not find surprising. It was a fairly lengthy statement, coming from a man with a newspaper.

"Consider Eloise," he said. He shook his head, which was his usual inclination while thinking of his sister. "How many men has she refused now?"

"At least three," Sophie said, "but that's not the point."

"What *is* the point, then?"

"*Posy.*"

"Right," he said slowly.

Sophie leaned forward, her eyes taking on an odd mix of bewilderment and determination. "I don't know why the gentlemen don't see how wonderful she is."

"She's an acquired taste," Benedict said, momentarily

forgetting that he wasn't supposed to offer a real opinion.

"*What?*"

"*You* said she's not for everyone."

"But you're not supposed to—" She slumped a bit in her seat. "Never mind."

"What were you going to say?"

"Nothing."

"*Sophie*," he prodded.

"Just that you weren't supposed to agree with me," she muttered. "But even I can recognize how ridiculous that is."

It was a splendid thing, Benedict had long since realized, to have a sensible wife.

Sophie didn't speak for some time, and Benedict would have resumed his perusal of the newspaper, except that it was too interesting watching her face. She'd chew on her lip, then let out a weary sigh, then straighten a bit, as if she'd got a good thought, then frown.

Really, he could have watched her all afternoon.

"Can *you* think of anyone?" she suddenly asked.

"For Posy?"

She gave him a look. A whom-else-might-I-be-speaking-of look.

He let out a breath. He should have anticipated the question, but he'd begun to think of the painting he was working on his studio. It was a portrait of Sophie, the fourth he'd done in their three years of marriage. He was beginning to think that he'd not got her mouth quite right. It wasn't the lips so much as the corners of her mouth. A good portraitist needed to understand the muscles of the human body, even those on the face, and—

"Benedict!"

"What about Mr. Folsom?" he said quickly.

"The solicitor?"

He nodded.

"He looks shifty."

She was right, he realized, now that he thought on it. "Sir Reginald?"

Sophie gave him another look, visibly disappointed with his selection. "He's *fat*."

"So is—"

"She is *not*," Sophie cut in. "She is pleasantly plump."

"I was going to say that so is Mr. Folsom," Benedict said, feeling the need to defend himself, "but that you had chosen to comment upon his shiftiness."

"Oh."

He allowed himself the smallest of smiles.

"Shiftiness is far worse than excess weight," she mumbled.

"I could not agree more," Benedict said. "What about Mr. Woodson?"

"Who?"

"The new vicar. The one you said—"

"—has a brilliant smile!" Sophie finished excitedly. "Oh, Benedict, that's perfect! Oh, I love you love you love you!" At that, she practically leapt across the low table between them and into his arms.

"Well, I love you, too," he said, and he congratulated himself on having had the foresight to shut the door to the drawing room earlier.

The newspaper flew over his shoulder, and all was right with the world.

The season drew to a close a few weeks later, and so Posy decided to accept Sophie's invitation for an extended visit. London was hot and sticky and rather smelly in the summer, and a sojourn in the country seemed just the thing. Besides, she had not seen either of her godsons in several months, and she had been *aghast* when Sophie had written to say that Alexander had already begun to lose some of his baby fat.

Oh, he was just the most squeezable, adorable thing. She had to go see him before he grew too thin. She simply had to.

And it would be nice to see Sophie, too. She'd written that she was still feeling a bit weak, and Posy did like to be a help.

A few days into the visit, she and Sophie were taking tea, and talk turned, as it occasionally did, to Araminta and Rosamund, whom Posy occasionally bumped into in London. After over a year of silence, her mother finally had begun to acknowledge her, but even so, conversation was brief and stilted. Which, Posy had decided, was for the best. Her mother might have had nothing to say to her, but she didn't have anything to say to her mother, either.

As far as epiphanies went, it had been rather liberating.

"I saw her outside the milliner," Posy said, fixing her tea just the way she liked it, with extra milk and no sugar. "She'd just come down the steps, and I couldn't avoid her, and then I realized I didn't want to avoid her. Not that I wished to speak with her, of course." She took a sip. "Rather, I didn't wish to expend the energy needed to hide."

Sophie nodded approvingly.

"And then we spoke, and said nothing, really, although she did manage to get in one of her clever little insults."

"I hate that."

"I know. She's *so* good at it."

"It's a talent," Sophie remarked. "Not a good one, but a talent nonetheless."

"Well," Posy continued, "I must say, I was rather

mature about the entire encounter. I let her say what she wished, and then I bid her goodbye. And then I had the most amazing realization."

"What is that?"

Posy gave a smile. "I like myself."

"Well, of course you do," Sophie said, blinking with confusion.

"No, no, you don't understand," Posy said. It was strange, because Sophie ought to have understood perfectly. She was the only person in the world who knew what it meant to live as Araminta's unfavored child. But there was something so sunny about Sophie. There always had been. Even when Araminta treated her as a virtual slave, Sophie had never seemed beaten. There had always been a singular spirit to her, a sparkle. It wasn't defiance; Sophie was the least defiant person Posy knew, except perhaps for herself.

Not defiance . . . resilience. Yes, that was it exactly.

At any rate, Sophie ought to have understood what Posy had meant, but she didn't, so Posy said, "I didn't always like myself. And why should I have done? My own mother didn't like me."

"Oh, Posy," Sophie said, her eyes brimming with tears, "you mustn't—"

"No, no," Posy said good-naturedly. "Don't think anything of it. It doesn't bother me."

Sophie just looked at her.

"Well, not anymore," Posy amended. She eyed the plate of biscuits sitting on the table between them. She really oughtn't to eat one. She'd had three, and she *wanted* three more, so maybe that meant that if she had one, she was really abstaining from two . . .

She twiddled her fingers against her leg. Probably she shouldn't have one. Probably she should leave them for Sophie, who had just had a baby and needed to regain her strength. Although Sophie did look perfectly recovered, and little Alexander was already four months old . . .

"Posy?"

She looked up.

"Is something amiss?"

Posy gave a little shrug. "I can't decide whether I wish to eat a biscuit."

Sophie blinked. "A biscuit? Really?"

"There are at least two reasons why I should not, and probably more than that." She paused, frowning.

"You looked quite serious," Sophie remarked. "Almost as if you were conjugating Latin."

"Oh, no, I should look far more at peace if I were conjugating Latin," Posy declared. "That would be quite simple, as I know nothing about it. Biscuits, on the other hand, I ponder endlessly." She sighed and looked down at her middle. "Much to my dismay."

"Don't be silly, Posy," Sophie scolded. "You are the loveliest woman of my acquaintance."

Posy smiled and took the biscuit. The marvelous thing about Sophie was that she wasn't lying. Sophie really did think her the loveliest woman of her acquaintance. But then again, Sophie had always been that sort of person. She saw kindness where others saw . . . Well, where others didn't even bother to look, to be frank.

Posy took a bite and chewed, deciding that it was absolutely worth it. Butter, sugar, and flour. What could be better?

"I received a letter from Lady Bridgerton today," Sophie remarked.

Posy looked up in interest. Technically, Lady Bridgerton could mean Sophie's sister-in-law, the wife of the current viscount. But they both knew she referred to Benedict's mother. To them, she would always be Lady Bridgerton. The other one was Kate. Which was just as well, as that was Kate's preference within the family.

"She said that Mr. Fibberly called." When Posy did not comment, Sophie added, "He was looking for you."

"Well, of course he was," Posy said, deciding to have that fourth biscuit after all. "Hyacinth is too young and Eloise terrifies him."

"Eloise terrifies me," Sophie admitted. "Or at least she

used to. Hyacinth I'm quite sure will terrify me to the grave."

"You just need to know how to manage her," Posy said with a wave. It was true, Hyacinth Bridgerton *was* terrifying, but the two of them had always got on quite well. It was probably due to Hyacinth's firm (some might say unyielding) sense of justice. When she'd found out that Posy's mother had never loved her as well as Rosamund . . .

Well, Posy had never told tales, and she wasn't going to begin now, but let it be said that Araminta had never again eaten fish.

Or chicken.

Posy had got this from the servants, and they always had the most accurate gossip.

"But you were about to tell me about Mr. Fibberly," Sophie said, still sipping at her tea.

Posy shrugged, even though she hadn't been about to do any such thing. "He's so dull."

"Handsome?"

Posy shrugged again. "I can't tell."

"One generally need only look at the face."

"I can't get past his dullness. I don't think he laughs."

"It can't be that bad."

"Oh, it can, I assure you." She reached out and took

another biscuit before she realized she hadn't meant to. Oh well, it was already in her hand now, she couldn't very well put it back. She waved it in the air as she spoke, trying to make her point. "He sometimes makes this dreadful noise like, 'Ehrm ehrm ehrm,' and I think he thinks he's laughing, but he's clearly not."

Sophie giggled even though she looked as if she thought she shouldn't.

"And he doesn't even look at my bosom!"

"Posy!"

"It's my *only* good feature."

"It is not!" Sophie glanced about the drawing room, even though there was precisely no one about. "I can't believe you said that."

Posy let out a frustrated exhale. "I can't say *bosom* in London and now I can't do so in Wiltshire, either?"

"Not when I'm expecting the new vicar," Sophie said.

A chunk of Posy's biscuit fell off and fell into her lap. "What?"

"I didn't tell you?"

Posy eyed her suspiciously. Most people thought Sophie was a poor liar, but that was only because she had such an angelic look about her. And she rarely lied. So everyone assumed that if she did, she'd be dreadful at it.

Posy, however, knew better. "No," she said, brushing off her skirts, "you did not tell me."

"How very unlike me," Sophie murmured. She picked up a biscuit and took a bite.

Posy stared at her. "Do you know what I'm not doing now?"

Sophie shook her head.

"I am not rolling my eyes, because I am trying to act in a fashion that befits my age and maturity."

"You do look very grave."

Posy stared her down a bit more. "He is unmarried, I assume."

"Er, yes."

Posy lifted her left brow, the arch expression possibly the only useful gift she'd received from her mother. "How old is this vicar?"

"I do not know," Sophie admitted, "but he has all of his hair."

"And it has come to this," Posy murmured.

"I thought of you when I met him," Sophie said, "because he smiles."

Because he *smiled*? Posy was beginning to think that Sophie was a bit cracked. "I beg your pardon?"

"He smiles so often. And so well." At that *Sophie* smiled. "I couldn't help but think of you."

Posy did roll her eyes this time, then followed it with an immediate "I have decided to forsake maturity."

"By all means."

"I shall meet your vicar," Posy said, "but you should know I have decided to aspire to eccentricity."

"I wish you the best with that," Sophie said, not without sarcasm.

"You don't think I can?"

"You're the least eccentric person I know."

It was true, of course, but if Posy had to spend her life as an old maid, she wanted to be the eccentric one with the large hat, not the desperate one with the pinched mouth.

"What is his name?" she asked.

But before Sophie could answer, they heard the front door opening, and then it was the butler giving her her answer as he announced, "Mr. Woodson is here to see you, Mrs. Bridgerton."

Posy stashed her half-eaten biscuit under a serviette and folded her hands prettily in her lap. She was a little miffed with Sophie for inviting a bachelor for tea without warning her, but still, there seemed little reason not to make a good impression. She looked expectantly at the doorway, waiting patiently as Mr. Woodson's footsteps drew near.

And then . . .

And then . . .

Honestly, it wouldn't do to try to recount it, because she remembered almost nothing of what followed.

She saw him, and it was as if, after twenty-five years of life, her heart finally began to beat.

Hugh Woodson had never been the most admired boy at school. He had never been the most handsome, or the most athletic. He had never been the cleverest, or the snobbiest, or the most foolish. What he had been, and what he had been all of his life, was the most well liked.

People liked him. They always had. He supposed it was because he liked most everybody in return. His mother swore he'd emerged from the womb smiling. She said so with great frequency, although Hugh suspected she did so only to give her father the lead-in for: "Oh, Georgette, you know it was just gas."

Which never failed to set the both of them into fits of giggles.

It was a testament to Hugh's love for them both, and his general ease with himself, that he usually laughed as well.

Nonetheless, for all his likeability, he'd never seemed to attract the females. They adored him, of course, and confided their most desperate secrets, but they always did so in a way that led Hugh to believe he was viewed as a jolly, dependable sort of creature.

The worst part of it was that every woman of his acquaintance was absolutely positive that she knew the *per-*

fect woman for him, or if not, then she was quite sure that a perfect woman did indeed exist.

That no woman ever thought *herself* the perfect woman had not gone unnoticed. Well, by Hugh, at least. Everyone else was oblivious.

But he carried on, because there could be no point in doing otherwise. And as he had always suspected that women were the cleverer sex, he still held out hope that the perfect woman was indeed out there.

After all, no fewer than four dozen women had said so. They couldn't *all* be wrong.

But Hugh was nearing thirty, and Miss Perfection had not yet seen fit to reveal herself. Hugh was beginning to think that he should take matters into his own hands, except that he hadn't the slightest idea how to do such a thing, especially as he'd just taken a living in a rather quiet corner of Wiltshire, and there didn't seem to be a single appropriately-aged unmarried female in his parish.

Remarkable but true.

Maybe he should wander over to Gloucestershire Sunday next. There was a vacancy there, and he'd been asked to pitch in and deliver a sermon or two until they found a new vicar. There had to be at least one unattached female. The whole of the Cotswolds couldn't be bereft.

But this wasn't the time to dwell on such things. He was just arriving for tea with Mrs. Bridgerton, an invitation for which he was enormously grateful. He was still familiarizing himself with the area and its inhabitants, but it had taken but one church service to know that Mrs. Bridgerton was universally liked and admired. She seemed quite clever and kind as well.

He hoped she liked to gossip. He really needed someone to fill him in on the neighborhood lore. One really couldn't tend to one's flock without knowing its history.

He'd also heard that her cook laid a very fine tea. The biscuits had been mentioned in particular.

"Mr. Woodson to see you, Mrs. Bridgerton."

Hugh stepped into the drawing room as the butler stated his name. He was rather glad he'd forgotten to eat lunch, because the house smelled heavenly and—

And then he quite forgot everything.

Why he'd come.

Who he was.

The color of the sky, even, and the smell of the grass.

Indeed, as he stood there in the arched doorway of the Bridgertons' drawing room, he knew one thing, and one thing only.

The woman on the sofa, the one with the extraordinary eyes who was not Mrs. Bridgerton, was Miss Perfection.

Sophie Bridgerton knew a thing or two about love at first sight. She had, once upon a time, been hit by its proverbial lightning bolt, struck dumb with breathless passion, heady bliss, and an odd tingling sensation across her entire body.

Or at least, that was how she remembered it.

She also remembered that while Cupid's arrow had, in her case, proven remarkably accurate, it had taken quite a while for her and Benedict to reach their happily ever after. So even though she wanted to bounce in her seat with glee as she watched Posy and Mr. Woodson stare at each other like a pair of lovesick puppies, another part of her—the ex tremely practical, born-on-the-wrong-side-of-the-blanket, I-am-well-aware-that-the-world-is-not-made-up-of-rainbows-and-angels part of her—was trying to hold back her excitement.

But the thing about Sophie was, no matter how awful her childhood had been (and parts of it had been quite dreadfully awful), no matter what cruelties and indigni-ties she'd faced in her life (and there, too, she'd not been fortunate), she was, at heart, an incurable romantic.

Which brought her to Posy.

It was true that Posy visited several times each year, and it was also true that one of those visits almost always coincided with the end of the season, but Sophie *might* have added a little extra entreaty to her recently ten-dered invitation. She might have exaggerated a bit when describing how quickly the children were growing, and there was a chance that she had actually lied when she said that she was feeling poorly.

But in this case, the ends absolutely justified the means. Oh, Posy had told her that she would be perfectly content to remain unmarried, but Sophie did not believe her for a second. Or to be more precise, Sophie believed that Posy believed that she would be perfectly content. But one had only to look at Posy snuggling little William and Alexander to know that she was a born mother, and that the world would be a much poorer place if Posy did not have a passel of children to call her own.

It was true that Sophie had, one time or twelve, made a point of introducing Posy to whichever unattached gentleman was to be found at the moment in Wiltshire, but *this time* . . .

This time Sophie knew.

This time it was love.

"Mr. Woodson," she said, trying not to grin like a madwoman, "may I introduce you to my dear sister, Miss Posy Reiling?"

Mr. Woodson looked as if he thought he was saying something, but the truth was, he was staring at Posy as if he'd just met Aphrodite.

"Posy," Sophie continued, "this is Mr. Woodson, our

new vicar. He is only recently arrived, what was it, three weeks ago?"

He had been in residence for nearly two months. Sophie knew this perfectly well, but she was eager to see if he'd been listening well enough to correct her.

He just nodded, never taking his eyes off Posy.

"Please, Mr. Woodson," Sophie murmured, "do sit down."

He managed to understand her meaning, and he lowered himself into a chair.

"Tea, Mr. Woodson?" Sophie inquired.

He nodded.

"Posy, will you pour?"

Posy nodded.

Sophie waited, and then when it became apparent that Posy wasn't going to do much of anything besides smile at Mr. Woodson, she said, "*Posy.*"

Posy turned to look at her, but her head moved so slowly and with such reluctance, it was as if a giant magnet had turned its force onto her.

"Will you pour Mr. Woodson's tea?" Sophie murmured, trying to restrict her smile to her eyes.

"Oh. Of course." Posy turned back to the vicar, that silly smile returning to her face. "Would you like some tea?"

Normally Sophie might have mentioned that she had already asked Mr. Woodson if he wanted tea, but there was nothing normal about this encounter, so she decided to simply sit back and observe.

"I would love some," Mr. Woodson said to Posy. "Above all else."

Really, Sophie thought, it was as if she weren't even there.

"How do you take it?" Posy asked.

"However you wish."

Oh now, this was too much. No man fell so blindingly into love that he no longer held a preference for his tea. This was England, for heaven's sake. More to the point, this was *tea*.

"We have both milk and sugar," Sophie said, unable to help herself. She'd intended to sit and watch, but really, even the most hopeless romantic couldn't have remained silent.

Mr. Woodson didn't hear her.

"Either of them would be appropriate in your cup," she added.

"You have the most extraordinary eyes," he said, and his voice was full of wonder, as if he couldn't quite believe that he was right there in this room, with Posy.

"Your smile," Posy said in return. "It's . . . lovely."

He leaned forward. "Do you like roses, Miss Reiling?"

Posy nodded.

"I must bring you some."

Sophie gave up trying to appear serene and finally let herself grin. It wasn't as if either of them was looking at her, anyway. "We have roses," she said.

No response.

"In the back garden."

Again, nothing.

"Where the two of you might go for a stroll."

It was as if someone had just stuck a pin in both of them.

"Oh, shall we?"

"I would be delighted."

"Please, allow me to—"

"Take my arm."

"I would—"

"You must—"

By the time Posy and Mr. Woodson were at the door, Sophie could hardly tell who was saying what. And not a drop of tea had entered Mr. Woodson's cup.

Sophie waited for a full minute, and then burst out laughing, clapping her hand over her mouth to stifle the sound, although she wasn't sure why she needed to. It was a laugh of pure delight. Pride, too, at having orchestrated the whole thing.

"What are you laughing about?" It was Benedict, wandering into the room, his fingers stained with paint. "Ah, biscuits. Excellent. I'm famished. Forgot to eat this morning." He took the last one and frowned. "You might have left more for me."

"It's Posy," Sophie said, grinning. "And Mr. Woodson. I predict a very short engagement."

Benedict's eyes widened. He turned to the door, then to the window. "Where are they?"

"In the back. We can't see them from here."

He chewed thoughtfully. "But we could from my studio."

For about two seconds neither moved. But only two seconds.

They ran for the door, pushing and shoving their way down the hall to Benedict's studio, which jutted out of the back of the house, giving it light from three directions. Sophie got there first, although not by entirely fair means, and let out a shocked gasp.

"What is it?" Benedict said from the doorway.

"They're kissing!"

He strode forward. "They are not."

"Oh, they are."

He drew up beside her, and his mouth fell open. "Well, I'll be damned."

And Sophie, who never cursed, responded, "I know. I *know*."

"And they only just met? Really?"

"You kissed me the first night we met," she pointed out.

"That was different."

Sophie managed to pull her attention from the kissing couple on the lawn for just long enough to demand, "How?"

He thought about that for a moment, then answered, "It was a masquerade."

"Oh, so it's all right to kiss someone if you don't know who they are?"

"Not fair, Sophie," he said, clucking as he shook his head. "I asked you, and you wouldn't tell me."

That was true enough to put an end to that particular branch of the conversation, and they stood there for another moment, shamelessly watching Posy and the vicar. They'd stopped kissing and were now talking—from the looks of it, a mile a minute. Posy would speak, and then Mr. Woodson would nod vigorously and interrupt her, and then she would interrupt him, and then he looked like he was giggling, of all things, and then Posy began to speak with such animation that her arms waved all about her head.

"What on earth could they be saying?" Sophie wondered.

"Probably everything they should have said before he kissed her." Benedict frowned, crossing his arms. "How long have they been at this, anyway?"

"You've been watching just as long as I have."

"No, I meant, when did he arrive? Did they even speak before . . ." He waved his hand toward the window, gesturing to the couple, who looked about ready to kiss again.

"Yes, of course, but . . ." Sophie paused, thinking. Both Posy and Mr. Woodson had been rather tongue-tied at their meeting. In fact, she couldn't recall a single substantive word that was spoken. "Well, not very much, I'm afraid."

Benedict nodded slowly. "Do you think I should go out there?"

Sophie looked at him, then at the window, and then back. "Are you mad?"

He shrugged. "She is my sister now, and it *is* my house . . ."

"Don't you dare!"

"So I'm not supposed to protect her honor?"

"It's her first kiss!"

He quirked a brow. "And here we are, spying on it."

"It's my right," Sophie said indignantly. "I arranged the whole thing."

"Oh you did, did you? I seem to recall that *I* was the one to suggest Mr. Woodson."

"But you didn't *do* anything about it."

"That's your job, darling."

Sophie considered a retort, because his tone was rather

annoying, but he did have a point. She did rather enjoy trying to find a match for Posy, and she was *definitely* enjoying her obvious success.

"You know," Benedict said thoughtfully, "we might have a daughter someday."

Sophie turned to him. He wasn't normally one for such non sequiturs. "I beg your pardon?"

He gestured to the lovebirds on the lawn. "Just that this could be excellent practice for me. I'm quite certain I wish to be an overbearingly protective father. I could storm out and tear him apart from limb to limb."

Sophie winced. Poor Mr. Woodson wouldn't stand a chance.

"Challenge him to a duel?"

She shook her head.

"Very well, but if he lowers her to the ground, I am interceding."

"He won't— Oh dear heavens!" Sophie leaned forward, her face nearly to the glass. "Oh my God."

And she didn't even cover her mouth in horror at having blasphemed.

Benedict sighed, then flexed his fingers. "I really don't want to injure my hands. I'm halfway through your portrait, and it's going so well."

Sophie had one hand on his arm, holding him back even though he wasn't really moving anywhere. "No," she said, "don't—" She gasped. "Oh, my. Maybe we should do something."

"They're not on the ground yet."

"Benedict!"

"Normally I'd say to call the priest," he remarked, "except that seems to be what got us into this mess in the first place."

Sophie swallowed. "Perhaps you can procure a special license for them? As a wedding gift?"

He grinned. "Consider it done."

It was a splendid wedding. And that kiss at the end . . .

No one was surprised when Posy produced a baby nine months later, and then at yearly intervals after that. She took great care in the naming of her brood, and Mr. Woodson, who was as beloved a vicar as he'd been in every other stage of his life, adored her too much to argue with any of her choices.

First there was Sophia, for obvious reasons, and then Benedict. The next would have been Violet, except that Sophie begged her not to. She'd always wanted the name for her daughter, and it would be far too confusing with the families living so close. So Posy went with Georgette, after Hugh's mother, whom she thought had just the *nicest* smile.

After that was John, after Hugh's father. For quite

some time it appeared that he would remain the baby of the family. After giving birth every June for four years in a row, Posy stopped getting pregnant. She wasn't doing anything differently, she confided in Sophie; she and Hugh were still very much in love. It just seemed that her body had decided it was through with childbearing.

Which was just as well. With two girls and two boys, all in the single digits, she had her hands full.

But then, when John was five, Posy rose from bed one morning and threw up on the floor. It could only mean one thing, and the following autumn, she delivered a girl.

Sophie was present at the birth, as she always was. "What shall you name her?" she asked.

Posy looked down at the perfect little creature in her arms. It was sleeping quite soundly, and even though she knew that newborns did not smile, the baby really did look as if it were rather pleased about something.

Maybe about being born. Maybe this one was going to attack life with a smile. Good humor would be her weapon of choice.

What a splendid human being she would be.

"Araminta," Posy said suddenly.

Sophie nearly fell over from the shock of it. "*What?*"

"I want to name her Araminta. I'm quite certain." Posy stroked the baby's cheek, then touched her gently under the chin.

Sophie could not seem to stop shaking her head. "But your mother . . . I can't believe you would—"

"I'm not naming her *for* my mother," Posy cut in gently. "I'm naming her *because* of my mother. It's different."

Sophie looked dubious, but she leaned over to get a closer peek at the baby. "She's really quite sweet," she murmured.

Posy smiled, never once taking her eyes off the baby's face. "I know."

"I suppose I could grow accustomed to it," Sophie said, her head bobbing from side to side in acquiescence. She wiggled her finger between the baby's hand and body, giving the palm a little tickle until the tiny fingers wrapped instinctively around her own. "Good evening, Araminta," she said. "Very nice to meet you."

"Minty," Posy said.

Sophie looked up. "What?"

"I'm calling her Minty. Araminta will do well in the family Bible, but I do believe she's a Minty."

Sophie pressed her lips together in an effort not to smile. "Your mother would hate that."

"Yes," Posy murmured, "she would, wouldn't she?"

"Minty," Sophie said, testing the sound on her tongue. "I like it. No, I think I love it. It suits her."

Posy kissed the top of Minty's head. "What kind of girl will you be?" she whispered. "Sweet and docile?"

Sophie chuckled at that. She had been present at twelve birthings—four of her own, five of Posy's, and three of Benedict's sister Eloise. Never had she heard a baby enter this world with as loud a cry as little Minty. "This one," she said firmly, "is going to lead you a merry chase."

And she did. But that, dear reader, is another story . . .

Romancing Mister Bridgerton

To say that a big secret was revealed in *Romancing Mister Bridgerton* would be a major understatement. But Eloise Bridgerton—one of the book's most important secondary characters—left town before all of London learned the truth about Lady Whistledown. Many of my readers expected a scene in the next book (*To Sir Phillip, With Love*) that showed Eloise "finding out," but there was no way to fit such a scene in the book. Eventually, however, Eloise would have to know, and that's where the 2nd epilogue comes in . . .

Romancing Mister Bridgerton:
The 2nd Epilogue

"You didn't tell her?"

Penelope Bridgerton would have said more, and in fact would have liked to say more, but words were difficult, what with her mouth hanging slack. Her husband had just returned from a mad dash across the south of England with his three brothers, in pursuit of his sister Eloise, who had, by all accounts, run off to elope with—

Oh, dear God.

"Is she married?" Penelope asked frantically.

Colin tossed his hat on a chair with a clever little twist of his wrist, one corner of his mouth lifting in a satisfied smile as it spun through the air on a perfect horizontal axis. "Not yet," he replied.

So she hadn't eloped. But she *had* run away. And she'd done it in secret. Eloise, who was Penelope's closest friend. Eloise, who told Penelope everything. Eloise, who apparently *didn't* tell Penelope everything, had run off to the home of a man none of them knew, leaving a note assuring her family that all would be well and not to worry.

Not to worry????

Good heavens, one would think Eloise Bridgerton knew her family better than that. They had been frantic, every last one of them. Penelope had stayed with her new mother-in-law while the men were searching for Eloise. Violet Bridgerton had put up a good front, but her skin was positively ashen, and Penelope could not help but notice the way her hands shook with every movement.

And now Colin was back, acting as if nothing was amiss, answering none of her questions to her satisfaction, and beyond all that—

"How could you not have told her?" she said again, dogging his heels.

He sprawled into a chair and shrugged. "There really wasn't an appropriate time."

"You were gone five days!"

"Yes, well, not all of them were with Eloise. A day's travel on either end, after all."

"But—but—"

Colin summoned just enough energy to glance about the room. "Don't suppose you ordered tea?"

"Yes, of course," Penelope said reflexively, since it had not taken more than a week of marriage to learn that when it came to her new husband, it was best to always have food at the ready. "But Colin——"

"I did hurry back, you know."

"I can see that," she said, taking in his dampened, windblown hair. "Did you ride?"

He nodded.

"From Gloucestershire?"

"Wiltshire, actually. We retired to Benedict's."

"But——"

He smiled disarmingly. "I missed you."

And Penelope was not so accustomed to his affection that she did not blush. "I missed you, too, but——"

"Come sit with me."

Where? Penelope almost demanded. Because the only flat surface was his lap.

His smile, which had been charm personified, grew more heated. "I'm missing you right now," he murmured.

Much to her extreme embarrassment, her gaze moved instantly to the front of his breeches. Colin let out a bark of laughter, and Penelope crossed her arms. "*Don't,* Colin," she warned.

"Don't what?" he asked, all innocence.

"Even if we weren't in the sitting room, and even if the draperies weren't open—"

"An easily remedied nuisance," he commented with a glance to the windows.

"And *even*," she ground out, her voice growing in depth, if not quite in volume, "were we not expecting a maid to enter at any moment, the poor thing staggering under the weight of your tea tray, the fact of the matter is—"

Colin let out a sigh.

"—you *have not answered my question*!"

He blinked. "I've quite forgotten what it was."

A full ten seconds elapsed before she spoke. And then: "I'm going to kill you."

"Of that, I'm certain," he said offhandedly. "Truly, the only question is when."

"Colin!"

"Might be sooner rather than later," he murmured. "But in truth, I thought I'd go in an apoplexy, brought on by bad behavior."

She stared at him.

"*Your* bad behavior," he clarified.

"I didn't have bad behavior before I met you," she retorted.

"Oh, ho, ho," he chortled. "Now *that* is rich."

And Penelope was forced to shut her mouth. Because, blast it all, he was right. And that was what all of this was about, as it happened. Her husband, after entering the hall, shrugging off his coat, and kissing her rather soundly on the lips (in front of the butler!), had blithely informed her, "Oh, and by the by, I never did tell her you were Whistledown."

And if there was anything that might count as bad behavior, it had to be ten years as the author of the now infamous *Lady Whistledown's Society Papers*. Over the past decade, Penelope had, in her pseudonymous guise, managed to insult just about everyone in society, even herself. (Surely, the *ton* would have grown suspicious if she had never poked fun at herself, and besides, she really did look like an overripe citrus fruit in the dreadful yellows and oranges her mother had always forced her to wear.)

Penelope had "retired" just before her marriage, but a blackmail attempt had convinced Colin that the best course of action was to reveal her secret in a grand gesture, and so he had announced her identity at his sister Daphne's ball. It had all been very romantic and very, well, *grand*, but by the end of the night it had become apparent that Eloise had disappeared.

Eloise had been Penelope's closest friend for years, but even she had not known Penelope's big secret. And now she still didn't. She'd left the party before Colin had announced it, and he apparently had not seen fit to say anything once he'd found her.

"Frankly," Colin said, his voice holding an uncharacteristic strain of irritability, "it's less than she deserved, after what she put us through."

"Well, yes," Penelope murmured, feeling rather disloyal even as she said it. But the entire Bridgerton clan had been mad with worry. Eloise had left a note, it was true, but it had somehow got mixed into her mother's correspondence, and an entire day had passed before the family was reassured that Eloise had not been abducted. And even then, no one's mind was set at ease; Eloise may have left of her own accord, but it had taken another day of tearing her bedchamber to bits before they found a letter from Sir Phillip Crane that indicated where she might have run off to.

Considering all that, Colin did have something of a point.

"We have to go back in a few days for the wedding," he said. "We'll tell her then."

"Oh, but we can't!"

He paused. Then he smiled. "And why is that?" he asked, his eyes resting on her with great appreciation.

"It will be her wedding day," Penelope explained, aware that he'd been hoping for a far more diabolical reason. "She must be the center of all attention. I cannot tell her something such as *this*."

"A bit more altruistic than I'd like," he mused, "but the end result is the same, so you have my approval—"

"I don't need your approval," Penelope cut in.

"But nonetheless, you have it," he said smoothly. "We shall keep Eloise in the dark." He tapped his fingertips together and sighed with audible pleasure. "It will be a most excellent wedding."

The maid arrived just then, carrying a heavily laden tea tray. Penelope tried not to notice that she let out a little grunt when she was finally able to set it down.

"You may close the door behind you," Colin said, once the maid had straightened.

Penelope's eyes darted to the door, then to her husband, who had risen and was shutting the draperies.

"Colin!" she yelped, because his arms had stolen around her, and his lips were on her neck, and she could feel herself going quite liquid in his embrace. "I thought you wanted food," she gasped.

"I do," he murmured, tugging on the bodice of her dress. "But I want you more."

And as Penelope sank to the cushions that had somehow found their way to the plush carpet below, she felt very loved indeed.

Several days later, Penelope was seated in a carriage, gazing out the window and scolding herself.

Colin was asleep.

She was a widgeon for feeling so nervous about seeing Eloise again. Eloise, for heaven's sake. They had been as close as sisters for over a decade. Closer. Except, maybe . . . not quite as close as either had thought. They had kept secrets, both of them. Penelope wanted to wring Eloise's neck for not telling her about her suitor, but really, she hadn't a leg to stand on. When Eloise found out that Penelope was Lady Whistledown . . .

Penelope shuddered. Colin might be looking forward to the moment—he was positively devilish in his glee— but she felt rather ill, quite frankly. She hadn't eaten all day, and she was *not* the sort to skip breakfast.

She wrung her hands, craned her neck to get a better view out the window—she thought they might have turned onto the drive for Romney Hall, but she wasn't precisely certain—then looked back to Colin.

He was still asleep.

She kicked him. Gently, of course, because she did not think herself overly violent, but really, it wasn't fair that he had slept like a baby from the moment the carriage had started rolling. He had settled into his seat, inquired after her comfort, and then, before she'd even managed the *you* in "Very well, thank you," his eyes were closed.

Thirty seconds later he was snoring.

It really wasn't fair. He always fell asleep before she did at night as well.

She kicked him again, harder this time.

He mumbled something in his sleep, shifted positions ever so slightly, and slumped into the corner.

Penelope scooted over. Closer, closer . . .

Then she organized her elbow in a sharp point and jabbed him in the ribs.

"Wha . . . ?" Colin shot straight awake, blinking and coughing. "What? What? What?"

"I think we're here," Penelope said.

He looked out the window, then back at her. "And you needed to inform of this by taking a weapon to my body?"

"It was my elbow."

He glanced down at her arm. "You, my dear, are in possession of exceedingly bony elbows."

Penelope was quite sure her elbows—or any part of her, for that matter—were not the least bit bony, but there seemed little to gain by contradicting him, so she said, again, "I think we're here."

Colin leaned toward the glass with a couple of sleepy blinks. "I think you're right."

"It's lovely," Penelope said, taking in the exquisitely maintained grounds. "Why did you tell me it was run-down?"

"It is," Colin replied, handing her her shawl. "Here," he said with a gruff smile, as if he weren't yet used to caring for another person's welfare in quite the way he did hers. "It will be chilly yet."

It was still fairly early in the morning; the inn at which they had slept was only an hour's ride away. Most of the family had stayed with Benedict and Sophie, but their home was not large enough to accommodate all of the Bridgertons. Besides, Colin had explained, they were newlyweds. They needed their privacy.

Penelope hugged the soft wool to her body and leaned against him to get a better look out the window. And, to be honest, just because she liked to lean against him. "I think it looks lovely," she said. "I have never seen such roses."

"It's nicer on the outside than in," Colin explained as the carriage drew to a halt. "But I expect Eloise will change that."

He opened the door himself and hopped out, then offered his arm to assist her down. "Come along, Lady Whistledown—"

"Mrs. Bridgerton," she corrected.

"Whatever you wish to call yourself," he said with a grand smile, "you're still mine. And this is your swan song."

As Colin stepped across the threshold of what was to be his sister's new home, he was struck by an unexpected sense of relief. For all his irritation with her, he loved his sister. They had not been particularly intimate while growing up; he had been much closer in age to Daphne, and Eloise had often seemed nothing so much as a pesky afterthought. But the previous year had brought them closer, and if it hadn't been for Eloise, he might never have discovered Penelope.

And without Penelope, he'd be . . .

It was funny. He couldn't imagine what he'd be without her.

He looked down at his new wife. She was glancing around the entry hall, trying not to be too obvious about it. Her face was impassive, but he knew she was taking everything in. And tomorrow, when they were musing about the events of the day, she would have remembered every last detail.

Mind like an elephant, she had. He loved it.

"Mr. Bridgerton," the butler said, greeting them with a little nod of his head. "Welcome back to Romney Hall."

"A pleasure, Gunning," Colin murmured. "So sorry about the last time."

Penelope looked to him in askance.

"We entered rather . . . suddenly," Colin explained.

The butler must have seen Penelope's expression of

alarm, because he quickly added, "I stepped out of the way."

"Oh," she started to say, "I'm so——"

"Sir Phillip did not," Gunning cut in.

"Oh." Penelope coughed awkwardly. "Is he going to be all right?"

"Bit of swelling around the throat," Colin said, unconcerned. "I expect he's improved by now." He caught her glancing down at his hands and let out a chuckle. "Oh, it wasn't me," he said, taking her arm to lead her down the hall. "I just watched."

She grimaced. "I think that might be worse."

"Quite possibly," he said with great cheer. "But it all turned out well in the end. I quite like the fellow now, and I rather——Ah, Mother, there you are."

And sure enough, Violet Bridgerton was bustling down the hall. "You're late," she said, even though Colin was fairly certain they were not. He bent down to kiss her proffered cheek, then stepped to the side as his mother came forward to take both of Penelope's hands in hers. "My dear, we need you in back. You are the matron of honor, after all."

Colin had a sudden vision of the scene—a gaggle of chatty females, all talking over one another about minutiae he couldn't begin to care about, much less understand. They told each other everything, and——

He turned sharply. "Don't," he warned, "say a word."

"I beg your pardon." Penelope let out a little huff of righteous indignation. "I'm the one who said we couldn't tell her on her wedding day."

"I was talking to my mother," he said.

Violet shook her head. "Eloise is going to kill us."

"She nearly killed us already, running off like an idiot," Colin said, with uncharacteristic shortness of temper. "I've already instructed the others to keep their mouths shut."

"Even Hyacinth?" Penelope asked doubtfully.

"Especially Hyacinth."

"Did you bribe her?" Violet asked. "Because it won't work unless you bribe her."

"Good Lord," Colin muttered. "One would think I'd joined this family yesterday. Of course I bribed her." He turned to Penelope. "No offense to recent additions."

"Oh, none taken," she said. "What did you give her?"

He thought about his bargaining session with his youngest sister and nearly shuddered. "Twenty pounds."

"Twenty pounds!" Violet exclaimed. "Are you mad?"

"I suppose you could have done better," he retorted. "And I've only given her half. I wouldn't trust that girl as far as I could throw her. But if she keeps her mouth shut, I'll be another ten pounds poorer."

"I wonder how far you *could* throw her," Penelope mused.

Colin turned to his mother. "I tried for ten, but she

wouldn't budge." And then to Penelope: "Not nearly far enough."

Violet sighed. "I ought to scold you for that."

"But you won't." Colin flashed her a grin.

"Heaven help me," was her only reply.

"Heaven help whatever chap is mad enough to marry her," he remarked.

"I think there is more to Hyacinth than the two of you allow," Penelope put in. "You ought not to underestimate her."

"Good Lord," Colin replied, "we don't do *that*."

"You're so sweet," Violet said, leaning forward to give Penelope an impromptu hug.

"It's only through sheer force of luck she hasn't taken over the world," Colin muttered.

"Ignore him," Violet said to Penelope. "And you," she added, turning to Colin, "must head immediately to the church. The rest of the men have already gone down. It's only a five-minute walk."

"You're planning to walk?" he asked doubtfully.

"Of course not," his mother replied dismissively. "And we certainly cannot spare a carriage for you."

"I wouldn't dream of asking for one," Colin replied, deciding that a solitary stroll through the fresh morning air was decidedly preferable to a closed carriage with his female relations.

He leaned down to kiss his wife's cheek. Right near her ear. "Remember," he whispered, "no telling."

"I can keep a secret," she replied.

"It's far easier to keep a secret from a thousand people than it is from just one," he said. "Far less guilt involved."

Her cheeks flushed, and he kissed her again near her ear. "I know you so well," he murmured.

He could practically hear her teeth gnashing as he left.

"Penelope!"

Eloise started to jump from her seat to greet her, but Hyacinth, who was supervising the dressing of her hair, jammed her hand on her shoulder with a low, almost menacing, "*Down.*"

And Eloise, who normally would have slain Hyacinth with a glare, meekly resumed her seat.

Penelope looked to Daphne, who appeared to be supervising Hyacinth.

"It has been a long morning," Daphne said.

Penelope walked forward, pushed gently past Hyacinth, and carefully embraced Eloise so as not to muss her coiffure. "You look beautiful," she said.

"Thank you," Eloise replied, but her lips were trembling, and her eyes were wet and threatening to spill over at any moment.

More than anything, Penelope wanted to take her aside

and tell her that everything was going to be all right, and she didn't *have* to marry Sir Phillip if she didn't want to, but when all was said and done, Penelope *didn't* know that everything was going to be all right, and she rather suspected that Eloise did have to marry her Sir Phillip.

She'd heard bits and pieces. Eloise had been in residence at Romney Hall for over a week without a chaperone. Her reputation would be in tatters if it got out, which it surely would. Penelope knew better than anyone the power and tenacity of gossip. Plus, Penelope had heard that Eloise and Anthony had had A Talk.

The matter of the wedding, it seemed, was final.

"I'm so glad you're here," Eloise said.

"Goodness, you know I would never miss your wedding."

"I know." Eloise's lips trembled, and then her face took on that expression one makes when one is trying to appear brave and actually thinks one might be succeeding. "I know," she said again, a little more evenly. "Of course you wouldn't. But that does not lessen my pleasure in seeing you."

It was an oddly stiff sentence for Eloise, and for a moment Penelope forgot her own secrets, her own fears and worries. Eloise was her dearest friend. Colin was her love, her passion, and her soul, but it was Eloise, more than anyone, who had shaped Penelope's adult life. Penelope could not imagine what the last decade would have been like without Eloise's smile, her laughter, and her indefatigable good cheer.

Even more than her own family, Eloise had loved her.

"Eloise," Penelope said, crouching down beside her so that she might put her arm around her shoulders. She cleared her throat, mostly because she was about to ask a question for which the answer probably did not matter. "Eloise," she said again, her voice dropping to a near whisper. "Do you want this?"

"Of course," Eloise replied.

But Penelope wasn't sure she believed her. "Do you lo—" She caught herself. And she did that little thing with her mouth that tried to be a smile. And she asked, "Do you like him? Your Sir Phillip?"

Eloise nodded. "He's . . . complicated."

Which made Penelope sit down. "You're joking."

"At a time like this?"

"Aren't you the one who always said that men were simple creatures?"

Eloise looked at her with an oddly helpless expression. "I thought they were."

Penelope leaned in, aware that Hyacinth's auditory skills were positively canine. "Does he like you?"

"He thinks I talk too much."

"You do talk too much," Penelope replied.

Eloise shot her a look. "You could at least smile."

"It's the truth. But I find it endearing."

"I think he does as well." Eloise grimaced. "Some of the time."

"Eloise!" called Violet from the doorway. "We really must be on our way."

"We wouldn't want the groom to think you've run off," Hyacinth quipped.

Eloise stood and straightened her shoulders. "I've done quite enough running off recently, wouldn't you say?" She turned to Penelope with a wise, wistful smile. "It's time I began running to and stopped running from."

Penelope looked at her curiously. "What did you say?"

But Eloise only shook her head. "It's just something I heard recently."

It was a curious statement, but this wasn't the time to delve further, so Penelope moved to follow the rest of the family. After she'd taken a few steps, however, she was halted by the sound of Eloise's voice.

"Penelope!"

Penelope turned. Eloise was still in the doorway, a good ten feet behind her. She had an odd look on her face, one that Penelope could not quite interpret. Penelope waited, but Eloise did not speak.

"Eloise?" Penelope said quietly, because it looked as if

Eloise *wished* to say something, just wasn't sure how. Or possibly what.

And then—

"*I'm sorry.*" Eloise blurted it out, the words rushing across her lips with a speed that was remarkable, even for her.

"You're sorry," Penelope echoed, mostly out of surprise. She hadn't really considered what Eloise might say in that moment, but an apology would not have topped the list. "For what?"

"For keeping secrets. That wasn't well-done of me."

Penelope swallowed. *Good Lord.*

"Forgive me?" Eloise's voice was soft, but her eyes were urgent, and Penelope felt like the worst sort of fraud.

"Of course," she stammered. "It is nothing." And it *was* nothing, at least when compared to her own secrets.

"I should have told you about my correspondence with Sir Phillip. I don't know why I didn't at the outset," Eloise continued. "But then, later, when you and Colin were falling in love . . . I think it was . . . I think it was just because it was *mine.*"

Penelope nodded. She knew a great deal about wanting something of one's own.

Eloise let out a nervous laugh. "And now look at me."

Penelope did. "You look beautiful." It was the truth.

Eloise was not a serene bride, but she was a glowing one, and Penelope felt her worries lift and lighten and finally disappear. All would be well. Penelope did not know if Eloise would experience the same bliss in her marriage as she'd found, but she would at least be happy and content.

And who was she to say that the new married couple wouldn't fall madly in love? Stranger things had happened.

She linked her arm through Eloise's and steered her out into the hall, where Violet had raised her voice to heretofore unimagined volumes.

"I think your mother wants us to make haste," Penelope whispered.

"Eloeeeeeeeeeeeese!" Violet positively bellowed. "NOW!"

Eloise's brows rose as she gave Penelope a sideways glance. "Whatever makes you think so?"

But they didn't hurry. Arm in arm they glided down the hall, as if it were the church aisle.

"Who would have thought we'd both marry within months of each other?" Penelope mused. "Weren't we meant to be old crones together?"

"We can still be old crones," Eloise replied gaily. "We shall simply be married old crones."

"It will be grand."

"Magnificent!"

"Stupendous!"

"We shall be leaders of crone fashion!"

"Arbiters of cronish taste."

"What," Hyacinth demanded, hands on hips, "are the two of you talking about?"

Eloise lifted her chin and looked down her nose at her. "You're far too young to understand."

And she and Penelope practically collapsed in a fit of giggles.

"They've gone mad, Mother," Hyacinth announced.

Violet gazed lovingly at her daughter and daughter-in-law, both of whom had reached the unfashionable age of twenty-eight before becoming brides. "Leave them alone, Hyacinth," she said, steering her toward the waiting carriage. "They'll be along shortly." And then she added, almost as an afterthought: "You're too young to understand."

After the ceremony, after the reception, and after Colin was able to assure himself once and for all that Sir Phillip Crane would indeed make an acceptable husband to his sister, he managed to find a quiet corner into which he could yank his wife and speak with her privately.

"Does she suspect?" he asked, grinning.

"You're terrible," Penelope replied. "It's her *wedding*."

Which was not one of the two customary answers to a yes-or-no question. Colin resisted the urge to let out an impatient breath, and instead offered a rather smooth and urbane "By this you mean . . . ?"

Penelope stared at him for a full ten seconds, and then she muttered, "I don't know what Eloise was talking about. Men are *abysmally* simple creatures."

"Well . . . *yes*," Colin agreed, since it had long been obvious to him that the female mind was an utter and complete mystery. "But what has that got to do with anything?"

Penelope glanced over both shoulders before dropping her voice to a harsh whisper. "Why would she even be thinking about Whistledown at a time like this?"

She had a point there, loath as Colin was to admit it. In his mind, this had all played out with Eloise somehow being aware that she was the only person who didn't know the secret of Lady Whistledown's identity.

Which was ridiculous to be sure, but still, a satisfying daydream.

"Hmmmm," he said.

Penelope looked at him suspiciously. "What are you thinking?"

"Are you certain we cannot tell her on her wedding day?"

"Colin . . ."

"Because if we *don't*, she's sure to find out from *some*-one, and it doesn't seem fair that we not be present to see her face."

"Colin, *no*."

"After all you've been through, wouldn't you say you deserve to see her reaction?"

"No," Penelope said slowly. "No. No, I wouldn't."

"Oh, you sell yourself too cheaply, my darling," he said, smiling benevolently at her. "And besides that, think of Eloise."

"I fail to see what else it is I have been doing all morning."

He shook his head. "She would be devastated. Hearing the awful truth from a complete stranger."

"It's not awful," Penelope shot back, "and how do you know it would be a stranger?"

"We've sworn my entire family to secrecy. Who else does she know out in this godforsaken county?"

"I rather like Gloucestershire," Penelope said, her teeth now charmingly clenched. "I find it delightful."

"Yes," he said equably, taking in her furrowed brow, pinched mouth, and narrowed eyes. "You look delighted."

"Weren't you the one who insisted we keep her in the dark for as long as humanly possible?"

"*Humanly possible* being the phrase of note," Colin replied. "*This* human"—he gestured rather unnecessarily to himself—"finding it quite impossible to maintain his silence."

"I can't believe you've changed your mind."

He shrugged. "Isn't it a man's prerogative?"

At that her lips parted, and Colin found himself wishing he'd found a corner as private as it was quiet, because she was practically begging to be kissed, whether she knew it or not.

But he was a patient man, and they did still have that comfortable room reserved at the inn, and there was still much mischief to be made right here at the wedding. "Oh, Penelope," he said huskily, leaning in more than was proper, even with one's wife, "don't you want to have some fun?"

She flushed scarlet. "Not *here*."

He laughed aloud at that.

"I wasn't talking about that," she muttered.

"Neither was I, as a matter of fact," he returned, completely unable to keep the humor off his face, "but I *am* pleased that it comes to mind so readily." He pretended to glance about the room. "When do you think it would be polite to leave?"

"Definitely not yet."

He pretended to ponder. "Mmmm, yes, you're probably correct at that. Pity. But"—at that he pretended to brighten—"it does leave us time to make mischief."

Again, she was speechless. He liked that. "Shall we?" he murmured.

"I don't know what I'm going to do with you."

"We need to work on this," he said, giving his head a shake. "I'm not sure you fully understand the mechanics of a yes-or-no question."

"I think you should sit down," she said, her eyes now taking on that glint of cautious exhaustion usually reserved for small children.

Or adult fools.

"And then," she continued, "I think you should remain in your seat."

"Indefinitely?"

"*Yes.*"

Just to torture her, he sat. And then—

"*Nooooo*, I think I'd rather make mischief."

Back to his feet he was, and striding off to find Eloise before Penelope could even attempt to lunge for him.

"Colin, *don't*!" she called out, her voice echoing off the walls of the reception room. She managed to yell—of course—at the precise moment when every other wedding guest paused to take a breath.

A roomful of Bridgertons. What were the odds?

Penelope jammed a smile on her face as she watched two dozen heads swivel in her direction. "Nothing about it," she said, her voice coming out strangled and chirpy. "So sorry to disturb."

And apparently Colin's family was well used to his embarking on something requiring the rejoinder "Colin, don't!" because they all resumed their conversations with barely another glance in her direction.

Except Hyacinth.

"Oh, blast," Penelope muttered under her breath, and she raced forward.

But Hyacinth was quick. "What's going on?" she asked, falling into stride beside Penelope with remarkable agility.

"Nothing," Penelope replied, because the last thing she wanted was Hyacinth adding to the disaster.

"He's going to tell her, isn't he?" Hyacinth persisted, let out an "*Euf*" and an "Excuse me," when she pushed past one of her brothers.

"No," Penelope said firmly, darting around Daphne's children, "he's not."

"He *is*."

Penelope actually stopped for a moment and turned. "Do any of you ever listen to anyone?"

"Not me," Hyacinth said cheerfully.

Penelope shook her head and moved forward, Hyacinth hot on her heels. When she reached Colin, he was standing next to the newlyweds and had his arms linked through Eloise's and was smiling down at her as if he had never once considered:

a. Teaching her to swim by tossing her in a lake.
b. Cutting off three inches of her hair while she slept.

or

c. Tying her to a tree so that she did not follow him to a local public inn.

Which of course he had, all three of them, and two he'd actually done. (Even Colin wouldn't have dared something so permanent as a shearing.)

"Eloise," Penelope said, somewhat breathless from trying to shake off Hyacinth.

"Penelope." But Eloise's voice sounded curious. Which did not surprise Penelope; Eloise was no fool, and she was well aware that her brother's normal modes of behavior did not include beatific smiles in her direction.

"Eloise," Hyacinth said, for no reason Penelope could deduce.

"Hyacinth."

Penelope turned to her husband. "Colin."

He looked amused. "Penelope. Hyacinth."

Hyacinth grinned. "Colin." And then: "Sir Phillip."

"Ladies." Sir Phillip, it seemed, favored brevity.

"Stop!" Eloise burst out. "What is going on?"

"A recitation of our Christian names, apparently," Hyacinth said.

"Penelope has something to say to you," Colin said.

"I don't."

"She does."

"I *do*," Penelope said, thinking quickly. She rushed

forward, taking Eloise's hands in her own. "Congratulations. I'm so happy for you."

"That's what you needed to say?" Eloise asked.

"Yes."

"*No.*"

And from Hyacinth: "I am enjoying myself immensely."

"Er, it's very kind of you to say so," Sir Phillip said, looking a bit perplexed at her sudden need to compliment the host. Penelope closed her eyes for a brief moment and let out a weary sigh; she was going to need to take the poor man aside and instruct him on the finer points of marrying into the Bridgerton family.

And because she did know her new relations so well, and she knew that there was no way she was going to avoid revealing her secret, she turned to Eloise and said, "Might I have a moment alone?"

"With me?"

It was enough to make Penelope wish to strangle someone. Anyone. "Yes," she said patiently, "with you."

"And me," Colin put in.

"And me," Hyacinth added.

"*Not* you," Penelope said, not bothering to look at her.

"But still me," Colin added, looping his free arm through Penelope's.

"Can this wait?" Sir Phillip asked politely. "This is

her wedding day, and I expect that she does not wish to miss it."

"I know," Penelope said wearily. "I'm so sorry."

"It's all right," Eloise said, breaking free of Colin's grasp and turning to her new husband. She murmured a few words to him that Penelope could not hear, then said, "There is a small salon just through that door. Shall we?"

She led the way, which suited Penelope because it gave her time to say to Colin, "You will say nothing."

He surprised her by nodding, and then, maintaining his silence, he held open the door for her as she entered the room behind Eloise.

"This won't take long," Penelope said apologetically. "At least, I hope it won't."

Eloise said nothing, just looked at her with an expression that was, Penelope had just enough presence of mind to notice, uncharacteristically serene.

Marriage must agree with her, Penelope thought, because the Eloise *she* knew would have been chomping at the bit at such a moment. A big secret, a mystery to be revealed—Eloise loved that sort of thing.

But she was just standing there, calmly waiting, a light smile touching her features. Penelope looked to Colin in confusion, but he was apparently taking her instructions to heart, and his mouth was clamped firmly shut.

"Eloise," Penelope began.

Eloise smiled. A bit. Just at the corners, as if she wanted to smile more. "Yes?"

Penelope cleared her throat. "Eloise," she said again, "there is something I must tell you."

"Really?"

Penelope's eyes narrowed. Surely the moment did not call for sarcasm. She took a breath, tamping down the urge to fire off an equally dry rejoinder, and said, "I did not wish to tell you on your wedding day"—at this she *speared* her husband with a glare—"but it seems I have no choice."

Eloise blinked a few times, but other than that, her placid demeanor did not change.

"I can think of no other way to say it," Penelope plodded on, feeling positively sick, "but while you were gone . . . That is to say, the night you left, as a matter of fact . . ."

Eloise leaned forward. The movement was slight, but Penelope caught it, and for a moment she thought— Well, she didn't think anything clearly, certainly nothing that she could have expressed in a proper sentence. But she did get a feeling of unease—a different sort of unease than the one she was already feeling. It was a suspicious sort of unease, and—

"I am Whistledown," she blurted out, because if she waited any longer she thought her brain might explode.

And Eloise said, "I know."

Penelope sat down on the nearest solid object, which happened to be a table. "You know."

Eloise shrugged. "I know."

"How?"

"Hyacinth told me."

"*What?*" This from Colin, looking fit to be tied. Or perhaps more accurately, fit to tie Hyacinth.

"I'm sure she's at the door," Eloise murmured, with a nod. "In case you want to—"

But Colin was one step ahead of her, wrenching open the door to the small salon. Sure enough, Hyacinth tumbled in.

"Hyacinth!" Penelope said disapprovingly.

"Oh, please," Hyacinth retorted, smoothing her skirts. "You didn't think I wouldn't eavesdrop, did you? You know me better than that."

"I'm going to wring your neck," Colin ground out. "We had an agreement."

Hyacinth shrugged. "I don't really need twenty pounds, as it happens."

"I already *gave* you ten."

"I know," Hyacinth said with a cheerful smile.

"Hyacinth!" Eloise exclaimed.

"Which isn't to say," Hyacinth continued modestly, "that I don't *want* the other ten."

"She told me last night," Eloise explained, her eyes narrowing dangerously, "but only after informing me that she knew who Lady Whistledown was, and in fact the whole of society knew, but that the knowledge would cost me twenty-*five* pounds."

"Did it not occur to you," Penelope asked, "that if the whole of society knew, that you could simply have asked someone else?"

"The whole of society wasn't in my bedchamber at two in the morning," Eloise snapped.

"I am thinking of buying a hat," Hyacinth mused. "Or maybe a pony."

Eloise shot her a nasty look, then turned to Penelope. "Are you really Whistledown?"

"I am," Penelope admitted. "Or rather—" She looked over at Colin, not exactly certain why she was doing so except that she loved him so much, and he knew her so well, and when he saw her helpless little wobbly smile, he would smile in return, no matter how irate he was with Hyacinth.

And he did. Somehow, amidst everything, he knew what she needed. He always did.

Penelope turned back to Eloise. "I *was*," she amended. "No longer. I've retired."

But of course Eloise already knew that. Lady W's letter of retirement had circulated long before Eloise had left town.

"For good," Penelope added. "People have asked, but I shan't be induced to pick up my quill again." She paused, thinking of the scribblings she'd embarked upon at home. "At least not as Whistledown." She looked at Eloise, who had sat down next to her on the table. Her face was somewhat blank, and she hadn't said anything in *ages*—well, ages for Eloise, at least.

Penelope tried to smile. "I am thinking of writing a novel, actually."

Still nothing from Eloise, although she was blinking quite rapidly, and her brow was scrunched up as if she were thinking quite hard.

And so Penelope took one of her hands and said the one thing she was really feeling. "I'm sorry, Eloise."

Eloise had been staring rather blankly at an end table, but at that, she turned, her eyes finding Penelope's. "You're sorry?" she echoed, and she sounded dubious, as if sorry couldn't possibly be the correct emotion, or at least, not *enough* of it.

Penelope's heart sank. "I'm so sorry," she said again. "I should have told you. I should have—"

"Are you *mad*?" Eloise asked, finally seeming to snap to attention. "Of *course* you should not have told me. I could never have kept this a secret."

Penelope thought it rather remarkable of her to admit it.

"I am so *proud* of you," Eloise continued. "Forget the writing for a moment—I cannot even fathom the logistics of it all, and someday—when it is not my wedding day—I shall insist upon hearing every last detail."

"You were surprised, then?" Penelope murmured.

Eloise gave her a rather dry look. "To put it mildly."

"I had to get her a chair," Hyacinth supplied.

"I was already sitting down," Eloise ground out.

Hyacinth waved her hand in the air. "Nevertheless."

"Ignore her," Eloise said, focusing firmly on Penelope. "Truly, I cannot begin to tell you how impressed I am—now that I've got over the shock, that is."

"Really?" It hadn't occurred to Penelope until that very moment just how much she'd wished for Eloise's approval.

"Keeping us all in the dark for so long," Eloise said, shaking her head with slow admiration. "From me. From *her*." She jabbed a finger in Hyacinth's direction. "It's really very well-done of you." At that she leaned forward and enveloped Penelope in a warm hug.

"You're not angry with me?"

Eloise moved back and opened her mouth, and Penelope could see that she'd been about to say, "No," probably to be followed by "Of course not."

But the words remained in Eloise's mouth, and she just

sat there, looking slightly thoughtful and surprised until she finally said . . . "No."

Penelope felt her brows lift. "Are you certain?" Because Eloise didn't sound certain. She didn't much sound like Eloise, to be honest.

"It would be different if I were still in London," Eloise said quietly, "with nothing else to do. But this——" She glanced around the room, gesturing rather vaguely toward the window. "*Here*. It's just not the same. It's a different life," she said quietly. "I'm a different person. A little bit, at least."

"Lady Crane," Penelope reminded her.

Eloise smiled. "Good of you to remind me of that, Mrs. Bridgerton."

Penelope almost laughed. "Can you believe it?"

"Of you, or me?" Eloise asked.

"Both."

Colin, who had been keeping a respectful distance—one hand firmly clamped around Hyacinth's arm to keep *her* at a respectful distance—stepped forward. "We should probably return," he said quietly. He held out his hand, and helped first Penelope, then Eloise, to her feet. "You," he said, leaning forward to kiss his sister on the cheek, "should *certainly* return."

Eloise smiled wistfully, the blushing bride once again, and nodded. With one last squeeze of Penelope's hands, she brushed past Hyacinth (rolling her eyes as she did so) and made her way back to her wedding party.

Penelope watched her go, linking her arm in Colin's and leaned gently into him. They both stood there in contented silence, idly watching the now empty doorway, listening to the sounds of the party wafting through the air.

"Do you think it would be polite if we left?" he murmured.

"Probably not."

"Do you think Eloise would mind?"

Penelope shook her head.

Colin's arms tightened around her, and she felt his lips gently brush her ear. "Let's go," he said.

She did not argue.

On the twenty-fifth of May, in the year 1824, precisely one day after the wedding of Eloise Bridgerton to Sir Phillip Crane, three missives were delivered to the room of Mr. and Mrs. Colin Bridgerton, guests at the Rose and Bramble Inn, near Tetbury, Gloucestershire. They arrived together; all were from Romney Hall.

"Which shall we open first?" Penelope asked, spreading them before her on the bed.

Colin yanked off the shirt he'd donned to answer the knock. "I defer to your good judgment as always."

"As always?"

He crawled back into bed beside her. She was remarkably adorable when she was being sarcastic. He couldn't think of another soul who could carry that off. "As whenever it suits me," he amended.

"Your mother, then," Penelope said, plucking one of the letters off the sheet. She broke open the seal and carefully unfolded the paper.

Colin watched as she read. Her eyes widened, then her brows rose, then her lips pinched slightly at the corners, as if she were smiling despite herself. "What does she have to say?" he asked.

"She forgives us."

"I don't suppose it would make any sense for me to ask for what."

Penelope gave him a stern look. "For leaving the wedding early."

"You told me Eloise wouldn't mind."

"And I'm sure she did not. But this is your *mother*."

"Write back and assure her that should she ever remarry, I will stay to the bitter end."

"I will do no such thing," Penelope replied, rolling her eyes. "I don't think she expects a reply, in any case."

"Really?" Now he was curious, because his mother always expected replies. "What did we do to earn her forgiveness, then?"

"Er, she mentioned something about the timely delivery of grandchildren."

Colin grinned. "Are you blushing?"

"No."

"You *are*."

She elbowed him in the ribs. "I'm not. Here, read it yourself if you are so inclined. I shall read Hyacinth's."

"I don't suppose she returned my ten pounds," Colin grumbled.

Penelope unfolded the paper and shook it out. Nothing fluttered down.

"That minx is lucky she's my sister," he muttered.

"What a bad sport you are," Penelope chided. "She bested you, and rather brilliantly, too."

"Oh, please," he scoffed. "I did not see *you* praising her cunning yesterday afternoon."

She waved off his protests. "Yes, well, some things are more easily seen in hindsight."

"What does she have to say?" Colin asked, leaning over her shoulder. Knowing Hyacinth, it was probably some scheme to extort more money from his pockets.

"It's rather sweet, actually," Penelope said. "Nothing nefarious at all."

"Did you read both sides?" Colin asked dubiously.

"She only wrote on one side."

"Uncharacteristically uneconomical of her," he added, with suspicion.

"Oh, heavens, Colin, it is just an account of the wedding after we left. And I must say, she has a superior eye for humor and detail. She would have made a fine Whistledown."

"God help us all."

The last letter was from Eloise, and unlike the other two, it was addressed to Penelope alone. Colin was curious, of course—who wouldn't be? But he moved away to allow Penelope her privacy. Her friendship with his sister was something he held in both awe and respect. He was close to his brothers—extremely so. But he had never seen a bond of friendship quite so deep as that between Penelope and Eloise.

"Oh!" Penelope let out, as she turned a page. Eloise's missive was a good deal longer than the previous two, and she'd managed to fill two sheets, front and back. "That minx."

"What did she do?" Colin asked.

"Oh, it was nothing," Penelope replied, even though her expression was rather peeved. "You weren't there, but the morning of the wedding she kept apologizing for keeping secrets, and it never even occurred to me that she was trying to get me to admit to keeping secrets of my own. Made me feel wretched, she did."

Her voice trailed off as she read through another page. Colin leaned back against the fluffy pillows, his eyes resting on his wife's face. He liked watching her eyes move from left to right, following the words. He liked watching her lips move as she smiled or frowned. It was rather amazing, actually, how contented he felt, simply watching his wife read.

Until she gasped, that was, and turned utterly white.

He shoved himself up on his elbows. "What is it?"

Penelope shook her head and groaned. "Oh, she is devious."

Privacy be damned. He grabbed the letter. "What did she say?"

"Down there," Penelope said, pointing miserably at the bottom. "At the end."

Colin brushed her finger away and began to read. "Good Lord, she's wordy," he muttered. "I can't make heads or tails of it."

"Revenge," Penelope said. "She says my secret was bigger than hers."

"It was."

"She says she's owed a boon."

Colin pondered that. "She probably is."

"To even the score."

He patted her hand. "I'm afraid that's how we Bridgertons think. You've never played a sporting game with us, have you?"

Penelope moaned. "She said she is going to consult *Hyacinth*."

Colin felt the blood leave his face.

"I know," Penelope said, shaking her head. "We'll never be safe again."

Colin slid his arm around her and pulled her close. "Didn't we say we wanted to visit Italy?"

"Or India."

He smiled and kissed her on the nose. "Or we could just stay here."

"At the Rose and Bramble?"

"We're supposed to depart tomorrow morning. It's the last place Hyacinth would look."

Penelope glanced up at him, her eyes growing warm and perhaps just a little bit mischievous. "I have no pressing engagements in London for at least a fortnight."

He rolled atop her, tugging her down until she was flat on her back. "My mother did say she would not forgive us unless we produced a grandchild."

"She did not put it in quite so uncompromising terms."

He kissed her, right on the sensitive spot behind her earlobe that always made her squirm. "Pretend she did."

"Well, in that case—oh!"

His lips slid down her belly. "Oh?" he murmured.

"We had best get to—oh!"

He looked up. "You were saying?"

"To work," she just barely managed to get out.

He smiled against her skin. "Your servant, Mrs. Bridgerton. Always."

To Sir Phillip, With Love

Rarely have I written such meddlesome children as Amanda and Oliver Crane, the lonely twin children of Sir Phillip Crane. It seemed impossible they could grow into well-adjusted, reasonable adults, but I figured if anyone could whip them into shape, it would be their new stepmother, Eloise (née Bridgerton) Crane. I had long wanted to try my hand at writing in the first person, so I decided to see the world through the eyes of a grown-up Amanda. She was going to fall in love, and Phillip and Eloise were going to have to watch it happen.

To Sir Phillip, With Love:
The 2nd Epilogue

I am not the most patient of individuals. And I have almost no tolerance for stupidity. Which was why I was proud of myself for holding my tongue this afternoon, while having tea with the Brougham family.

The Broughams are our neighbors, and have been for the past six years, since Mr. Brougham inherited the property from his uncle, also named Mr. Brougham. They have four daughters and one extremely spoiled son. Luckily for me the son is five years younger than I am, which means I shall not have to entertain notions of marrying him. (Although my sisters Penelope and Georgiana, nine and ten years my junior, will not be so lucky.) The Brougham daughters are all one year apart, beginning two years ahead of me and ending two behind. They are perfectly pleasant, if perhaps a touch too sweet and gentle for my taste. But lately they have been too much to bear.

This is because I, too, have a brother, and he is not five years younger than they are. In fact, he is my twin, which makes him a matrimonial possibility for any of them.

Unsurprisingly, Oliver did not elect to accompany my mother, Penelope, and me to tea.

But here is what happened, and here is why I am pleased with myself for not saying what I wished to say, which was: *Surely you must be an idiot.*

I was sipping my tea, trying to keep the cup at my lips for as long as possible so as to avoid questions about Oliver, when Mrs. Brougham said, "It must be so very intriguing to be a twin. Tell me, dear Amanda, how is it different than not being one?"

I should hope that I do not have to explain why this question was so asinine. I could hardly tell her what the difference was, as I have spent approximately one hundred percent of my life as a twin and thus have precisely zero experience at not being one.

I must have worn my disdain on my face because my mother shot me one of her legendary warning looks the moment my lips parted to reply. Because I did not wish to embarrass my mother (and not because I felt any need to make Mrs. Brougham feel cleverer than she actually was), I said, "I suppose one always has a companion."

"But your brother is not here now," one of the Brougham girls said.

"My father is not always with my mother, and I would imagine that she considers him to be her companion," I replied.

"A brother is hardly the same as a husband," Mrs. Brougham trilled.

"One would hope," I retorted. Truly, this was one of the more ridiculous conversations in which I had taken part. And Penelope looked as if she would have questions when we returned home.

My mother gave me another look, one that said she knew exactly what sort of questions Penelope would have, and she did not wish to answer them. But as my mother had always said she valued curiosity in females . . .

Well, she'd be hoisted by her own petard.

I should mention that, petard hoistings aside, I am convinced that I have the finest mother in England. And unlike being a non-twin, about which I have no knowledge, I do know what it's like to have a different mother, so I am fully qualified, in my opinion, to make the judgment.

My mother, Eloise Crane, is actually my stepmother,

although I only refer to her as such when required to for purposes of clarification. She married my father when Oliver and I were eight years old, and I am quite certain she saved us all. It is difficult to explain what our lives were like before she entered them. I could certainly describe events, but the *tone* of it all, the feeling in our house . . .

I don't really know how to convey it.

My mother—my original mother—killed herself. For most of my life I did not know this. I thought she died of a fever, which I suppose is true. What no one told me was that the fever was brought on because she tried to drown herself in a lake in the dead of winter.

I have no intention of taking my own life, but I must say, this would not be my chosen method.

I know I should feel compassion and sympathy for her. My current mother was a distant cousin of hers and tells me that she was sad her entire life. She tells me that some people are like that, just as others are unnaturally cheerful all the time. But I can't help but think that if she was going to kill herself, she might as well have done it earlier. Perhaps when I was a toddler. Or better yet, an infant. It certainly would have made my life easier.

I asked my uncle Hugh (who is not really my uncle, but he is married to the stepsister of my current mother's brother's wife *and* he lives quite close *and* he's a vicar) if

I would be going to hell for such a thought. He said no, that frankly, it made a lot of sense to him.

I do think I prefer his parish to my own.

But the thing is, now I have memories of her. Marina, my first mother. I don't *want* memories of her. The ones I have are hazy and muddled. I can't recall the sound of her voice. Oliver says that might be because she hardly spoke. I can't remember whether she spoke or not. I can't remember the exact shape of her face, and I can't remember her smell.

Instead I remember standing outside her door, feeling very small and frightened. And I remember tiptoeing a great deal, because we knew we mustn't make noise. I remember always feeling rather nervous, as if I knew something bad were about to happen.

And indeed it did.

Shouldn't a memory be specific? I would not mind a memory of a moment, or of a face, or a sound. Instead I have vague feelings, and not even happy ones at that.

I once asked Oliver if he had the same memories, and he just shrugged and said he didn't really think about her. I am not sure if I believe him. I suppose I probably do; he does not often think deeply about such things. Or perhaps more accurately, he does not think deeply about anything. One can only hope that when he marries (which surely will not come soon enough for the sisters

Brougham) that he will choose a bride with a similar lack of thoughtfulness and sensibility. Otherwise, she shall be miserable. He won't be, of course; he wouldn't even notice her misery.

Men are like that, I'm told.

My father, for example, is remarkably unobservant. Unless, of course, you happen to be a plant, and then he notices everything. He is a botanist and could happily toddle about in his greenhouse all day. He seems to me a most unlikely match for my mother, who is vivacious and outgoing and never at a loss for words, but when they are together it is obvious that they love each other very much. Last week I caught them kissing in the garden. I was aghast. Mother is nearly forty, and Father older than that.

But I have digressed. I was speaking of the Brougham family, more specifically of Mrs. Brougham's foolish query about not being a twin. I was, as previously mentioned, feeling rather pleased with myself for not having been rude, when Mrs. Brougham said something that *was* of interest.

"My nephew comes to visit this afternoon."

Every one of the Brougham girls popped straighter in her seat. I swear, it was like some children's game with snaps. Bing bing bing bing . . . Up they went, from perfect posture to preternaturally erect.

From this I immediately deduced that Mrs. Brougham's nephew must be of marriageable age, probably of good fortune, and perhaps of pleasing features.

"You did not mention that Ian was coming to visit," one of the daughters said.

"He's not," replied Mrs. Brougham. "He is still at Oxford, as you well know. Charles is coming."

Poof. The daughters Brougham deflated, all at once.

"Oh," said one of them. "Charlie."

"Today, you say," said another, with a remarkable lack of enthusiasm.

And then the third said, "I shall have to hide my dolls."

The fourth said nothing. She just resumed drinking her tea, looking rather bored by the whole thing.

"Why do you have to hide your dolls?" Penelope asked. In all truth, I was wondering the same thing, but it seemed too childish a question for a lady of nineteen years.

"That was twelve years ago, Dulcie," Mrs. Brougham said. "Good heavens, you've a memory of an elephant."

"One does not forget what he did to my dolls," Dulcie said darkly.

"What did he do?" Penelope asked.

Dulcie made a slashing motion across her throat. Penelope gasped, and I must confess, there was something rather gruesome in Dulcie's expression.

"He is a beast," said one of Dulcie's sisters.

"He is *not* a beast," Mrs. Brougham insisted.

The Brougham girls all looked at us, shaking their heads in silent agreement, as if to say, *Do not listen to her.*

"How old is your nephew now?" my mother asked.

"Two and twenty," Mrs. Brougham replied, looking rather grateful for the question. "He was graduated from Oxford last month."

"He is a year older than Ian," explained one of the girls.

I nodded, even though I could hardly use Ian—whom I had never met—as a reference point.

"He's not as handsome."

"Or as nice."

I looked at the last Brougham daughter, awaiting her contribution. But all she did was yawn.

"How long will he be staying?" my mother asked politely.

"Two weeks," Mrs. Brougham answered, but she really only got out "Two wee" before one of her daughters howled with dismay.

"Two weeks! An entire fortnight!"

"I was hoping he could accompany us to the local assembly," Mrs. Brougham said.

This was met by more groans. I must say, I was beginning to grow curious about this Charles fellow. Anyone who could inspire such dread among the Brougham daughters must have something to recommend him.

Not, I hasten to add, that I dislike the Brougham daughters. Unlike their brother, none of them was granted every wish and whim, and thus they are not at all unbearable. But they are—how shall I say it—placid and biddable, and therefore not a natural sort of companion for me (about whom such adjectives have never been applied). Truthfully, I don't think I had ever known any of them to express a strong opinion about anything. If all four of them detested someone that much—well, if nothing else, he would be interesting.

"Does your nephew like to ride?" my mother asked.

Mrs. Brougham got a crafty look in her eye. "I believe so."

"Perhaps Amanda would consent to showing him the area." With that, my mother smiled a most uncharacteristically innocent and sweet smile.

Perhaps I should add that one of the reasons I am convinced that mine is the finest mother in England is that she is rarely innocent and sweet. Oh, do not misunderstand—she has a heart of gold and would do anything for her family. But she grew up the fifth in a family of eight, and she can be marvelously devious and underhanded.

Also, she cannot be bested in conversation. Trust me, I have tried.

So when she offered me up as a guide, I could do nothing but say yes, even as three out of four Brougham sisters began to snicker. (The fourth still looked bored. I was beginning to wonder if there might be something wrong with her.)

"Tomorrow," Mrs. Brougham said delightedly. She clapped her hands together and beamed. "I shall send him over tomorrow afternoon. Will that do?"

Again, I could say nothing but yes, and so I did, wondering what exactly I had just consented to.

The following afternoon I was dressed in my best riding habit and was lolling about the drawing room, wondering if the mysterious Charles Brougham would actually make an appearance. If he didn't, I thought, he'd be entirely within his rights. It would be rude, of course, as he was breaking a commitment made on his behalf by his aunt, but all the same, it wasn't as if he'd asked to be saddled with the local gentry.

Pun unintended.

My mother had not even tried to deny that she was playing matchmaker. This surprised me; I would have thought she'd put up at least a feeble protest. But instead she reminded me that I had refused a season in London and then began to expound upon the lack of appropriately aged, eligible gentlemen here in our corner of Gloucestershire.

I reminded her that she had not found *her* husband in London.

She then said something that began with "Be that as it may" and then veered off so quickly and with such twists and turns that I could not follow a thing she said.

Which I am fairly certain was her intention.

My mother wasn't precisely upset that I had said no to a season; she was rather fond of our life in the country, and heaven knows my father would not survive in town for more than a week. Mother called me unkind for saying so, but I believe that she secretly agreed with me—Father would get distracted by a plant in the park, and we'd never find him again. (He's a bit distractable, my father.)

Or, and I confess this is more likely, he would say something utterly inappropriate at a party. Unlike my mother, my father does not have the gift of polite conversation, and he certainly does not see the need for double entendre or cunning twists of phrase. As far as he is concerned, a body ought to say what a body means.

I do love my father, but it is clear that he should be kept away from town.

I could have had a season in London, if I wished. My

mother's family is extremely well connected. Her brother is a viscount, and her sisters married a duke, an earl, and a baron. I should be admitted to all of the most exclusive gatherings. But I really didn't wish to go. I should have no freedom whatsoever. Here I may take walks or go for a ride by myself so long as I tell someone where I am going. In London a young lady may not so much as touch her toe to her front steps without a chaperone.

I think it sounds dreadful.

But back to my mother. She did not mind that I had refused the season because this meant that she would not have to be apart from my father for several months. (Since, as we have determined, he would have to be left at home.) But at the same time, she was genuinely concerned for my future. To that end, she had launched into a bit of a crusade. If I would not go to the eligible gentlemen, she would bring them to me.

Hence Charles Brougham.

At two o'clock he had still not arrived, and I must confess, I was growing irritable. It was a hot day, or at least as hot as it gets in Gloucestershire, and my dark green habit, which had felt so stylish and jaunty when I had donned it, was beginning to itch.

I was beginning to wilt.

Somehow my mother and Mrs. Brougham had forgotten to set a time for the nephew's arrival, so I had been obligated to be dressed and ready at noon precisely.

"What time would you say marks the end of the afternoon?" I asked, fanning myself with a folded-up newspaper.

"Hmmm?" My mother was writing a letter—presumably to one of her many siblings—and wasn't really listening. She looked quite lovely sitting there by the window. I have no idea what my original mother would have looked like as an older woman, since she did not deign to live that long, but Eloise had not lost any of her beauty. Her hair was still a rich, chestnut color and her skin unlined. Her eyes are difficult to describe—rather changeable in color, actually.

She tells me that she was never considered a beauty when she was young. No one thought she was unattractive, and she was in fact quite popular, but she was never designated a diamond of the first water. She tells me that women of intelligence age better.

I find this interesting, and I do hope it bodes well for my own future.

But at present I was not concerned for any future outside that of the next ten minutes, after which I was convinced I would perish from the heat. "The afternoon," I repeated. "When would you say it ends? Four o'clock? Five? Please say it isn't six."

She finally glanced up. "What are you talking about?"

"Mr. Brougham. We did say the afternoon, did we not?"

She looked at me blankly.

"I may stop waiting for him once the afternoon passes into evening, may I not?"

Mother paused for a moment, her quill suspended in air. "You should not be so impatient, Amanda."

"I'm not," I insisted. "I'm *hot*."

She considered that. "It is warm in here, isn't it?"

I nodded. "My habit is made of wool."

She grimaced, but I noticed she did not suggest that I change. She was not going to sacrifice a potential suitor for anything as inconsequential as the weather. I resumed fanning myself.

"I don't think his name is Brougham," Mother said.

"I beg your pardon?"

"I believe he is related to Mrs. Brougham, not mister. I don't know what her family name is."

I shrugged.

She went back to her letter. My mother writes an inordinate number of letters. About what, I cannot imagine. I would not call our family dull, but we are certainly ordinary. Surely her sisters have grown bored of *Georgiana has mastered French conjugation* and *Frederick has skinned his knee*.

But Mother likes to receive letters, and she says that

one must send to receive, so there she is at her desk, nearly every day, recounting the boring details of our lives.

"Someone is coming," she said, just as I was beginning to nod off on the sofa. I sat up and turned toward the window. Sure enough, a carriage was rolling up the drive.

"I thought we were meant to go for a ride," I said, somewhat irritably. Had I sweltered in my riding habit for nothing?

"You were," Mother murmured, her brow knitting together as she watched the carriage draw near.

I did not think that Mr. Brougham—or whoever was in the carriage—could see into the drawing room through the open window, but just in case, I maintained my dignified position on the sofa, tilting my head ever so slightly so that I could observe the events in the front drive.

The carriage came to a halt and a gentleman hopped down, but his back was to the house and I could see nothing of him other than his height (average) and his hair (dark). He then reached up and assisted a lady down.

Dulcie Brougham!

"What is she doing here?" I said indignantly.

And then, once Dulcie had both feet safely on the ground, the gentleman aided another young lady, and then another. And then another.

"Did he bring all of the Brougham girls?" my mother asked.

"Apparently so."

"I thought they hated him."

I shook my head. "Apparently not."

The reason for the sisters' about face became clear a few moments later, when Gunning announced their arrival.

I do not know what Cousin Charles *used* to look like, but now . . . well, let us just say that any young lady would find him pleasing. His hair was thick and with a bit of wave, and even from across the room I could see that his eyelashes were ridiculously long. His mouth was the sort that always looks as if it is about to smile, which in my opinion is the best sort of mouth to have.

I am not saying that I felt anything other than polite interest, but the Brougham sisters were falling all over themselves to be the one on his arm.

"Dulcie," my mother said, walking forth with a welcoming smile. "And Antonia. And Sarah." She took a breath. "And Cordelia, too. What a pleasant surprise to see all of you."

It is a testament to my mother's skills as a hostess that she did indeed sound pleased.

"We could not let dear Cousin Charles come over by himself," Dulcie explained.

"He does not know the way," added Antonia.

It could not have been a simpler journey—one had only to ride into the village, turn right at the church, and it was only another mile until our drive.

But I did not say this. I did, however, look over at Cousin Charles with some sympathy. It could not have been an entertaining drive.

"Charles, dear," Dulcie was saying, "this is Lady Crane, and Miss Amanda Crane."

I bobbed a curtsy, wondering if I was going to have to climb into that carriage with all five of them. I hoped not. If it was hot in here, it would be beastly in the carriage.

"Lady Crane, Amanda," Dulcie continued, "my dear cousin Charles, Mr. Farraday."

I cocked my head at that. My mother was correct—his name was not Brougham. Oh dear, did that mean he was related to *Mrs.* Brougham? I found Mr. Brougham the more sensible of the two.

Mr. Farraday bowed politely, and for the briefest of moments, his eyes caught mine.

I should say at this point that I am not a romantic. Or at least I do not think I am a romantic. If I were, I would have gone to London for that season. I would have spent my days reading poetry and my nights dancing and flirting and making merry.

I certainly do not believe in love at first sight. Even my

parents, who are as much in love as anyone I know, tell me that they did not love each other instantly.

But when my eyes met Mr. Farraday's . . .

As I said, it was not love at first sight, since I do not believe in such things. It was not anything at first sight, really, but there was something . . . a shared recognition . . . a sense of humor. I'm not certain how to describe it.

I suppose, if pressed, that I would say it was a sense of knowing. That somehow I already knew him. Which was of course ridiculous.

But not as ridiculous as his cousins, who were trilling and frilling and fluttering about. Clearly they had decided that Cousin Charles was no longer a beast, and if anyone was going to marry him, it was going to be one of them.

"Mr. Farraday," I said, and I could feel the corners of my mouth pinching in an attempt to hold back a smile.

"Miss Crane," he said, wearing much the same expression. He bent over my hand and kissed it, much to the consternation of Dulcie, who was standing right next to me.

Again, I *must* stress that I am not a romantic. But my insides did a little flip when his lips touched my skin.

"I am afraid that I am dressed for a ride," I told him, motioning to my riding habit.

"So you are."

I glanced ruefully at his cousins, who were most assuredly not dressed for any sort of athletic endeavor. "It's such a lovely day," I murmured.

"Girls," my mother said, looking squarely at the Brougham sisters, "why don't you join me while Amanda and your cousin go for a ride? I did promise your mother that she would show him the area."

Antonia opened her mouth to protest, but she was no match for Eloise Crane, and indeed she did not make even a sound before my mother added, "Oliver will be down shortly."

That settled it. They sat, all four of them, in a neat row on the sofa, descending as one, with identically placid smiles on their faces.

I almost felt sorry for Oliver.

"I did not bring my mount," Mr. Farraday said regretfully.

"That is no matter," I replied. "We have an excellent stables. I'm certain we can find something suitable."

And off we went, out the drawing room door, then out of the house, then around the corner to the back lawn, and then—

Mr. Farraday sagged against the wall, laughing. "Oh, thank you," he said, with great feeling. "Thank you. Thank you."

I was not sure if I should feign ignorance. I could hardly acknowledge the sentiment without insulting his cousins, which I did not wish to do. As I have mentioned, I do not dislike the Brougham sisters, even if I found them a bit ridiculous that afternoon.

"Tell me you can ride," he said.

"Of course."

He motioned to the house. "None of them can."

"That's not true," I replied, puzzled. I knew I had seen them on horseback at some point.

"They can sit in a saddle," he said, his eyes flashing with what could only be a dare, "but they cannot ride."

"I see," I murmured. I considered my options and said, "I can."

He looked at me, one corner of his mouth tilted up. His eyes were a rather nice shade of green, mossy with little brown flecks. And again, I got that odd sense of being in accord.

I hope I am not being immodest when I say that there are a few things I do quite well. I can shoot with a pistol (although not with a rifle, and not as well as my mother, who is freakishly good). I can add up sums twice as quickly as Oliver, provided I have pen and paper. I can fish, and I can swim, and above all, I can ride.

"Come with me," I said, motioning toward the stables.

He did, falling into step beside me. "Tell me, Miss Crane," he said, his voice laced with amusement, "with what were you bribed for your presence this afternoon?"

"You think your company was not enough reward?"

"You did not know me," he pointed out.

"True." We turned onto the path toward the stables, and I was happy to feel that the breeze was picking up. "As it happens, I was outmaneuvered by my mother."

"You admit to being outmaneuvered," he murmured. "Interesting."

"You don't know my mother."

"No," he assured me, "I am impressed. Most people would not confess to it."

"As I said, you don't know my mother." I turned to him and smiled. "She is one of eight siblings. Besting her in any sort of devious matter is nothing short of a triumph."

We reached the stables, but I paused before entering. "And what about you, Mr. Farraday?" I asked. "With what were you bribed for your presence this afternoon?"

"I, too, was thwarted," he said. "I was told I'd escape my cousins."

I let out a snort of laughter at that. Inappropriate, yes, but unavoidable.

"They attacked just as I was departing," he told me grimly.

"They are a fierce lot," I said, utterly deadpan.

"I was outnumbered."

"I thought they didn't like you," I said.

"So did I." He planted his hands on his hips. "It was the only reason I consented to the visit."

"What exactly did you do to them when you were children?" I asked.

"The better question would be—what did they do to me?"

I knew better than to claim that he held the upper hand because of his gender. Four girls could easily trounce one boy. I had gone up against Oliver countless times as a child, and although he would never admit it, I bested him more often than not.

"Frogs?" I asked, thinking of my own childhood pranks.

"That was me," he admitted sheepishly.

"Dead fish?"

He didn't speak, but his expression was clearly one of guilt.

"Which one?" I asked, trying to imagine Dulcie's horror.

"All of them."

I sucked in my breath. "At the same time?"

He nodded.

I was impressed. I suppose most ladies would not find such things attractive, but I have always had an unusual sense of humor. "Have you ever done a flour ghosting?" I asked.

His eyebrows rose, and he actually leaned forward. "Tell me more."

And so I told him about my mother, and how Oliver and I had tried to scare her off before she'd married my father. We'd been utter beasts. Truly. Not just mischievous children, but utter and complete blights on the face of humanity. It's a wonder my father hadn't shipped us off to a workhouse. The most memorable of our stunts was when we'd rigged a bucket of flour above her door so that it would dust her when she stepped out into the hall.

Except that we'd filled the bucket quite high, so it was more of a coating than a dusting, and in fact more of a deluge than anything else.

We also hadn't counted on the bucket hitting her on the head.

When I said that my current mother's entry into our lives had saved us all, I meant it quite literally. Oliver and I were so desperate for attention, and our father, as lovely as he is now, had no idea how to manage us.

I told all this to Mr. Farraday. It was the strangest thing. I have no idea why I spoke so long and said so much. I thought it must be that he was an extraordinary listener, except that he later told me that he is not, that in fact he is a dreadful listener and usually interrupts too often.

But he didn't with me. He listened, and I spoke, and then I listened and he spoke, and he told me of his brother Ian, with his angelic good looks and courtly manners. How everyone fawns over him, even though Charles is the elder. How Charles never could manage to hate him, though, because when all was said and done, Ian was a rather fine fellow.

"Do you still want to go for a ride?" I asked, when I noticed that the sun had already begun to dip in the sky. I could not imagine how long we had been standing there, talking and listening, listening and talking.

To my great surprise Charles said no, let's walk instead.

And we did.

It was still warm later that night, and so after supper was done I took myself outside. The sun had sunk below the horizon, but it was not yet completely dark. I sat on the steps of the back patio, facing west so I could watch the last hints of daylight turn from lavender to purple to black.

I love this time of the night.

I sat there for quite some time, long enough so that the stars began to appear, long enough so that I had to hug my arms to my body to ward off the chill. I hadn't brought a shawl. I suppose I hadn't thought I'd be sitting outside for so long. I was just about to head back inside when I heard someone approaching.

It was my father, on his way home from his greenhouse. He was holding a lantern and his hands were dirty. Something about the sight of him made me feel like a child again. He was a big bear of a man, and even before he'd married Eloise, back when he didn't seem to know what to say to his own children, he'd always made me feel safe. He was my father, and he would protect me. He didn't need to say it, I just knew.

"You're out late," he said, sitting beside me. He set his lantern down and brushed his hands against his work trousers, shaking off the loose dirt.

"Just thinking," I replied.

He nodded, then leaned his elbows on his thighs and looked out at the sky. "Any shooting stars tonight?"

I shook my head even though he wasn't facing me. "No."

"Do you need one?"

I smiled to myself. He was asking if I had any wishes to be made. We used to wish on stars together all the time when I was small, but somehow we'd got out of the habit.

"No," I said. I was feeling introspective, thinking about Charles and wondering what it meant that I'd spent the whole of the afternoon with him and now could not wait to see him again tomorrow. But I didn't feel as if I needed any wishes granted. At least, not yet.

"I always have wishes," he remarked.

"You do?" I turned to him, my head tilting to the side as I took in his profile. I know that he'd been terribly unhappy before he'd met my current mother, but that was all well behind him. If ever a man had a happy and fulfilled life, it was he.

"What do you wish for?" I asked.

"The health and happiness of my children, first and foremost."

"That doesn't count," I said, feeling myself smile.

"Oh, you don't think so?" He looked at me, and there was more than a hint of amusement in his eyes. "I assure you, it's the first thing I think about in the morning, and the last before I lay myself down to sleep."

"Really?"

"I have five children, Amanda, and every one of them is healthy and strong. And as far as I know, you're all happy. It's probably dumb luck that you've all turned out so well, but I'm not going to tempt any fates by wishing for something else."

I thought about that for a moment. It had never occurred to me to wish for something I already had. "Is it scary being a parent?" I asked.

"The most terrifying thing in the world."

I don't know what I thought he might say, but it wasn't that. But then I realized—he was speaking to me as an adult. I don't know if he'd ever really done so before. He was still my father, and I was still his daughter, but I'd crossed some mysterious threshold.

It was thrilling and sad at the same time.

We sat together for a few minutes more, pointing out constellations and not saying anything of import. And then, just when I was about to head back inside he said, "Your mother said that you had a gentleman caller this afternoon."

"And four of his female cousins," I quipped.

He looked over at me with arched brows, a silent scolding for making light of the topic.

"Yes," I said. "I did."

"Did you like him?"

"Yes." I felt myself grow a bit light, as if my insides had gone fizzy. "I did."

He digested that, then said, "I'm going to have to get a very large stick."

"What?"

"I used to say to your mother that when you were old enough to be courted, I was going to have to beat away the gentlemen."

There was something almost sweet about that. "Really?"

"Well, not when you were very small. Then you were such a nightmare I despaired of anyone ever wanting you."

"Father!"

He chuckled. "Don't say you don't know it's true."

I couldn't contradict.

"But when you were a bit older, and I started to see the first hints of the woman you would become . . ." He sighed. "Good Lord, if ever being a parent is terrifying . . ."

"And now?"

He thought about that for a moment. "I suppose now I can only hope I raised you well enough to make sensible decisions." He paused. "And of course, if anyone even thinks about mistreating you, I shall still have that stick."

I smiled, then scooted over slightly, so that I could rest my head on his shoulder. "I love you, Father."

"I love you, too, Amanda." He turned and kissed me on the top of my head. "I love you, too."

I did marry Charles, by the way, and my father never once had to brandish a stick. The wedding occurred six months later, after a proper courtship and slightly improper engagement. But I am certainly not going to put into writing any of the events that made the engagement improper.

My mother insisted upon a premarital chat, but this was conducted the night before the wedding, by which time the information was no longer exactly timely, but I did not let on. I did, however, get the impression that she and my father might also have anticipated their marriage vows. I was shocked. Shocked. It seems most unlike them. Now that I have experienced the physical aspects of love, the mere thought of my parents . . .

It is too much to bear.

Charles's family home is in Dorset, rather close to the sea, but as his father is very much alive, we have let a home in Somerset, halfway between his family and mine. He dislikes town as much as I do. He is thinking of beginning a breeding program for horses, and it's the oddest thing, but apparently the breeding of plants and the breeding of animals are not entirely dissimilar. He and my father have become great friends, which is lovely, except that now my father visits quite often.

Our new home is not large and all of the bedrooms are quite near to one another. Charles has devised a new game he calls "See how quiet Amanda can be."

Then he proceeds to do all measure of wicked things to me—all whilst my father sleeps across the hall!

He is a devil, but I adore him. I can't help it. Especially when he . . .

Oh, wait, I wasn't going to put any such things in writing, was I?

Just know that I am smiling very broadly as I remember it.

And that it was *not* covered in my mother's premarital chat.

I suppose I should admit that last night I lost the game. I was not quiet at all.

My father did not say a word. But he departed rather unexpectedly that afternoon, citing some sort of botanical emergency.

I don't know that plants *have* emergencies, but as soon as he left, Charles insisted upon inspecting our roses for whatever it was my father said was wrong with his.

Except that for some reason he wanted to inspect the roses that were already cut and arranged in a vase in our bedroom.

"We're going to play a new game," he whispered in my ear. "See how noisy Amanda can be."

"How do I win?" I asked. "And what is the prize?"

I can be quite competitive, and so can he, but I think it is safe to say that we both won that time.

And the prize was lovely, indeed.

When He Was Wicked

I will confess that when I wrote the final words of *When He Was Wicked*, it didn't even occur to me to wonder whether Francesca and Michael would have children. Their love story had been so moving and so complete that I felt I had closed the book on them, so to speak. But within days of the book's publication, I began to hear from readers, and everybody wanted to know the same thing: Had Francesca ever had that baby she so desperately wanted? When I sat down to write the 2nd epilogue, I knew that this was the question I must answer . . .

When He Was Wicked:
The 2nd Epilogue

She was counting again.

Counting, always counting.

Seven days since her last menses.

Six until she might be fertile.

Twenty-four to thirty-one until she might expect to bleed again, provided she didn't conceive.

Which she probably wouldn't.

It had been three years since she'd married Michael. Three years. She'd suffered through her courses thirty-three times. She'd counted them, of course; made depressing little hatch marks on a piece of paper she kept tucked away in her desk, in the far back corner of the middle drawer, where Michael wouldn't see.

It would pain him. Not because he wanted a child, which he did, but rather because *she* wanted one so desperately.

And he wanted it for her. Maybe even more than he wanted one himself.

She tried to hide her sorrow. She tried to smile at the breakfast table and pretend that it didn't *matter* that she'd a wad of cloth between her legs, but Michael always saw it in her eyes, and he seemed to hold her closer through the day, kiss her brow more often.

She tried to tell herself that she should count her blessings. And she did. Oh, how she did. Every day. She was Francesca Bridgerton Stirling, Countess of Kilmartin, blessed with two loving families—the one she'd been born into, and the one she'd acquired—twice—through marriage.

She had a husband most women only dreamed of. Handsome, funny, intelligent, and as desperately in love with her as she was with him. Michael made her laugh. He made her days a joy and her nights an adventure. She loved to talk with him, to walk with him, to simply sit in the same room with him and steal glances while they were each pretending to read a book.

She was happy. Truly, she was. And if she never had a baby, at least she had this man—this wonderful, marvelous, miraculous man who understood her in a way that left her breathless.

He knew her. He knew every inch of her, and still, he never ceased to amaze and challenge her.

She loved him. With every breath in her body, she loved him.

And most of the time, it was enough. Most of the time, it was more than enough.

But late at night, after he'd fallen asleep, and she still lay awake, curled up against him, she felt an emptiness that she feared neither of them could ever fill. She would touch her abdomen, and there it was, flat as always, mocking her with its refusal to do the one thing she wanted more than anything else.

And that was when she cried.

There had to be a name for it, Michael thought as he stood at his window, watching Francesca disappear over the hillside toward the Kilmartin family plot. There had to be a name for this particular brand of pain, of torture, really. All he wanted in the world was to make her happy. Oh, for certain there were other things—peace, health, prosperity for his tenants, right-minded men in the seat of prime minister for the next hundred years. But when all was said and done, what he wanted was Francesca's happiness.

He loved her. He always had. It was, or at least it should have been, the most uncomplicated thing in the world.

He loved her. Period. And he would have moved heaven and earth, if it were only in his power, to make her happy.

Except the one thing she wanted most of all, the one thing she craved so desperately and fought so valiantly to hide her pain about, he could not seem to give her.

A child.

And the funny thing was, he was beginning to feel the same pain.

At first, he had felt it just for her. She wanted a child, and therefore he wanted one as well. She wanted to be a mother, and therefore he wanted her to be one. He wanted to see her holding a child, not because it would be his child, but because it would be hers.

He wanted her to have what she desired. And selfishly, he wanted to be the man to give it to her.

But lately, he'd felt the pangs himself. They would visit one of her many brothers or sisters and be immediately surrounded by the next generation of offspring. They would tug on his leg, shriek, "Uncle Michael!" and howl with laughter when he would toss them in the air, always begging for one more minute, one more twirl, one more secret peppermint candy.

The Bridgertons were marvelously fertile. They all seemed to produce exactly the number of offspring they desired. And then perhaps one more, just for good measure.

Except Francesca.

Five hundred and eighty-four days later, Francesca stepped out of the Kilmartin carriage and breathed the fresh, clean air of the Kent countryside. Spring was well under way, and the sun was warm on her cheeks, but when the wind blew, it carried with it the last hints of winter. Francesca didn't mind, though. She'd always liked the tingle of a cold wind on her skin. It drove Michael mad—he was always complaining that he'd never quite readjusted to life in a cold climate after so many years in India.

She was sorry he had not been able to accompany her on the long ride down from Scotland for the christening of Hyacinth's baby daughter, Isabella. He would be there, of course; she and Michael never missed the christening of any of their nieces and nephews. But affairs in Edinburgh had delayed his arrival. Francesca could have delayed her trip as well, but it had been many months since she had seen her family, and she missed them.

It was funny. When she was younger, she'd always been so eager to get away, to set up her own household, her own identity. But now, as she watched her nieces and nephews grow, she found herself visiting more often. She didn't want to miss the milestones. She had just happened to be visiting when Colin's daughter Agatha had taken her first steps. It had been breathtaking. And although she had wept quietly in her bed that night, the tears in her eyes as she'd watched Aggie lurch forward and laugh had been ones of pure joy.

If she wasn't going to be a mother, then by God, at least she would have those moments. She couldn't bear to think of life without them.

Francesca smiled as she handed her cloak to a footman and walked down the familiar corridors of Aubrey Hall. She'd spent much of her childhood here, and at Bridgerton House in London. Anthony and his wife had made some changes, but much was still just as it had always been. The walls were still painted the same creamy white, with the barest undertone of peach. And the Fragonard her father had bought her mother for her thirtieth birthday still hung over the table just outside the door to the rose salon.

"Francesca!"

She turned. It was her mother, rising from her seat in the salon.

"How long have you been standing out there?" Violet asked, coming to greet her.

Francesca embraced her mother. "Not long. I was admiring the painting."

Violet stood beside her and together they regarded the

Fragonard. "It's marvelous, isn't it?" she murmured, a soft, wistful smile touching her face.

"I love it," Francesca said. "I always have. It makes me think of Father."

Violet turned to her in surprise. "It does?"

Francesca could understand her reaction. The painting was of a young woman holding a bouquet of flowers with a note attached. Not a very masculine subject. But she was looking over her shoulder, and her expression was a little bit mischievous, as if, given the correct provocation, she might laugh. Francesca could not remember much of her parents' relationship; she had been but six at the time of her father's death. But she remembered the laughter. The sound of her father's deep, rich chuckle—it lived within her.

"I think your marriage must have been like that," Francesca said, motioning to the painting.

Violet took a half step back and cocked her head to the side. "I think you're right," she said, looking rather delighted by the realization. "I never thought of it quite that way."

"You should take the painting back with you to London," Francesca said. "It's yours, isn't it?"

Violet blushed, and for a brief moment, Francesca saw the young girl she must have been shining out from her eyes. "Yes," she said, "but it belongs here. This was where he gave it to me. And this"—she motioned to its spot of honor on the wall—"was where we hung it together."

"You were very happy," Francesca said. It wasn't a question, just an observation.

"As are you."

Francesca nodded.

Violet reached out and took her hand, patting it gently as they both continued to study the painting. Francesca knew exactly what her mother was thinking about—her infertility, and the fact that they seemed to have unspoken agreement never to talk about it, and really, why should they? What could Violet possibly say that would make it better?

Francesca couldn't say anything, because that would just make her mother feel even worse, and so instead they stood there as they always did, thinking the same thing but never speaking of it, wondering which of them hurt more.

Francesca thought it might be her—hers was the barren womb, after all. But maybe her mother's pain was more acute. Violet was her *mother*, and she was grieving for the lost dreams of her child. Wouldn't that be painful? And the irony was, Francesca would never know. She'd never know what it felt like to hurt for a child because she'd never know what it was to be a mother.

She was almost three and thirty. She did not know any

married lady who had reached that age without conceiving a child. It seemed that children either arrived right away or not at all.

"Has Hyacinth arrived?" Francesca asked, still looking at the painting, still staring at the twinkle in the woman's eye.

"Not yet. But Eloise will be here later this afternoon. She—"

But Francesca heard the catch in her mother's voice before she'd cut herself off. "Is she expecting, then?" she asked.

There was a beat of silence, and then: "Yes."

"That's wonderful." And she meant it. She did, with every last bit of her being. She just didn't know how to make it sound that way.

She didn't want to look at her mother's face. Because then she would cry.

Francesca cleared her throat, tilting her head to the side as if there were an inch of the Fragonard she hadn't yet perused. "Anyone else?" she queried.

She felt her mother stiffen slightly beside her, and she wondered if Violet was deciding whether it was worth it to pretend that she didn't know exactly what she meant.

"Lucy," her mother said quietly.

Francesca finally turned and faced Violet, pulling her hand out of her mother's grasp. "Again?" she asked. Lucy and Gregory had been married for less than two years, but this would be their second child.

Violet nodded. "I'm sorry."

"Don't say that," Francesca said, horrified by how thick her voice sounded. "Don't say you're sorry. It's not something to be sorry about."

"No," her mother said quickly. "That wasn't what I meant."

"You should be delighted for them."

"I am!"

"More delighted for them than you are sorry for me," Francesca choked out.

"Francesca . . ."

Violet tried to reach for her, but Francesca pulled away. "Promise me," she said. "You have to promise me that you will always be more happy than you are sorry."

Violet looked at her helplessly, and Francesca realized that her mother did not know what to say. For her entire life, Violet Bridgerton had been the most sensitive and wonderful of mothers. She always seemed to know what her children needed, exactly when they needed it—whether it was a kind word or a gentle prod, or even a giant proverbial kick in the breeches.

But now, in this moment, Violet was lost. And Francesca was the one who had done it to her.

"I'm sorry, Mother," she said, the words spilling out. "I'm so sorry, I'm so sorry."

"No." Violet rushed forward to embrace her, and this time Francesca did not pull away. "No, darling," Violet said again, softly stroking her hair. "Don't say that, please don't say that."

She shushed and she crooned, and Francesca let her mother hold her. And when Francesca's hot, silent tears fell on her mother's shoulder, neither one of them said a word.

By the time Michael arrived two days later, Francesca had thrown herself into the preparations for little Isabella's christening, and her conversation with her mother was, if not forgotten, at least not at the forefront of her mind. It wasn't as if any of this was new, after all. Francesca was just as barren as she'd been every time she came to England to see her family. The only difference this time was that she'd actually talked to someone about it. A little bit.

As much as she was able.

And yet, somehow, something had been lifted from her. When she'd stood there in the hall, her mother's arms around her, something had poured out from her along with her tears.

And while she still grieved for the babies she would never have, for the first time in a long time, she felt unreservedly happy.

It was strange and wonderful, and she positively refused to question it.

"Aunt Francesca! Aunt Francesca!"

Francesca smiled as she looped her arm through that of her niece. Charlotte was Anthony's youngest, due to turn eight in a month's time. "What is it, poppet?"

"Did you see the baby's dress? It's so *long*."

"I know."

"And frilly."

"Christening dresses are meant to be frilly. Even the boys are covered in lace."

"It seems a waste," Charlotte said with a shrug. "Isabella doesn't *know* she's wearing anything so pretty."

"Ah, but we do."

Charlotte pondered this for a moment. "But I don't care, do you?"

Francesca chuckled. "No, I don't suppose I do. I should love her no matter what she was wearing."

The two of them continued their stroll through the gardens, picking the grape hyacinths to decorate the chapel. They had nearly filled the basket when they heard the unmistakable sound of a carriage coming down the drive.

"I wonder who it is now," Charlotte said, rising to her toes as if that might actually help her see the carriage any better.

"I'm not sure," Francesca replied. Any number of relations were due that afternoon.

"Uncle Michael, maybe."

Francesca smiled. "I hope so."

"I *adore* Uncle Michael," Charlotte said with a sigh, and Francesca almost laughed, because the look in her niece's eye was one she'd seen a thousand times before.

Women adored Michael. It seemed even seven-year-old girls were not immune to his charm.

"Well, he is very handsome," Francesca demurred.

Charlotte shrugged. "I suppose."

"You suppose?" Francesca replied, trying very hard not to smile.

"*I* like him because he tosses me in the air when Father isn't looking."

"He does like to bend the rules."

Charlotte grinned. "I know. It's why I don't tell Father."

Francesca had never thought of Anthony as particularly stern, but he had been the head of the family for over twenty years, and she supposed the experience had endowed him with a certain love of order and tidiness.

And it had to be said—he *did* like to be in charge.

"It shall be our secret," Francesca said, leaning down to whisper in her niece's ear. "And anytime you wish to come visit us in Scotland, you may. We bend rules all the time."

Charlotte's eyes grew huge. "You do?"

"Sometimes we have breakfast for supper."

"Brilliant."

"And we walk in the rain."

Charlotte shrugged. "Everybody walks in the rain."

"Yes, I suppose, but sometimes we *dance*."

Charlotte stepped back. "May I go back with you *now*?"

"That's up to your parents, poppet." Francesca laughed and reached for Charlotte's hand. "But we can dance right now."

"Here?"

Francesca nodded.

"Where everyone can see?"

Francesca looked around. "I don't see anyone watching. And even if there were, who cares?"

Charlotte's lips pursed, and Francesca could practically *see* her mind at work. "Not me!" she announced, and she linked her arm through Francesca's. Together they did a little jig, followed by a Scottish reel, twisting and twirling until they were both breathless.

"Oh, I wish it would rain!" Charlotte laughed.

"Now what would be the fun in that?" came a new voice.

"Uncle Michael!" Charlotte shrieked, launching herself at him.

"And I am instantly forgotten," Francesca said with a wry smile.

Michael looked at her warmly over Charlotte's head. "Not by me," he murmured.

"Aunt Francesca and I have been dancing," Charlotte told him.

"I know. I saw you from inside the house. I especially enjoyed the new one."

"What new one?"

Michael pretended to look confused. "The new dance you were doing."

"We weren't doing any new dances," Charlotte replied, her brows knitting together.

"Then what was that one that involved throwing yourself on the grass?"

Francesca bit her lip to keep from smiling.

"We *fell*, Uncle Michael."

"No!"

"We did!"

"It was a vigorous dance," Francesca confirmed.

"You must be exceptionally graceful, then, because it looked *completely* as if you'd done it on purpose."

"We didn't! We didn't!" Charlotte said excitedly. "We really did just fall. By accident!"

"I suppose I will believe you," he said with a sigh, "but only because I know you are far too trustworthy to lie."

She looked him in the eye with a melting expression. "I would never lie to you, Uncle Michael," she said.

He kissed her cheek and set her down. "Your mother says it's time for dinner."

"But you just got here!"

"I'm not going anywhere. You need your sustenance after all the dancing."

"I'm not hungry," she offered.

"Pity, then," he said, "because I was going to teach you to waltz this afternoon, and you certainly cannot do that on an empty stomach."

Charlotte's eyes grew to near circles. "Really? Father said I cannot learn until I am ten."

Michael gave her one of those devastating half smiles that still made Francesca tingle. "We don't have to tell him, do we?"

"Oh, Uncle Michael, I *love* you," she said fervently, and then, after one extremely vigorous hug, Charlotte ran off to Aubrey Hall.

"And another one falls," Francesca said with a shake of her head, watching her niece dash across the fields.

Michael took her hand and tugged her toward him. "What is that supposed to mean?"

Francesca grinned a little and sighed a little and said, "I would *never* lie to you."

He kissed her soundly. "I certainly hope not."

She looked up into his silvery eyes and let herself ease against the warmth of his body. "It seems no woman is immune."

"How lucky I am, then, that I fall under the spell of only one."

"Lucky for *me*."

"Well, yes," he said with affected modesty, "but I wasn't going to say it."

She swatted him on the arm.

He kissed her in return. "I missed you."

"I missed you, too."

"And how is the clan Bridgerton?" he asked, linking his arm through hers.

"Rather wonderful," Francesca replied. "I am having a splendid time, actually."

"Actually?" he echoed, looking vaguely amused.

Francesca steered him away from the house. It had been over a week since she'd had his company, and she didn't wish to share him just then. "What do you mean?" she asked.

"You said 'actually.' As if you were surprised."

"Of course not," she said. But then she thought. "I

always have a lovely time when I visit my family," she said carefully.

"But . . ."

"But it's better this time." She shrugged. "I don't know why."

Which wasn't precisely the truth. That moment with her mother—there had been magic in those tears.

But she couldn't tell him that. He'd hear the bit about crying and nothing else, and then he'd worry, and she'd feel terrible for worrying him, and she was *tired* of all that.

Besides, he was a man. He'd never understand, anyway.

"I feel happy," she announced. "Something in the air."

"The sun *is* shining," he observed.

She gave him a jaunty, single-shouldered shrug and leaned back against a tree. "Birds are singing."

"Flowers blooming?"

"Just a few," she admitted.

He regarded the landscape. "All the moment needs is a cherubic little bunny hopping across the field."

She smiled blissfully and leaned into him for a kiss. "Bucolic splendor is a marvelous thing."

"Indeed." His lips found hers with familiar hunger. "I missed you," he said, his voice husky with desire.

She let out a little moan as he nipped her ear. "I know. You said that."

"It bears repeating."

Francesca meant to say something witty about never tiring of hearing it, but at that moment she found herself pressed rather breathlessly against the tree, one of her legs lifted up around his hips.

"You wear *far* too many clothes," he growled.

"We're a little too close to the house," she gasped, her belly clenching with need as he pressed more intimately against her.

"How far," he murmured, one his hands stealing under her skirts, "is 'not too close'?"

"Not far."

He drew back and gazed at her. "Really?"

"Really." Her lips curved, and she felt devilish. She felt powerful. And she wanted to take charge. Of him. Of her life. Of everything.

"Come with me," she said impulsively, and she grabbed his hand and ran.

Michael had missed his wife. At night, when she was not beside him, the bed felt cold, and the air felt empty. Even when he was tired, and his body was not hungry for her, he craved her presence, her scent, her warmth.

He missed the sound of her breathing. He missed the way the mattress moved differently when there was a second body on it.

He knew, even though she was more reticent than he, and far less likely to use such passionate words, that she felt the same way. But even so, he was pleasantly surprised to be racing across a field, letting her take the lead, knowing that in a few short minutes he would be buried deep within her.

"Here," she said, skidding to a halt at the bottom of a hill.

"Here?" he asked dubiously. There was no cover of trees, nothing to block them from sight should anyone stroll by.

She sat. "No one comes this way."

"No one?"

"The grass is very soft," she said seductively, patting a spot beside her.

"I'm not even going to ask how you know that," he muttered.

"Picnics," she said, her expression delightfully outraged, "with my *dolls*."

He took off his coat and laid it like a blanket on the grass. The ground was softly sloped, which he would imagine would be more comfortable for her than horizontal.

He looked at her. He looked at the coat. She didn't move.

"You," she said.

"Me?"

"Lie down," she ordered.

He did. With alacrity.

And then, before he'd had time to make a comment, to tease or cajole, or even really to breathe, she'd straddled him.

"Oh, dear G—" he gasped, but he couldn't finish. She was kissing him now, her mouth hot and hungry and aggressive. It was all deliciously familiar—he loved knowing every little bit of her, from the slope of her breast to the rhythm of her kisses—and yet this time, she felt a little . . .

New.

Renewed.

One of his hands moved to the back of her head. At home he liked to pull the pins out one by one, watching each lock tumble from her coiffure. But today he was too needy, too urgent, and he didn't have patience for—

"What was that for?" he asked. She had yanked his hand away.

Her eyes narrowed languidly. "I'm in charge," she whispered.

His body tightened. More. Dear God, she was going to kill him.

"Don't go slow," he gasped.

But he didn't think she was listening. She was taking her time, undoing his breeches, letting her hands flutter along his belly until she found him.

"Frannie . . ."

One finger. That's all she gave him. One featherlight finger along his shaft.

She turned, looked at him. "This is fun," she remarked.

He just focused on trying to breathe.

"I love you," she said softly, and he felt her rise. She hoisted her skirts to her thighs as she positioned herself, and then, with one spectacularly swift stroke, she took him within her, her body coming to rest against his, leaving him embedded to the hilt.

He wanted to move then. He wanted to thrust up, or flip her over and pound until they were both nothing but dust, but her hands were firm on his hips, and when he looked up at her, her eyes were closed, and she almost looked as if she were concentrating.

Her breathing was slow and steady, but it was loud, too, and with each exhale she seemed to bear down on him just a little bit heavier.

"Frannie," he groaned, because he didn't know what else to do. He wanted her to move faster. Or harder. Or something, but all she did was rock and back and forth, her hips arching and curving in delicious torment. He clutched her hips, intending to move her up and down, but she opened her eyes and shook her head with a soft, blissful smile.

"I like it this way," she said.

He wanted something different. He *needed* something

different, but when she looked down at him, she looked so damned happy that he could deny her nothing. And then, sure enough, she began to shudder, and it was strange, because he knew the feel of her climax so well, and yet this time it seemed softer . . . and stronger, at the same time.

She swayed, and she rocked, and then she let out a little scream and sagged against him.

And then, to his utter and complete surprise, he came. He hadn't thought he was ready. He hadn't thought he was remotely near climax, not that it would have taken long had he been able to move beneath her. But then, without warning, he had simply exploded.

They lay that way for some time, the sun falling gently on them. She burrowed her face in his neck, and he held her, wondering how it was possible that such moments existed.

Because it was perfect. And he would have stayed there forever, had he been able. And even though he didn't ask her, he knew she felt the same.

They'd meant to go home two days after the christening, Francesca thought as she watched one of her nephews tackle the other to the ground, but here it was, three weeks out, and they had not even begun to pack.

"No broken bones, I hope."

Francesca smiled up at her sister Eloise, who had also elected to stay on at Aubrey Hall for an extended visit. "No," she answered, wincing slightly when the future Duke of Hastings—otherwise known as Davey, aged eleven—let out a war whoop as he jumped from a tree. "But it's not for lack of trying."

Eloise took a seat beside her and tilted her face to the sun. "I'll put my bonnet on in a minute, I swear it," she said.

"I can't quite determine the rules of the game," Francesca remarked.

Eloise didn't bother to open her eyes. "That's because there are none."

Francesca watched the chaos with fresh perspective. Oliver, Eloise's twelve-year-old stepson, had grabbed hold of a ball—since when had there been a ball?—and was racing across the lawn. He appeared to reach his goal—not that Francesca would ever be sure whether that was the giant oak stump that had been there since she was a child or Miles, Anthony's second son, who had been sitting cross-legged and cross-armed since Francesca had come outside ten minutes earlier.

But whichever was the case, Oliver must have won a point, because he slammed the ball against the ground and then jumped up and down with a triumphant cry. Miles must have been on his team—this was the first indication Francesca had that there were teams—because he hopped to his feet and celebrated in kind.

Eloise opened one eye. "My child didn't kill anyone, did he?"

"No."

"No one killed him?"

Francesca smiled. "No."

"Good." Eloise yawned and resettled into her chaise.

Francesca thought about her words. "Eloise?"

"Mmmm?"

"Do you ever . . ." She frowned. There really wasn't any right way to ask this. "Do you ever love Oliver and Amanda . . ."

"Less?" Eloise supplied.

"Yes."

Eloise sat up straighter and opened her eyes. "No."

"Really?" It wasn't that Francesca didn't believe her. She loved her nieces and nephews with every breath in her body; she would have laid down her life for any one of them—Oliver and Amanda included—without even a moment's hesitation. But she hadn't ever given birth. She had never carried a child in her womb—not for long, anyway—and didn't know if somehow that made it different. Made it more.

If she had a baby, one of her own, born of her blood and Michael's, would she suddenly realize that this love she felt now for Charlotte and Oliver and Miles and all the others—Would it suddenly feel like a wisp next to what was in her heart for her own child?

Did it make a difference?

Did she want it to make a difference?

"I thought it would," Eloise admitted. "Of course I loved Oliver and Amanda long before I had Penelope. How could I not? They are pieces of Phillip. And," she continued, her face growing thoughtful, as if she had never quite delved into this before, "they are . . . themselves. And I am their mother."

Francesca smiled wistfully.

"But even so," Eloise continued, "before I had Penelope, and even when I was carrying her, I thought it would be different." She paused. "It *is* different." She paused again. "But it's not less. It's not a question of levels or amounts, or even . . . really . . . the nature of it." Eloise shrugged. "I can't explain it."

Francesca looked back to the game, which had resumed with new intensity. "No," she said softly, "I think you did."

There was a long silence, and then Eloise said, "You don't . . . talk about it much."

Francesca shook her head gently. "No."

"Do you want to?"

She thought about that for a moment. "I don't know." She turned to her sister. They had been at sixes and sevens for much of their childhood, but in so many ways Eloise was like the other half of her coin. They looked so alike, save for the color of their eyes, and they even shared the same birthday, just one year apart.

Eloise was watching her with a tender curiosity, a sympathy that, just a few weeks ago, would have been heartbreaking. But now it was simply comforting. Francesca didn't feel pitied, she felt loved.

"I'm happy," Francesca said. And she was. She really was. For once she didn't feel that aching emptiness hiding underneath. She'd even forgotten to count. She didn't know how many days it had been since her last menses, and it felt so bloody *good*.

"I hate numbers," she muttered.

"I beg your pardon?"

She bit back a smile. "Nothing."

The sun, which had been obscured behind a thin layer of cloud, suddenly popped into the open. Eloise shaded her eyes with her hand as she sat back. "Good heavens," she remarked. "I think Oliver just *sat* on Miles."

Francesca laughed, and then, before she even knew what she was about, stood. "Do you think they'll let me play?"

Eloise looked at her as if she'd gone mad, which, Francesca thought with a shrug, perhaps she had.

Eloise looked at Francesca, and then at the boys, and then back at Francesca. And then she stood. "If you do it, I'll do it."

"You can't do it," Francesca said. "You're pregnant."

"Barely," Eloise said with a scoff. "Besides, Oliver wouldn't dare sit on *me*." She held out her arm. "Shall we?"

"I believe we shall." Francesca linked her arm through her sister's, and together they ran down the hill, shouting like banshees and loving every minute of it.

"I heard you made quite a scene this afternoon," Michael said, perching on the edge of the bed.

Francesca did not move. Not even an eyelid. "I'm exhausted" was all she said.

He took in the dusty hem of her dress. "And dirty, too."

"Too tired to wash."

"Anthony said that Miles said that he was quite impressed. Apparently you throw quite well for a girl."

"It would have been brilliant," she replied, "had I been informed that I wasn't meant to use my hands."

He chuckled. "What game, exactly, were you playing?"

"I have no idea." She let out an exhausted little moan. "Would you rub my feet?"

He pushed himself farther onto the bed and slid her dress up to mid-calf. Her feet were filthy. "Good Lord," he exclaimed. "Did you go barefoot?"

"I couldn't very well play in my slippers."

"How did Eloise fare?"

"She, apparently, throws like a boy."

"I thought you weren't meant to use your hands."

At that, she pushed herself indignantly up on her elbows. "I *know*. It depended on what end of the field one was at. Whoever heard of such a thing."

He took her foot in his hands, making a mental note to wash them later—his hands that was, she could take care of her own feet. "I had no idea you were so competitive," he remarked.

"It runs in the family," she mumbled. "No, no, there. Yes, right there. Harder. Ooooooohhhh . . ."

"Why do I feel as if I heard this before," he mused, "except that I was having much more fun?"

"Just be quiet and keep rubbing my feet."

"At your service, Your Majesty," he murmured, smiling when she realized she was perfectly content to be referred to as such. After a minute or two of silence, save for the occasional moan from Francesca, he asked, "How much longer do you wish to stay?"

"Are you eager to return home?"

"I do have matters to attend to," he replied, "but nothing that cannot wait. I'm rather enjoying your family, actually."

She quirked a brow—and a smile. "Actually?"

"Indeed. Although it was a bit daunting when your sister beat me at the shooting match."

"She beats everyone. She always has. Shoot with Gregory next time. He can't hit a tree."

Michael moved on to the other foot. Francesca looked so happy and relaxed. Not just now, but at the supper table, and in the drawing room, and when she was chasing her nieces and nephews, and even at night, when he was making love to her in their huge four-poster bed. He was ready to go home, back to Kilmartin, which was ancient and drafty but indelibly theirs. But he'd happily remain here forever, if it meant Francesca would always look like this.

"I think you're right," she said.

"Of course," he replied, "but about what, exactly?"

"It's time to go home."

"I didn't say that it was. I merely inquired as to your intentions."

"You didn't have to say it," she said.

"If you want to stay—"

She shook her head. "I don't. I want to go home. Our home." With a stiff groan, she sat up all the way, curling her legs beneath her. "This has been lovely, and I have had such a wonderful time, but I miss Kilmartin."

"Are you certain?"

"I miss you."

He lifted his brows. "I'm right here."

She smiled and leaned forward. "I miss having you to myself."

"You need only say the word, my lady. Anytime, anywhere. I'll whisk you off and let you have your way with me."

She chuckled. "Perhaps right now."

He thought that was an excellent idea, but chivalry forced him to say, "I thought you were sore."

"Not that sore. Not if you do all the work."

"That, my dear, is not a problem." He pulled his shirt over his head and lay down beside her, giving her a long, delicious kiss. He pulled back with a contented sigh and then just gazed at her. "You're beautiful," he whispered. "More than ever."

She smiled—that lazy, warm smile that meant she'd been recently pleasured, or knew she was about to be.

He loved that smile.

He went to work on the buttons at the back of her frock and was halfway down when all of a sudden a thought popped into his head. "Wait," he said. "Can you?"

"Can I what?"

He stopped, frowning as he tried to count it out in his head. Oughtn't she be bleeding? "Isn't it your time?" he asked.

Her lips parted, and she blinked. "No," she said, sounding a little bit startled—not by his question but by her answer. "No, I'm not."

He shifted position, moving back a few inches so that he could better see her face. "Do you think . . . ?"

"I don't know." She was blinking rapidly now, and he could hear that her breathing had grown more rapid. "I suppose. I could . . ."

He wanted to whoop with joy, but he dared not. Not yet. "When do you think—"

"—I'll know? I don't know. Maybe—"

"—in a month? Two?"

"Maybe two. Maybe sooner. I don't know." Her hand flew to her belly. "It might not take."

"It might not," he said carefully.

"But it might."

"It might."

He felt laughter bubbling within him, a strange giddiness in his belly, growing and tickling until it burst from his lips.

"We can't be sure," she warned, but he could see that she was excited, too.

"No," he said, but somehow he knew they were.

"I don't want to get my hopes up."

"No, no, of course we mustn't."

Her eyes grew wide, and she placed both hands on her belly, still absolutely, completely flat.

"Do you feel anything?" he whispered.

She shook her head. "It would be too early, anyway."

He knew that. He knew that he knew that. He didn't know why he'd asked.

And then Francesca said the damnedest thing. "But he's there," she whispered. "I know it."

"Frannie . . ." If she was wrong, if her heart was broken again—he just didn't think he could bear it.

But she was shaking her head. "It's true," she said, and she wasn't insisting. She wasn't trying to convince him, or even herself. He could hear it in her voice. Somehow she knew.

"Have you been feeling ill?" he asked.

She shook her head.

"Have you— Good God, you shouldn't have been playing with the boys this afternoon."

"Eloise did."

"Eloise can do what she damned well pleases. She isn't *you*."

She smiled. Like a Madonna, she smiled, he would have sworn it. And she said, "I won't break."

He remembered when she'd miscarried years ago. It had not been his child, but he had felt her pain, hot and searing, like a fist around his heart. His cousin—her first husband—had been dead a scant few weeks, and they were both reeling from that loss. When she'd lost John's baby . . .

He didn't think either one of them could survive another loss like that.

"Francesca," he said urgently, "you must take care. *Please*."

"It won't happen again," she said, shaking her head.

"How do you *know*?"

She gave him a bewildered shrug. "I don't know. I just do."

Dear God, he prayed she was not deluding herself. "Do you want to tell your family?" he asked quietly.

She shook her head. "Not yet. Not because I have any fears," she hastened to add. "I just want—" Her lips pressed together in the most adorably giddy little smile. "I just want it to be mine for a little while. Ours."

He brought her hand to his lips. "How long is a little while?"

"I'm not sure." But her eyes were growing crafty. "I'm not quite sure . . ."

One year later . . .

Violet Bridgerton loved all her children equally, but she loved them *differently* as well. And when it came to missing them, she did so in what she considered a most logical manner. Her heart pined the most for the one she'd seen the least. And that was why, as she waited in the draw-ing room at Aubrey Hall, waiting for a carriage bearing the Kilmartin crest to roll down the drive, she found her-self fidgety and eager, jumping up every five minutes to watch through the window.

"She wrote that they would arrive today," Kate re-assured her.

"I know," Violet replied with a sheepish smile. "It's just that I haven't seen her for an entire year. I know Scotland is far, but I've never gone an entire year without seeing one of my children before."

"Really?" Kate asked. "That's remarkable."

"We all have our priorities," Violet said, deciding there was no point in trying to pretend she wasn't jumping at the bit. She set down her embroidery and moved to the window, craning her neck when she thought she saw something glinting in the sunlight.

"Even when Colin was traveling so much?" Kate asked.

"The longest he was gone was three hundred and forty-two days," Violet replied. "When he was traveling in the Mediterranean."

"You counted?"

Violet shrugged. "I can't help myself. I like to count." She thought of all the counting she'd done when her chil-dren were growing up, making sure she had as many offspring at the end of an outing as she'd had at the beginning. "It helps to keep track of things."

Kate smiled as she reached down and rocked the cradle at her feet. "I shall never complain about the logistics of managing four."

Violet crossed the room to peek down at her newest grandchild. Little Mary had been a bit of a surprise, coming so many years after Charlotte. Kate had thought herself done with childbearing, but then, ten months earlier, she'd got out bed, walked calmly to the chamber pot, emptied the contents of her stomach, and announced to Anthony, "I believe we're expecting again."

Or so they'd told Violet. She made it a point to stay out of her grown children's bedrooms except in the case of illness or childbirth.

"I never complained," Violet said softly. Kate didn't hear, but Violet hadn't meant her to. She smiled down at Mary, sleeping sweetly under a purple blanket. "I think your mother would have been delighted," she said, looking up at Kate.

Kate nodded, her eyes misting over. Her mother—actually her stepmother, but Mary Sheffield had raised her from a little girl—had passed away a month before Kate realized that she was pregnant. "I know it makes no sense," Kate said, leaning down to examine her child's face more closely, "but I would swear she looks a bit like her."

Violet blinked and tilted her head to the side. "I think you're right."

"Something about the eyes."

"No, it's the nose."

"Do you think? I rather thought—Oh look!" Kate pointed toward the window. "Is that Francesca?"

Violet straightened and rushed to the window. "It is!" she exclaimed. "Oh, and the sun is shining. I'm going to wait outside."

With nary a backward glance she grabbed her shawl off a side table and dashed into the hall. It had been so long since she'd seen Frannie, but that wasn't the only reason she was so eager to see her. Francesca had changed during her last visit, back at Isabella's christening. It was hard to explain, but Violet had sensed that something had shifted within her.

Of all her children, Francesca had always been the most quiet, the most private. She loved her family, but she also loved being apart from them, forging her own identity, making her own life. It was not surprising that she had never chosen to share her feelings about the most painful corner of her life—her infertility. But last time, even though they had not spoken about it explicitly, something had still passed within them, and Violet had almost felt as if she'd been able to absorb some of her grief.

When Francesca had departed, the clouds behind her

eyes had been lifted. Violet didn't know whether she had finally accepted her fate, or whether she had simply learned how to rejoice in what she had, but Francesca had seemed, for the first time in Violet's recent memory, unreservedly happy.

Violet ran through the hall—really, at her age!—and pushed open the front door so that she could wait in the drive. Francesca's carriage was nearly there, starting the final turn so that one of the doors would be facing the house.

Violet could see Michael through the window. He waved. She beamed.

"Oh, I've missed you!" she exclaimed, hurrying forward as he hopped down. "You must promise never to wait so long again."

"As if I could refuse you anything," he said, leaning down to kiss her cheek. He turned then, holding his arm out to assist Francesca.

Violet embraced her daughter, then stepped back to look at her. Frannie was . . .

Glowing.

She was positively radiant.

"I missed you, Mother," she said.

Violet would have made a reply, but she found herself unexpectedly choked up. She felt her lips press together, then twitch at the corners as she fought to contain her tears. She didn't know why she was so emotional. Yes, it had been over a year, but hadn't she gone three hundred and forty-two days before? This was not so very different.

"I have something for you," Francesca said, and Violet could have sworn her eyes were glistening, too.

Francesca turned back to the carriage and held out her arms. A maid appeared in the doorway, holding some sort of bundle, which she then handed down to her mistress.

Violet gasped. Dear God, it couldn't be . . .

"Mother," Francesca said softly, cradling the precious little bundle, "this is John."

The tears, which had been waiting patiently in Violet's eyes, began to roll. "Frannie," she whispered, taking the baby into her arms, "why didn't you tell me?"

And Francesca—her maddening, inscrutable third daughter—said, "I don't know."

"He's beautiful," Violet said, not caring that she'd been kept in the dark. She didn't care about anything in that moment—nothing but the tiny boy in her arms, gazing up at her with an impossibly wise expression.

"He has your eyes," Violet said, looking up at Francesca.

Frannie nodded, and her smile was almost silly, as if she couldn't quite believe it. "I know."

"And your mouth."

"I think you're right."

"And your—oh, my, I think he has your nose as well."

"I'm told," Michael said in an amused voice, "that I was involved in his creation, too, but I have yet to see any evidence."

Francesca looked at him with so much love that it nearly took Violet's breath away. "He has your charm," she said.

Violet laughed, and then she laughed again. There was too much happiness inside of her—she couldn't possibly hold it in. "I think it's time we introduced this little fellow to his family," she said. "Don't you?"

Francesca held out her arms to take the baby, but Violet turned away. "Not just yet," she said. She wanted to hold him a while longer. Maybe until Tuesday.

"Mother, I think he might be hungry."

Violet assumed an arch expression. "He'll let us know."

"But—"

"I know a thing or two about babies, Francesca Bridgerton Stirling." Violet grinned down at John. "They adore their grandmamas, for example."

He gurgled and cooed, and then—she was positive—he smiled.

"Come with me, little one," she whispered, "I have so much to tell you."

And behind her, Francesca turned to Michael and said,

"Do you think we'll get him back for the duration of the visit?"

He shook his head, then added, "It'll give us more time to see about getting the little fellow a sister."

"Michael!"

"Listen to the man," Violet called, not bothering to turn around.

"Good heavens," Francesca muttered.

But she did listen.

And she did enjoy.

And nine months later, she said good morning to Janet Helen Stirling.

Who looked *exactly* like her father.

It's In His Kiss

If ever there was an ending in one of my books that read-ers howled about, it was the one in *It's In His Kiss*, when Hyacinth's daughter finds the diamonds for which Hya-cinth has been searching for more than a decade . . . and then puts them back. I thought this was exactly what a daughter of Hyacinth and Gareth would do, and really, wasn't it poetic justice that Hyacinth (a character whom I can only call "a piece of work") should have a daughter who is just like her?

But in the end, I agreed with readers: Hyacinth de-served to find those diamonds . . . eventually.

It's In His Kiss:
The 2nd Epilogue

1847, and all has come full circle. Truly.

Hmmph.

It was official, then.

She had become her mother.

Hyacinth St. Clair fought the urge to bury her face in her hands as she sat on the cushioned bench at Mme. Langlois, Dressmaker, by far the most fashionable modiste in all London.

She counted to ten, in three languages, and then, just for good measure, swallowed and let out an exhale. Because, really, it would not do to lose her temper in such a public setting.

No matter how desperately she wanted to *throttle* her daughter.

"Mummy." Isabella poked her head out from behind the curtain. Hyacinth noted that the word had been a statement, not a question.

"Yes?" she returned, affixing onto her face an expression of such placid serenity she might have qualified for one of those pietà paintings they had seen when last they'd traveled to Rome.

"Not the pink."

Hyacinth waved a hand. Anything to refrain from speaking.

"Not the purple, either."

"I don't believe I suggested purple," Hyacinth murmured.

"The blue's not right, and nor is the red, and frankly, I just don't understand this insistence society seems to have upon white, and well, if I might express my opinion—"

Hyacinth felt herself slump. Who knew motherhood could be so tiring? And really, shouldn't she be *used* to this by now?

"—a girl really ought to wear the color that most complements her complexion, and not what some over-important ninny at Almack's deems fashionable."

"I agree wholeheartedly," Hyacinth said.

"You do?" Isabella's face lit up, and Hyacinth's breath positively caught, because she looked so like her own mother in that moment it was almost eerie.

"Yes," Hyacinth said, "but you're still getting at least one in white."

"But—"

"No buts!"

"But—"

"Isabella."

Isabella muttered something in Italian.

"I heard that," Hyacinth said sharply.

Isabella smiled, a curve of lips so sweet that only her own mother (certainly *not* her father, who freely admitted himself wound around her finger) would recognize the deviousness underneath. "But did you understand it?" she asked, blinking three times in rapid succession.

And because Hyacinth knew that she would be trapped by her lie, she gritted her teeth and told the truth. "No."

"I didn't think so," Isabella said. "But if you're interested, what I said was—"

"Not—" Hyacinth stopped, forcing her voice to a lower volume; panic at what Isabella might say had caused her outburst to come out overly loud. She cleared her throat. "Not now. Not here," she added meaningfully. Good heavens, her daughter had no sense of propriety. She had such opinions, and while Hyacinth was always in favor of a female with opinions, she was even more in favor of a female who knew *when* to share such opinions.

Isabella stepped out of her dressing room, clad in a lovely gown of white with sage green trimming that Hyacinth knew she'd turn her nose up at, and sat beside her on the bench. "What are you whispering about?" she asked.

"I wasn't whispering," Hyacinth said.

"Your lips were moving."

"Were they?"

"They were," Isabella confirmed.

"If you must know, I was sending off an apology to your grandmother."

"Grandmama Violet?" Isabella asked, looking around. "Is she here?"

"No, but I thought she was deserving of my remorse, nonetheless."

Isabella blinked and cocked her head to the side in question. "Why?"

"All those times," Hyacinth said, hating how tired her voice sounded. "All those times she said to me, 'I hope you have a child *just like you* . . .'"

"And you do," Isabella said, surprising her with a light kiss to the cheek. "Isn't it just delightful?"

Hyacinth looked at her daughter. Isabella was nineteen. She'd made her debut the year before, to grand success. She was, Hyacinth thought rather objectively, far prettier than she herself had ever been. Her hair was a breathtaking strawberry blond, a throwback to some long-forgotten ancestor on heaven knew which side of the family. And the curls—oh, my, they were the bane of Isabella's existence, but Hyacinth adored them. When Isabella had been a toddler, they'd bounced in perfect little ringlets, completely untamable and always delightful.

And now . . . Sometimes Hyacinth looked at her and saw the woman she'd become, and she couldn't even breathe, so powerful was the emotion squeezing across her chest. It was a love she couldn't have imagined, so fierce and so tender, and yet at the same time the girl drove her positively batty.

Right now, for example.

Isabella was smiling innocently at her. Too innocently, truth be told, and then she looked down at the slightly poufy skirt on the dress Hyacinth loved (and Isabella would hate) and picked absently at the green ribbon trimmings.

"Mummy?" she said.

It was a question this time, not a statement, which meant that Isabella wanted something, and (for a change) wasn't quite certain how to go about getting it.

"Do you think this year—"

"No," Hyacinth said. And this time she really did send up a silent apology to her mother. Good heavens, was this what Violet had gone through? *Eight* times?

"You don't even know what I was going to ask."

"Of course I know what you were going to ask. When will you learn that I *always* know?"

"Now that is not true."

"It's more true than it is untrue."

"You can be quite supercilious, did you know that?"

Hyacinth shrugged. "I'm your mother."

Isabella's lips clamped into a line, and Hyacinth enjoyed a full four seconds of peace before she asked, "But this year, do you think we can—"

"We are not traveling."

Isabella's lips parted with surprise. Hyacinth fought the urge to let out a triumphal shout.

"How did you kn—"

Hyacinth patted her daughter's hand. "I told you, I always know. And much as I'm sure we would all enjoy a bit of travel, we will remain in London for the season, and you, my girl, will smile and dance and look for a husband."

Cue the bit about becoming her mother.

Hyacinth sighed. Violet Bridgerton was probably laughing about this, this very minute. In fact, she'd been laughing about it for nineteen years. "Just like you,"

Violet liked to say, grinning at Hyacinth as she tousled Isabella's curls. "Just like you."

"Just like you, Mother," Hyacinth murmured with a smile, picturing Violet's face in her mind. "And now I'm just like you."

An hour or so later. Gareth, too, has grown and changed, although, we soon shall see, not in any of the ways that matter . . .

Gareth St. Clair leaned back in his chair, pausing to savor his brandy as he glanced around his office. There really was a remarkable sense of satisfaction in a job well-done and completed on time. It wasn't a sensation he'd been used to in his youth, but it was something he'd come to enjoy on a near daily basis now.

It had taken several years to restore the St. Clair fortunes to a respectable level. His father—he'd never quite got 'round to calling him anything else—had stopped his systematic plundering and eased into a vague sort of neglect once he learned the truth about Gareth's birth. So Gareth supposed it could have been a great deal worse.

But when Gareth had assumed the title, he discovered that he'd inherited debts, mortgages, and houses that had been emptied of almost all valuables. Hyacinth's dowry, which had increased with prudent investments upon their marriage, went a long way toward fixing the situation, but still, Gareth had had to work harder and with more diligence than he'd ever dreamed possible to wrench his family out of debt.

The funny thing was, he'd enjoyed it.

Who would have thought that he, of all people, would find such satisfaction in hard work? His desk was spotless, his ledgers neat and tidy, and he could put his fingers on any important document in under a minute. His accounts always summed properly, his properties were thriving, and his tenants were healthy and prosperous.

He took another sip of his drink, letting the mellow fire roll down his throat. Heaven.

Life was perfect. Truly. Perfect.

George was finishing up at Cambridge, Isabella would surely choose a husband this year, and Hyacinth . . .

He chuckled. Hyacinth was still Hyacinth. She'd become a bit more sedate with age, or maybe it was just that motherhood had smoothed off her rough edges, but she was still the same outspoken, delightful, perfectly wonderful Hyacinth.

She drove him crazy half the time, but it was a *nice* sort of crazy, and even though he sometimes sighed to his friends and nodded tiredly when they all complained about their wives, secretly he knew he was the luckiest man in London. Hell, England even. The world.

He set his drink down, then tapped his fingers against the elegantly wrapped box sitting on the corner of his desk. He'd purchased it that morning at Mme. LaFleur, the dress shop he knew Hyacinth did not frequent, in order to spare her the embarrassment of having to deal with salespeople who knew every piece of lingerie in her wardrobe.

French silk, Belgian lace.

He smiled. Just a little bit of French silk, trimmed with a minuscule amount of Belgian lace.

It would look heavenly on her.

What there was of it.

He sat back in his chair, savoring the daydream. It was going to be a long, lovely night. Maybe even . . .

His eyebrows rose as he tried to remember his wife's schedule for the day. Maybe even a long, lovely afternoon. When *was* she due home? And would she have either of the children with her?

He closed his eyes, picturing her in various states of undress, followed by various interesting poses, followed by various *fascinating* activities.

He groaned. She was going to have to return home *very* soon, because his imagination was far too active not to be satisfied, and—

"*Gareth!*"

Not the most mellifluous of tones. The lovely erotic

haze floating about his head disappeared entirely. Well, almost entirely. Hyacinth might not have looked the least bit inclined for a bit of afternoon sport as she stood in the doorway, her eyes narrowed and jaw clenched, but she was *there*, and that was half the battle.

"Shut the door," he murmured, rising to his feet.

"Do you know what your daughter did?"

"Your daughter, you mean?"

"Our daughter," she ground out. But she shut the door.

"Do I want to know?"

"Gareth!"

"Very well," he sighed, followed by a dutiful "What did she do?"

He'd had this conversation before, of course. Countless times. The answer usually had something to do with something involving marriage and Isabella's somewhat unconventional views on the subject. And of course, Hyacinth's frustration with the whole situation.

It rarely varied.

"Well, it wasn't so much what she did," Hyacinth said.

He hid his smile. This was also not unexpected.

"It's more what she won't do."

"Jump to your bidding?"

"*Gareth.*"

He halved the distance between them. "Aren't I enough?"

"I beg your pardon?"

He reached out, tugged at her hand, pulled her gently against him. "I always jump to your bidding," he murmured.

She recognized the look in his eye. "Now?" She twisted around until she could see the closed door. "Isabella is upstairs."

"She won't hear."

"But she could——"

His lips found her neck. "There's a lock on the door."

"But she'll know——"

He started working on the buttons on her frock. He was *very* good at buttons. "She's a smart girl," he said, stepping back to enjoy his handiwork as the fabric fell away. He *loved* when his wife didn't wear a chemise.

"Gareth!"

He leaned down and took one rosy-tipped breast into his mouth before she could object.

"Oh, Gareth!" And her knees went weak. Just enough for him to scoop her up and take her to the sofa. The one with the extra-deep cushions.

"More?"

"God, yes," she groaned.

He slid his hand under her skirt until he could tickle her senseless. "Such token resistance," he murmured. "Admit it. You always want me."

"Twenty years of marriage isn't admission enough?"

"Twenty-two years, and I want to hear it from your lips."

She moaned when he slipped a finger inside of her. "Almost always," she conceded. "I almost always want you."

He sighed for dramatic effect, even as he smiled into her neck. "I shall have to work harder, then."

He looked up at her. She was gazing down at him with an arch expression, clearly over her fleeting attempt at uprightness and respectability.

"Much harder," she agreed. "And a bit faster, too, while you're at it."

He laughed out loud at that.

"Gareth!" Hyacinth might be a wanton in private, but she was always aware of the servants.

"Don't worry," he said with a smile. "I'll be quiet. I'll be very, very quiet." With one easy movement, he bunched her skirts well above her waist and slid down until his head was between her legs. "It's you, my darling, who will have to control your volume."

"Oh. Oh. Oh . . ."

"More?"

"Definitely more."

He licked her then. She tasted like heaven. And when she squirmed, it was always a treat.

"Oh my heavens. Oh my . . . Oh my . . ."

He smiled against her, then swirled a circle on her until she let out a quiet little shriek. He loved doing this to her, loved bringing her, his capable and articulate wife, to senseless abandon.

Twenty-two years. Who would have thought that after twenty-two years he'd still want this one woman, this one woman only, and this one woman so intensely?

"Oh, Gareth," she was panting. "Oh, Gareth . . . More, Gareth . . ."

He redoubled his efforts. She was close. He knew her so well, knew the curve and shape of her body, the way she moved when she was aroused, the way she breathed when she wanted him. She was close.

And then she was gone, arching and gasping until her body went limp.

He chuckled to himself as she batted him away. She always did that when she was done, saying she couldn't bear one more touch, that she'd surely die if she wasn't given the chance to float down to normalcy.

He moved, curling against her body until he could see her face. "That was nice," she said.

He lifted a brow. "Nice?"

"Very nice."

"Nice enough to reciprocate?"

Her lips curved. "Oh, I don't know if it was *that* nice."

His hand went to his trousers. "I shall have to offer a repeat engagement, then."

Her lips parted in surprise.

"A variation on a theme, if you will."

She twisted her neck to look down. "What are you doing?"

He grinned lasciviously. "Enjoying the fruits of my labors." And then she gasped as he slid inside of her, and he gasped from the sheer pleasure of it all, and then he thought how very much he loved her.

And then he thought nothing much at all.

The following day. We didn't really think that Hyacinth would give up, did we?

Late afternoon found Hyacinth back at her second favorite pastime. Although *favorite* didn't seem quite the right adjective, nor was *pastime* the correct noun. *Compulsion* probably fit the description better, as did *miserable*, or perhaps *unrelenting*. *Wretched?*

Inevitable.

She sighed. Definitely inevitable. An inevitable compulsion.

How long had she lived in this house? Fifteen years?

Fifteen years. Fifteen years and a few months atop that, and she was still searching for those bloody jewels.

One would think she'd have given up by now. Certainly, anyone else would have given up by now. She was, she had to admit, the most ridiculously stubborn person of her own acquaintance.

Except, perhaps, her own daughter. Hyacinth had never told Isabella about the jewels, if only because she knew that Isabella would join in the search with an unhealthy fervor to rival her own. She hadn't told her son, George, either, because he would tell Isabella. And Hyacinth would never get that girl married off if she thought there was a fortune in jewels to be found in her home.

Not that Isabella would want the jewels for fortune's sake. Hyacinth knew her daughter well enough to realize that in some matters—possibly most—Isabella was exactly like her. And Hyacinth's search for the jewels had never been about the money they might bring. Oh, she freely admitted that she and Gareth could use the money (and could have done with it even more so a few years back). But it wasn't about that. It was the principle. It was the glory.

It was the desperate need to finally clutch those bloody rocks in her hand and shake them before her husband's face and say, "See? See? I haven't been mad all these years!"

Gareth had long since given up on the jewels. They probably didn't even exist, he told her. Someone had surely found them years earlier. They'd lived in Clair House for *fifteen years*, for heaven's sake. If Hyacinth was going to find them, she'd have located them by now, so why did she continue to torture herself?

An excellent question.

Hyacinth gritted her teeth together as she crawled across the washroom floor for what was surely the eight hundredth time in her life. She knew all that. Lord help her, she knew it, but she couldn't give up now. If she gave up now, what did that say about the past fifteen years? Wasted time? All of it, wasted time?

She couldn't bear the thought.

Plus, she really wasn't the sort to give up, was she? If she did, it would be so completely at odds with everything she knew about herself. Would that mean she was getting old?

She wasn't ready to get old. Perhaps that was the curse of being the youngest of eight children. One was never quite ready to be old.

She leaned down even lower, planting her cheek against the cool tile of the floor so that she could peer under the tub. No old lady would do *this*, would she? No old lady would—

"Ah, there you are, Hyacinth."

It was Gareth, poking his head in. He did not look the least bit surprised to find his wife in such an odd position. But he did say, "It's been several months since your last search, hasn't it?"

She looked up. "I thought of something."

"Something you hadn't already thought of?"

"Yes," she ground out, lying through her teeth.

"Checking behind the tile?" he queried politely.

"Under the tub," she said reluctantly, moving herself into a seated position.

He blinked, shifting his gaze to the large claw-footed tub. "Did you move that?" he asked, his voice incredulous.

She nodded. It was amazing the sort of strength one could summon when properly motivated.

He looked at her, then at the tub, then back again. "No," he said. "It's not possible. You didn't—"

"I did."

"You couldn't—"

"I could," she said, beginning to enjoy herself. She didn't get to surprise him these days nearly as often as she would have liked. "Just a few inches," she admitted.

He looked back over at the tub.

"Maybe just one," she allowed.

For a moment she thought he would simply shrug his shoulders and leave her to her endeavors, but then he surprised her by saying, "Would you like some help?"

It took her a few seconds to ascertain his meaning. "With the tub?" she asked.

He nodded, crossing the short distance to the edge of its basin. "If you can move it an inch by yourself," he said, "surely the two of us can triple that. Or more."

Hyacinth rose to her feet. "I thought you didn't believe that the jewels are still here."

"I don't." He planted his hands on his hips as he surveyed the tub, looking for the best grip. "But you do, and surely this must fall within the realm of husbandly duties."

"Oh." Hyacinth swallowed, feeling a little guilty for thinking him so unsupportive. "Thank you."

He motioned for her to grab a spot on the opposite side. "Did you lift?" he asked. "Or shove?"

"Shove. With my shoulder, actually." She pointed to a narrow spot between the tub and the wall. "I wedged myself in there, then hooked my shoulder right under the lip, and—"

But Gareth was already holding his hand up to stop her. "No more," he said. "Don't tell me. I beg of you."

"Why not?"

He looked at her for a long moment before answering, "I don't really know. But I don't want the details."

"Very well." She went to the spot he'd indicated and grabbed the lip. "Thank you, anyway."

"It's my—" He paused. "Well, it's not my pleasure. But it's something."

She smiled to herself. He really was the best of husbands.

Three attempts later, however, it became apparent that they were not going to budge the tub in that manner. "We're going to have to use the wedge and shove method," Hyacinth announced. "It's the only way."

Gareth gave her a resigned nod, and together they squeezed into the narrow space between the tub and the wall.

"I have to say," he said, bending his knees and planting the soles of his boots against the wall, "this is all very undignified."

Hyacinth had nothing to say to that, so she just grunted. He could interpret the noise any way he wished.

"This should really count for something," he murmured.

"I beg your pardon?"

"This." He motioned with his hand, which could have meant just about anything, as she wasn't quite certain whether he was referring to the wall, the floor, the tub, or some particle of dust floating through the air.

"As gestures go," he continued, "it's not too terribly grand, but I would think, should I ever forget your birthday, for example, that this ought to go some distance in restoring myself to your good graces."

Hyacinth lifted a brow. "You couldn't do this out of the goodness of your heart?"

He gave her a regal nod. "I could. And in fact, I am. But one never knows when one——"

"Oh, for heaven's sake," Hyacinth muttered. "You do live to torture me, don't you?"

"It keeps the mind sharp," he said affably. "Very well. Shall we have at it?"

She nodded.

"On my count," he said, bracing his shoulders. "One, two . . . *three*."

With a heave and a groan, they both put all of their weight into the task, and the tub slid recalcitrantly across the floor. The noise was horrible, all scraping and squeaking, and when Hyacinth looked down she saw unattractive white marks arcing across the tile. "Oh, dear," she murmured.

Gareth twisted around, his face creasing into a peeved expression when he saw that they'd moved the tub a mere four inches. "I would have thought we'd have made a bit more progress than that," he said.

"It's heavy," she said, rather unnecessarily.

For a moment he did nothing but blink at the small sliver of floor they'd uncovered. "What do you plan to do now?" he asked.

Her mouth twisted slightly in a somewhat stumped expression. "I'm not sure," she admitted. "Check the floor, I imagine."

"You haven't done so already?" And then, when she didn't answer in, oh, half a second, he added, "In the fifteen years since you moved here?"

"I've *felt* along the floor, of course," she said quickly, since it was quite obvious that her arm fit under the tub. "But it's just not the same as a visual inspection, and—"

"Good luck," he cut in, rising to his feet.

"You're leaving?"

"Did you wish for me to stay?"

She hadn't expected him to stay, but now that he was here . . . "Yes," she said, surprised by her own answer. "Why not?"

He smiled at her then, and the expression was so warm, and loving, and best of all, familiar. "I could buy you a diamond necklace," he said softly, sitting back down.

She reached out, placed her hand on his. "I know you could."

They sat in silence for a minute, and then Hyacinth scooted herself closer to her husband, letting out a comfortable exhale as she eased against his side, letting her head rest on his shoulder. "Do you know why I love you?" she said softly.

His fingers laced through hers. "Why?"

"You could have bought me a necklace," she said. "And you could have hidden it." She turned her head so that she could kiss the curve of his neck. "Just so that I could have found it, you could have hidden it. But you didn't."

"I—"

"And don't say you never thought of it," she said, turning back so that she was once again facing the wall, just a few inches away. But her head was on his shoulder, and he was facing the same wall, and even though they weren't looking at each other, their hands were still entwined, and somehow the position was everything a marriage should be.

"Because I know you," she said, feeling a smile growing inside. "I know you, and you know me, and it's just the loveliest thing."

He squeezed her hand, then kissed the top of her head. "If it's here, you'll find it."

She sighed. "Or die trying."

He chuckled.

"That shouldn't be funny," she informed him.

"But it is."

"I know."

"I love you," he said.

"I know."

And really, what more could she want?

Meanwhile six feet away . . .

Isabella was quite used to the antics of her parents. She accepted the fact that they tugged each other into dark corners with far more frequency than was seemly. She thought nothing of the fact that her mother was one of the most outspoken women in London or that her father was still so handsome that her own friends sighed and stammered in his presence. In fact, she rather enjoyed being the daughter of such an unconventional couple. Oh, on the outside they were all that was proper, to be sure, with only the nicest sort of reputation for high-spiritedness.

But behind the closed doors of Clair House . . . Isabella knew that her friends were not encouraged to share their opinions as she was. Most of her friends were not even encouraged to have opinions. And certainly most young ladies of her acquaintance had not been given the opportunity to study modern languages, nor to delay a social debut by one year in order to travel on the continent.

So, when all was said and done, Isabella thought herself quite fortunate as pertained to her parents, and if that meant overlooking the occasional episodes of Not Acting

One's Age—well, it was worth it, and she'd learned to ignore much of their behavior.

But when she'd sought out her mother this afternoon—to acquiesce on the matter of the white gown with the dullish green trim, she might add—and instead found her parents on the washroom floor pushing a *bathtub* . . .

Well, really, that was a bit much, even for the St. Clairs.

And who would have faulted her for remaining to eavesdrop?

Not her mother, Isabella decided as she leaned in. There was no way Hyacinth St. Clair would have done the right thing and walked away. One couldn't live with the woman for nineteen years without learning *that*. And as for her father—well, Isabella rather thought he would have stayed to listen as well, especially as they were making it so *easy* for her, facing the wall as they were, with their backs to the open doorway, indeed with bathtub between them.

"What do you plan to do now?" her father was asking, his voice laced with that particular brand of amusement he seemed to reserve for her mother.

"I don't know," her mother replied, sounding uncharacteristically . . . well, not *un*sure, but certainly not as sure as usual. "Check the floor, I imagine."

Check the floor? What on earth were they talking about? Isabella leaned forward for a better listen, just in time to hear her father ask, "You haven't done so already? In the fifteen years since you moved here?"

"I've felt along the floor," her mother retorted, sounding much more like herself. "But it's not the same as a visual inspection, and—"

"Good luck," her father said, and then—*Oh, no! He was leaving!*

Isabella started to scramble, but then something must have happened because he sat back down. She inched back toward the open doorway—

Carefully, carefully now, he could get up at any moment. Holding her breath, she leaned in, unable to take her eyes off of the backs of her parents' heads.

"I could buy you a diamond necklace," her father said.

A diamond necklace?

A diamond . . .

Fifteen years.

Moving a tub?

In a washroom?

Fifteen years.

Her mother had searched for fifteen years.

For a diamond necklace?

A diamond necklace.

A diamond . . .

Oh. Dear. God.

What was she going to do? What was she going to do?

She knew what she must do, but good God, *how* was she supposed to do it?

And what could she say? What could she possibly say to—

Forget that for now. Forget it because her mother was talking again and she was saying, "You could have bought me a necklace. And you could have hidden it. Just so that I could have found it, you could have hidden it. But you didn't."

There was so much love in her voice it made Isabella's heart ache. And something about it seemed to sum up everything that her parents were. To themselves, to each other.

To their children.

And suddenly the moment was too personal to spy upon, even for her. She crept from the room, then ran to her own chamber, sagging into a chair just as soon as she closed the door.

Because she knew what her mother had been looking for for so very long.

It was sitting in the bottom drawer of her desk. And it was more than a necklace. It was an entire parure—a necklace, bracelet, and ring, a veritable shower of diamonds, each stone framed by two delicate aquamarines. Isabella had found them when she was ten, hidden in a small cavity behind one of the Turkish tiles in the nursery washroom. She *should* have said something about them. She knew that she should. But she hadn't, and she wasn't even sure why.

Maybe it was because she had found them. Maybe because she loved having a secret. Maybe it was because she hadn't thought they belonged to anyone else, or indeed, that anyone even knew of their existence. Certainly she hadn't thought that her mother had been searching for fifteen years.

Her mother!

Her mother was the last person anyone would imagine was keeping a secret. No one would think ill of Isabella for not thinking, when she'd discovered the diamonds—*Oh, surely my mother must be looking for these and has chosen, for her own devious reasons, not to tell me about it.*

Truly, when all was said and done, this was really her mother's fault. If Hyacinth had *told* her that she was searching for jewels, Isabella would immediately have confessed. Or if not immediately, then soon enough to satisfy everyone's conscience.

And now, speaking of consciences, hers was beating a nasty little tattoo in her chest. It was a most unpleasant—and unfamiliar—feeling.

It wasn't that Isabella was the soul of sweetness and light, all sugary smiles and pious platitudes. Heavens, no, she avoided such girls like the plague. But by the same token, she rarely did anything that was likely to make her feel guilty afterward, if only because perhaps—and only perhaps—her notions of propriety and morality were ever-so-slightly flexible.

But now she had a lump in the pit of her stomach, a lump with peculiar talent for sending bile up her throat. Her hands were shaking, and she felt ill. Not feverish, not even aguey, just ill. With herself.

Letting out an uneven breath, Isabella rose to her feet and crossed the room to her desk, a delicate rococo piece her namesake great-grandmother had brought over from Italy. She'd put the jewels there three years back, when she'd finally moved out of the top-floor nursery. She'd discovered a secret compartment at the back of the bottom drawer. This hadn't particularly surprised her; there seemed to be an uncommon number of secret compartments in the furniture at Clair House, much of which had been imported from Italy. But it *was* a boon and rather convenient, and so one day, when her family was off at some *ton* function they had deemed Isabella too young to attend, she'd sneaked back up to the nursery, retrieved the jewels from their hiding place behind the tile (which she had rather resourcefully plastered back up), and moved them to her desk.

They'd remained there ever since, except for the odd occasion when Isabella took them out and tried them on, thinking how nice they would look with her new gown, but *how* was she to explain their existence to her parents?

Now it seemed that no explanation would have been necessary. Or perhaps just a different sort of explanation.

A very different sort.

Settling into the desk chair, Isabella leaned down and retrieved the jewels from the secret compartment. They were still in the same corded velvet bag in which she'd found them. She slid them free, letting them pool luxuriously on the desktop. She didn't know much about jewels, but surely these had to be of the finest quality. They caught the sunlight with an indescribable magic, almost as if each stone could somehow capture the light and then send it showering off in every direction.

Isabella didn't like to think herself greedy or materialistic, but in the presence of such treasure, she understood how diamonds could make a man go a little bit mad. Or why women longed so desperately for one more piece, one more stone that was bigger, more finely cut than the last.

But these did not belong to her. Maybe they belonged to no one. But if anyone had a right to them, it was most definitely her mother. Isabella didn't know how or why Hyacinth knew of their existence, but that didn't seem to matter. Her mother had some sort of connection to the jewels, some sort of important knowledge. And if they belonged to anyone, they belonged to her.

Reluctantly, Isabella slid them back into the bag and tightened the gold cord so that none of the pieces could slip out. She knew what she had to do now. She knew exactly what she had to do.

But after that . . .

The torture would be in the waiting.

One year later

It had been two months since Hyacinth had last searched for the jewels, but Gareth was busy with some sort of estate matter, she had no good books to read, and, well, she just felt . . . itchy.

This happened from time to time. She'd go months without searching, weeks and days without even thinking about the diamonds, and then something would happen to remind her, to start her wondering, and there she was again—obsessed and frustrated, sneaking about the house so that no one would realize what she was up to.

And the truth was, she was embarrassed. No matter how one looked at it, she was at least a little bit of a fool. Either the jewels were hidden away at Clair House and she hadn't found them despite sixteen years of searching, or they weren't hidden, and she'd been chasing a delusion. She couldn't even imagine how she might explain this to her children, the servants surely thought her more than a little bit mad (they'd all caught her snooping about a washroom at one point or another), and Gareth—well, he was sweet and he humored her, but all the same, Hyacinth kept her activities to herself.

It was just better that way.

She'd chosen the nursery washroom for the afternoon's search. Not for any particular reason, of course, but she'd finished her systematic search of all of the servants' washrooms (always an endeavor that required some sensitivity and finesse), and before that she'd done her own washroom, and so the nursery seemed a good choice. After this she'd move to some of the second floor washrooms. George had moved into his own lodgings and if there really was a merciful God, Isabella would be married before long, and Hyacinth would not have to worry about anyone stumbling upon her as she poked, pried, and quite possibly pulled the tiles from the walls.

Hyacinth put her hands on her hips and took a deep breath as she surveyed the small room. She'd always liked it. The tiling was, or at least appeared to be, Turkish, and Hyacinth had to think that the Eastern peoples must enjoy far less sedate lives than the British, because the colors never failed to put her in a splendid mood—all royal blues and dreamy aquas, with streaks of yellow and orange.

Hyacinth had been to the south of Italy once, to the beach. It looked exactly like this room, sunny and sparkly in ways that the shores of England never seemed to achieve.

She squinted at the crown molding, looking for cracks or indentations, then dropped to her hands and knees for her usual inspection of the lower tiles.

She didn't know what she hoped to find, what might have suddenly made an appearance that she hadn't detected during the other, oh, at least a dozen previous searches.

But she had to keep going. She had to because she simply had no choice. There was something inside of her that just would not let go. And—

She stopped. Blinked. What was that?

Slowly, because she couldn't quite believe that she'd found anything new—it had been over a decade since any of her searches had changed in any measurable manner—she leaned in.

A crack.

It was small. It was faint. But it was definitely a crack, running from the floor to the top of the first tile, about six inches up. It wasn't the sort of thing most people would notice, but Hyacinth wasn't most people, and sad as it sounded, she had practically made a career of inspecting washrooms.

Frustrated with her inability to get really close, she shifted to her forearms and knees, then laid her cheek against the floor. She poked the tile to the right of the crack, then the left.

Nothing happened.

She stuck her fingernail at the edge of the crack, and dug it in. A tiny piece of plaster lodged under her nail.

A strange excitement began to build in her chest, squeezing, fluttering, rendering her almost incapable of drawing breath.

"Calm down," she whispered, even those words coming out on a shake. She grabbed the little chisel she always took with her on her searches. "It's probably nothing. It's probably—"

She jammed the chisel in the crack, surely with more force than was necessary. And then she twisted. If one of the tiles was loose, the torque would cause it to press outward, and—

"Oh!"

The tile quite literally popped out, landing on the floor with a clatter. Behind it was a small cavity.

Hyacinth squeezed her eyes shut. She'd waited her entire adult life for this moment, and now she couldn't even bring herself to look. "Please," she whispered. "*Please.*"

She reached in.

"Please. Oh, please."

She touched something. Something soft. Like velvet.

With shaking fingers she drew it out. It was a little bag, held together with a soft, silky cord.

Hyacinth straightened slowly, crossing her legs so that she was sitting Indian style. She slid one finger inside the bag, widening the mouth, which had been pulled tight.

And then, with her right hand, she upended it, sliding the contents into her left.

Oh my G—

"Gareth!" she shrieked. "Gareth!"

"I did it," she whispered, gazing down at the pool of jewels now spilling from her left hand. "I did it."

And then she bellowed it.

"I DID IT!!!!"

She looped the necklace around her neck, still clutching the bracelet and ring in her hand.

"I did it, I did it, I did it." She was singing it now, hopping up and down, almost dancing, almost crying. "I did it!"

"Hyacinth!" It was Gareth, out of breath from taking four flights of stairs two steps at a time.

She looked at him, and she could swear she could feel

her eyes shining. "I did it!" She laughed, almost crazily. "I did it!"

For a moment he could do nothing but stare. His face grew slack, and Hyacinth thought he might actually lose his footing.

"I did it," she said again. "I did it."

And then he took her hand, took the ring, and slipped it onto her finger. "So you did," he said, leaning down to kiss her knuckles. "So you did."

Meanwhile, one floor down . . .

"*Gareth!*"

Isabella looked up from the book she was reading, glancing toward the ceiling. Her bedchamber was directly below the nursery, rather in line with the washroom, actually.

"*I did it!*"

Isabella turned back to her book.

And she smiled.

On the Way to the Wedding

In writing the 2nd epilogues, I have tried to answer readers' lingering questions. In the case of *On the Way to the Wedding*, the question I heard the most post-publication was: What did Gregory and Lucy name all those babies? I'll admit that even I don't know how to craft a story revolving around the naming of nine infants (not all at once, thank heavens), so I decided to start the 2nd epilogue right where the first one ends—with Lucy giving birth for the last time. And because everyone—even the Bridgertons—must face hardship, I didn't make it easy . . .

On the Way to the Wedding:
The 2nd Epilogue

21 *June 1840*
Cutbank Manor
Nr Winkfield, Berks.

My dearest Gareth—

*I hope this letter finds you well. I can hardly believe
it has been almost a fortnight since I departed Clair
House for Berkshire. Lucy is quite enormous; it seems
impossible that she has not delivered yet. If I had
grown so large with George or Isabella, I am sure I
should have been complaining endlessly.*

(I am also sure that you will not remind me of any complaints I may have uttered whilst in a similar state.)

Lucy does claim that this feels quite unlike her previous confinements. I find I must believe her. I saw her right before she gave birth to Ben, and I swear she was dancing a jig. I would confess to an intense jealousy, but it would be uncouth and unmaternal to admit to such an emotion, and as we know, I am Always Couth. And occasionally maternal.

Speaking of our progeny, Isabella is having a fine time. I do believe she would be content to remain with her cousins throughout the summer. She has been teaching them how to curse in Italian. I made a feeble effort to scold her, but I'm sure she realized I was secretly delighted. Every woman should know how to curse in another language since polite society has deemed English unavailable to us.

I am not certain when I will be home. At this rate, I should not be surprised if Lucy holds out until July. And then of course I have promised to remain for a bit of time after the baby arrives. Perhaps you should send George out for a visit? I don't think anyone would notice if one more child was added to the current horde.

Your devoted wife,
Hyacinth

> *Postscript—'Tis a good thing I did not seal the letter*
> *yet. Lucy just delivered twins. Twins! Good heavens,*
> *what on earth are they going to do with two more*
> *children? The mind boggles.*

"I can't do this again."

Lucy Bridgerton had said it before, seven times, to be precise, but this time she really meant it. It wasn't so much that she had given birth to her ninth child just thirty minutes earlier; she'd grown rather expert at delivering babies and could pop one out with a minimum of discomfort. It was just that . . . Twins! Why hadn't anyone told her she might be carrying twins? No wonder she'd been so bloody uncomfortable these last few months. She'd had two babies in her belly, clearly engaged in a boxing match.

"Two girls," her husband was saying. Gregory looked over at her with a grin. "Well, that tips the scales. The boys will be disappointed."

"The boys will get to own property, vote, and wear trousers," said Gregory's sister Hyacinth, who had come to help Lucy toward the end of her confinement. "They shall endure."

Lucy managed a small chuckle. Trust Hyacinth to get to the heart of the matter.

"Does your husband know you've become a crusader?" Gregory asked.

"My husband supports me in all things," Hyacinth said sweetly, not taking her eyes off the tiny swaddled infant in her arms. "Always."

"Your husband is a saint," Gregory remarked, cooing at his own little bundle. "Or perhaps merely insane. Either way, we are eternally grateful to him for marrying you."

"*How* do you put up with him?" Hyacinth asked, leaning over Lucy, who was really beginning to feel quite strange. Lucy opened her mouth to make a reply, but Gregory beat her to it.

"I make her life an endless delight," he said. "Full of sweetness and light, and everything perfect and good."

Hyacinth looked as if she might like to throw up.

"You are simply jealous," Gregory said to her.

"Of what?" Hyacinth demanded.

With a wave of his hand, he dismissed the inquiry as inconsequential. Lucy closed her eyes and smiled, enjoying the interplay. Gregory and Hyacinth were always poking fun at each other—even now that they were both nearing their fortieth birthdays. Still, despite the constant needling—or maybe because of it—there was a rock-solid bond between them. Hyacinth in particular was viciously loyal; it had taken her two years to warm to Lucy after her marriage to Gregory.

Lucy supposed Hyacinth had had some just cause. Lucy had come so close to marrying the wrong man. Well, no, she *had* married the wrong man, but luckily for her, the combined influence of a viscount and an earl (along with a hefty donation to the Church of England) had made an annulment possible when, technically speaking, it shouldn't have been.

But that was all water under the bridge. Hyacinth was now a sister to her, as were all of Gregory's sisters. It had been marvelous marrying into a large family. It was probably why Lucy was so delighted that she and Gregory had ended up having such a large brood themselves.

"Nine," she said softly, opening her eyes to look at the two bundles that still needed names. And hair. "Who would have thought we'd have nine?"

"My mother will surely say that any sensible person would have stopped at eight," Gregory said. He smiled down at Lucy. "Would you like to hold one?"

She felt that familiar rush of maternal bliss wash over her. "Oh, yes."

The midwife helped her into a more upright position, and Lucy held out her arms to hold one of her new daughters. "She's very pink," she murmured, nestling the little bundle close to her chest. The tiny girl was screaming like a banshee. It was, Lucy decided, a marvelous sound.

"Pink is an excellent color," Gregory declared. "My lucky hue."

"This one has quite a grip," Hyacinth remarked, turning to the side so that everyone could see her little finger, captured in the baby's tiny fist.

"They are both very healthy," the midwife said. "Twins often aren't, you know."

Gregory leaned down to kiss Lucy on her forehead. "I am a very fortunate man," he murmured.

Lucy smiled weakly. She felt fortunate, too, almost miraculously so, but she was simply too tired to say anything other than "I think we must be done. Please tell me we're done."

Gregory smiled lovingly. "We're done," he declared. "Or at least as done as I can ensure."

Lucy nodded gratefully. She, too, was not willing to give up the comforts of the marital bed, but truly, there had to be something they could do to end the constant stream of babies.

"What shall we name them?" Gregory asked, making silly eyes at the baby in Hyacinth's arms.

Lucy nodded at the midwife and handed her the baby so that she could lie back down. Her arms were feeling shaky, she didn't trust herself to safely hold the baby, even here on her bed. "Didn't you want Eloise?" she murmured, closing her eyes. They'd named all of their children for their siblings: Katharine, Richard, Hermione, Daphne,

Anthony, Benedict, and Colin. Eloise was the obvious next choice for a girl.

"I know," Gregory said, and she could hear his smile in his voice. "But I wasn't planning for *two*."

At that, Hyacinth turned around with a gasp. "You're going to name the other one Francesca," she accused.

"Well," Gregory said, sounding perhaps just a little bit smug, "she *is* next in line."

Hyacinth stood openmouthed, and Lucy would not have been at all surprised if steam began to shoot forth from her ears. "I can't believe it," she said, now positively glaring at Gregory. "You will have named your children after every possible sibling except me."

"It's a happy accident, I assure you," Gregory said. "I thought for sure that Francesca would be left out as well."

"Even Kate got a namesake!"

"Kate was rather instrumental in our falling in love," Gregory reminded her. "Whereas you attacked Lucy at the church."

Lucy would have snorted with laughter, had she the energy.

Hyacinth, however, was unamused. "She was *marrying* someone else."

"You do hold a grudge, dear sister." Gregory turned to Lucy. "She just can't let go, can she?" He was holding one of the babies again, although which one, Lucy had no idea. He probably didn't know, either. "She's beautiful," he said, looking up to smile at Lucy. "Small, though. Smaller than the others were, I think."

"Twins are always small," the midwife said.

"Oh, of course," he murmured.

"They didn't feel small," Lucy said. She tried to push herself back up so she could hold the other baby, but her arms gave out. "I'm so tired," she said.

The midwife frowned. "It wasn't such a long labor."

"There were two babies," Gregory reminded her.

"Yes, but she's had so many before," the midwife replied in a brisk voice. "Birthing does get easier the more babies one has."

"I don't feel right," Lucy said.

Gregory handed the baby to a maid and peered over at her. "What's wrong?"

"She looks pale," Lucy heard Hyacinth say.

But she didn't sound the way she ought. Her voice was tinny, and it sounded as if she were speaking through a long, skinny tube.

"Lucy? Lucy?"

She tried to answer. She thought she was answering. But if her lips were moving, she couldn't tell, and she definitely did not hear her own voice.

"Something's wrong," Gregory said. He sounded sharp. He sounded scared. "Where's Dr. Jarvis?"

"He left," the midwife answered. "There was another baby . . . the solicitor's wife."

Lucy tried to open her eyes. She wanted to see his face, to tell him that she was fine. Except that she wasn't fine. She didn't hurt, exactly; well, not any more than a body usually hurt after delivering a baby. She couldn't really describe it. She simply felt *wrong*.

"Lucy?" Gregory's voice fought its way through her haze. "Lucy!" He took her hand, squeezed it, then shook it.

She wanted to reassure him, but she felt so far away. And that wrong feeling was spreading throughout, sliding from her belly to her limbs, straight down to her toes.

It wasn't so bad if she kept herself perfectly still. Maybe if she slept . . .

"What's wrong with her?" Gregory demanded. Behind him the babies were squalling, but at least they were wriggling and pink, whereas Lucy—

"Lucy?" He tried to make his voice urgent, but to him it just sounded like terror. "Lucy?"

Her face was pasty; her lips, bloodless. She wasn't exactly unconscious, but she wasn't responsive, either.

"What is *wrong* with her?"

The midwife hurried to the foot of the bed and looked under the covers. She gasped, and when she looked up, her face was nearly as pale as Lucy's.

Gregory looked down, just in time to see a crimson stain seeping along the bedsheet.

"Get me more towels," the midwife snapped, and Gregory did not think twice before doing her bidding.

"I'll need more than this," she said grimly. She shoved several under Lucy's hips. "Go, go!"

"I'll go," Hyacinth said. "You stay."

She dashed out to the hall, leaving Gregory standing at the midwife's side, feeling helpless and incompetent. What kind of man stood still while his wife bled?

But he didn't know what to do. He didn't know how to do anything except hand the towels to the midwife, who was jamming them against Lucy with brutal force.

He opened his mouth to say . . . something. He might have got a word out. He wasn't sure. It might have just been a sound, an awful, terrified sound that burst up from deep within him.

"Where are the towels?" the midwife demanded.

Gregory nodded and ran into the hall, relieved to be given a task. "Hyacinth! Hya—"

Lucy screamed.

"Oh my God." Gregory swayed, holding the frame of

the door for support. It wasn't the blood; he could handle the blood. It was the scream. He had never heard a human being make such a sound.

"What are you doing to her?" he asked. His voice was shaky as he pushed himself away from the wall. It was hard to watch, and even harder to hear, but maybe he could hold Lucy's hand.

"I'm manipulating her belly," the midwife grunted. She pressed down hard, then squeezed. Lucy let out another scream and nearly took off Gregory's fingers.

"I don't think that's such a good idea," he said. "You're pushing out her blood. She can't lose—"

"You'll have to trust me," the midwife said curtly. "I have seen this before. More times than I care to count."

Gregory felt his lips form the question—*Did they live?* But he didn't ask it. The midwife's face was far too grim. He didn't want to know the answer.

By now Lucy's screams had disintegrated into moans, but somehow this was even worse. Her breath was fast and shallow, her eyes squeezed shut against the pain of the midwife's jabs. "Please, make her stop," she whimpered.

Gregory looked frantically at the midwife. She was now using both hands, one reaching up—

"Oh, God." He turned back. He couldn't watch. "You have to let her help you," he said to Lucy.

"I have the towels!" Hyacinth said, bursting into the

room. She stopped short, staring at Lucy. "Oh my God." Her voice wavered. "Gregory?"

"Shut *up*." He didn't want to hear his sister. He didn't want to talk to her, he didn't want to answer her questions. He didn't *know*. For the love of God, couldn't she see that he didn't know what was happening?

And to force him to admit that out loud would have been the cruelest sort of torture.

"It hurts," Lucy whimpered. "It *hurts*."

"I know. I know. If I could do it for you, I would. I swear to you." He clutched her hand in both of his, willing some of his own strength to pass into her. Her grip was growing feeble, tightening only when the midwife made a particularly vigorous movement.

And then Lucy's hand went slack.

Gregory stopped breathing. He looked over at the midwife in horror. She was still standing at the base of the bed, her face a mask of grim determination as she worked. Then she stopped, her eyes narrowing as she took a step back. She didn't say anything.

Hyacinth stood frozen, the towels still stacked up in her arms. "What . . . what . . ." But her voice wasn't even a whisper, lacking the strength to complete her thought.

The midwife reached a hand out, touching the bloodied bed near Lucy. "I think . . . that's all," she said.

Gregory looked down at his wife, who lay terrifyingly

still. Then he turned back to the midwife. He could see her chest rise and fall, taking in all the great gulps of air she hadn't allowed herself while she was working on Lucy.

"What do you mean," he asked, barely able to force the words across his lips, " 'that's all'?"

"The bleeding's done."

Gregory turned slowly back to Lucy. The bleeding was done. What did that mean? Didn't all bleeding stop . . . eventually?

Why was the midwife just standing there? Shouldn't she be doing something? Shouldn't *he* be doing something? Or was Lucy—

He turned back to the midwife, his anguish palpable.

"She's not dead," the midwife said quickly. "At least I don't think so."

"You don't *think* so?" he echoed, his voice rising in volume.

The midwife staggered forward. She was covered with blood, and she looked exhausted, but Gregory didn't give a sodding damn if she was ready to drop. "*Help her*," he demanded.

The midwife took Lucy's wrist and felt for a pulse. She gave him a quick nod when she found one, but then she said, "I've done everything I can."

"No," Gregory said, because he refused to believe that

this was it. There was always something one could do. "No," he said again. "*No!*"

"Gregory," Hyacinth said, touching his arm.

He shook her off. "Do something," he said, taking a menacing step toward the midwife. "You have to do something."

"She's lost a great deal of blood," the midwife said, sagging back against the wall. "We can only wait. I have no way of knowing which way she'll go. Some women recover. Others . . ." Her voice trailed off. It might have been because she didn't want to say it. Or it might have been the expression on Gregory's face.

Gregory swallowed. He didn't have much of a temper; he'd always been a reasonable man. But the urge to lash out, to scream or beat the walls, to find some way to gather up all that blood and push it back into her . . .

He could barely breathe against the force of it.

Hyacinth moved quietly to his side. Her hand found his, and without thinking he entwined his fingers in hers. He waited for her to say something like: *She's going to be fine.* Or: *All will be well, just have faith.*

But she didn't. This was Hyacinth, and she never lied. But she was here. Thank God she was here.

She squeezed his hand, and he knew she would stay however long he needed her.

He blinked at the midwife, trying to find his voice.

"What if—" *No.* "What *when*," he said haltingly. "What do we do *when* she wakes up?"

The midwife looked at Hyacinth first, which for some reason irritated him. "She'll be very weak," she said.

"But she'll be all right?" he asked, practically jumping on top of her words.

The midwife looked at him with an awful expression. It was something bordering on pity. With sorrow. And resignation. "It's hard to say," she finally said.

Gregory searched her face, desperate for something that wasn't a platitude or half answer. "What the devil does that mean?"

The midwife looked somewhere that wasn't quite his eyes. "There could be an infection. It happens frequently in cases like this."

"Why?"

The midwife blinked.

"Why?" he practically roared. Hyacinth's hand tightened around his.

"I don't know." The midwife backed up a step. "It just does."

Gregory turned back to Lucy, unable to look at the midwife any longer. She was covered in blood—Lucy's blood—and maybe this wasn't her fault—maybe it wasn't anyone's fault—but he couldn't bear to look at her for another moment.

"Dr. Jarvis must return," he said in a low voice, picking up Lucy's limp hand.

"I will see to it," Hyacinth said. "And I will have someone come for the sheets."

Gregory did not look up.

"I will be going now as well," the midwife said.

He did not reply. He heard feet moving along the floor, followed by the gentle click of the door closing, but he kept his gaze on Lucy's face the whole time.

"Lucy," he whispered, trying to force his voice into a teasing tone. "La la la Lucy." It was a silly refrain, one their daughter Hermione had made up when she was four. "La la la Lucy."

He searched her face. Did she just smile? He thought he saw her expression change a touch.

"La la la Lucy." His voice wobbled, but he kept it up. "La la la Lucy."

He felt like an idiot. He *sounded* like an idiot, but he had no idea what else to say. Normally, he was never at a loss for words. Certainly not with Lucy. But now . . . what did one say at such a time?

So he sat there. He sat there for what felt like hours. He sat there and tried to remember to breathe. He sat there and covered his mouth every time he felt a huge choking sob coming on, because he didn't want her to hear it. He sat there and tried desperately not to think about what his life might be without her.

She had been his entire world. Then they had children, and she was no longer everything to him, but still, she was at the center of it all. The sun. His sun, around which everything important revolved.

Lucy. She was the girl he hadn't realized he adored until it was almost too late. She was so perfect, so utterly his other half that he had almost overlooked her. He'd been waiting for a love fraught with passion and drama; it hadn't even occurred to him that true love might be something that was utterly comfortable and just plain easy.

With Lucy he could sit for hours and not say a word. Or they could chatter like magpies. He could say something stupid and not care. He could make love to her all night or go several weeks spending his nights simply snuggled up to next to her.

It didn't matter. None of it mattered because they both *knew.*

"I can't do it without you," he blurted out. Bloody hell, he went an hour without speaking and *this* was the first thing he said? "I mean, I can, because I would have to, but it'll be awful, and honestly, I won't do such a good job. I'm a good father, but only because you are such a good mother."

If she died . . .

He shut his eyes tightly, trying to banish the thought. He'd been trying so hard to keep those three words from his mind.

Three words. "Three words" was supposed to mean *I love you*. Not—

He took a deep, shuddering breath. He had to stop thinking this way.

The window had been cracked open to allow a slight breeze, and Gregory heard a joyful shriek from outside. One of his children—one of the boys from the sound of it. It was sunny, and he imagined they were playing some sort of racing game on the lawn.

Lucy loved to watch them run about outside. She loved to run *with* them, too, even when she was so pregnant that she moved like a duck.

"Lucy," he whispered, trying to keep his voice from shaking. "Don't leave me. Please don't leave me.

"They need you more," he choked out, shifting his position so that he could hold her hand in both of his. "The children. They need *you* more. I know you know that. You would never say it, but you know it. And *I* need you. I think you know that, too."

But she didn't reply. She didn't move.

But she breathed. At least, thank God, she breathed.

"Father?"

Gregory started at the voice of his eldest child, and he quickly turned away, desperate for a moment to compose himself.

"I went to see the babies," Katharine said as she entered the room. "Aunt Hyacinth said I could."

He nodded, not trusting himself to speak.

"They're very sweet," Katharine said. "The babies, I mean. Not Aunt Hyacinth."

To his utter shock, Gregory felt himself smile. "No," he said, "no one would call Aunt Hyacinth sweet."

"But I do love her," Katharine said quickly.

"I know," he replied, finally turning to look at her. Ever loyal, his Katharine was. "I do, too."

Katharine took a few steps forward, pausing near the foot of the bed. "Why is Mama still sleeping?"

He swallowed. "Well, she's very tired, pet. It takes a great deal of energy to have a baby. Double for two."

Katharine nodded solemnly, but he wasn't sure if she believed him. She was looking at her mother with a furrowed brow—not quite concerned, but very, very curious. "She's pale," she finally said.

"Do you think so?" Gregory responded.

"She's white as a sheet."

His opinion precisely, but he was trying not to sound worried, so he merely said, "Perhaps a little more pale than usual."

Katharine regarded him for a moment, then took a seat in the chair next to him. She sat straight, her hands folded neatly in her lap, and Gregory could not help marveling at the miracle of her. Almost twelve years ago Katharine Hazel Bridgerton had entered this world, and he had become a father. It was, he had realized the instant she had been put into his arms, his one true vocation. He was a younger son; he was not going to hold a title, and he was not suited for the military or the clergy. His place in life was to be a gentleman farmer.

And a father.

When he'd looked down at baby Katharine, her eyes still that dark baby gray that all of his children had had when they were tiny, he knew. Why he was here, what he was meant for . . . that was when he knew. He existed to shepherd this miraculous little creature to adulthood, to protect her and keep her well.

He adored all of his children, but he would always have a special bond with Katharine, because she was the one who had taught him who he was meant to be.

"The others want to see her," she said. She was looking down, watching her right foot as she kicked it back and forth.

"She still needs her rest, pet."

"I know."

Gregory waited for more. She wasn't saying what she

was really thinking. He had a feeling that it was Katharine who wanted to see her mother. She wanted to sit on the side of the bed and laugh and giggle and then explain every last nuance of the nature walk she'd undertaken with her governess.

The others—the littler ones—were probably oblivious.

But Katharine had always been incredibly close to Lucy. They were like two peas in a pod. They looked nothing alike; Katharine was remarkably like her namesake, Gregory's sister-in-law, the current Viscountess Bridgerton. It made absolutely no sense, as theirs was not a blood connection, but both Katharines had the same dark hair and oval face. The eyes were not the same color, but the shape was identical.

On the inside, however, Katharine—*his* Katharine— was just like Lucy. She craved order. She needed to see the pattern in things. If she were able to tell her mother about yesterday's nature walk, she would have started with which flowers they'd seen. She would not have remembered all of them, but she would definitely have known how many there had been of each color. And Gregory would not be surprised if the governess came to him later and said that Katharine had insisted they go for an extra mile so that the "pinks" caught up with the "yellows."

Fairness in all things, that was his Katharine.

"Mimsy says the babies are to be named after Aunt Eloise and Aunt Francesca," Katharine said, after kicking her foot back and forth thirty-two times.

(He'd counted. Gregory could not believe he'd counted. He was growing more like Lucy every day.)

"As usual," he replied, "Mimsy is correct." Mimsy was the children's nanny and nurse, and a candidate for sainthood if he'd ever met one.

"She did not know what their middle names might be."

Gregory frowned. "I don't think we got 'round to deciding upon that."

Katharine looked at him with an unsettlingly direct gaze. "Before Mama needed her nap?"

"Er, yes," Gregory replied, his gaze sliding from hers. He was not proud that he'd looked away, but it was his only choice if he wanted to keep from crying in front of his child.

"I think one of them ought to be named Hyacinth," Katharine announced.

He nodded. "Eloise Hyacinth or Francesca Hyacinth?"

Katharine's lips pressed together in thought, then she said, rather firmly, "Francesca Hyacinth. It has a lovely ring to it. Although . . ."

Gregory waited for her to finish her thought, and when she did not he prompted, "Although . . . ?"

"It *is* a little flowery."

"I'm not certain how one can avoid that with a name like Hyacinth."

"True," Katharine said thoughtfully, "but what if she does not turn out to be sweet and delicate?"

"Like your Aunt Hyacinth?" he murmured. Some things really did beg to be said.

"She *is* rather fierce," Katharine said, without an ounce of sarcasm.

"Fierce or fearsome?"

"Oh, only fierce. Aunt Hyacinth is not at all fearsome."

"Don't tell *her* that."

Katharine blinked with incomprehension. "You think she wants to be fearsome?"

"*And* fierce."

"How odd," she murmured. Then she looked up with especially bright eyes. "I think Aunt Hyacinth is going to love having a baby named after her."

Gregory felt himself smile. A real one, not something conjured to make his child feel safe. "Yes," he said quietly, "she will."

"She probably thought she wasn't going to get one," Katharine continued, "since you and Mama were going in order. We all knew it would be Eloise for a girl."

"And who would have expected twins?"

"Even so," Katharine said, "there is Aunt Francesca to consider. Mama would have had to have had triplets for one to be named after Aunt Hyacinth."

Triplets. Gregory was not a Catholic, but it was difficult to suppress the urge to cross himself.

"And they would have all had to have been girls," Katharine added, "which does seem to be a mathematical improbability."

"Indeed," he murmured.

She smiled. And he smiled. And they held hands.

"I was thinking . . ." Katharine began.

"Yes, pet?"

"If Francesca is to be Francesca Hyacinth, then Eloise ought to be Eloise Lucy. Because Mama is the very best of mothers."

Gregory fought against the lump rising in his throat. "Yes," he said hoarsely, "she is."

"I think Mama would like that," Katharine said. "Don't you?"

Somehow, he managed to nod. "She would probably say that we should name the baby for someone else. She's quite generous that way."

"I know. That's why we must do it while she is still asleep. Before she has a chance to argue. Because she will, you know."

Gregory chuckled.

"She'll say we shouldn't have done it," Katharine said, "but secretly she will be delighted."

Gregory swallowed another lump in his throat, but this one, thankfully, was born of paternal love. "I think you're right."

Katharine beamed.

He ruffled her hair. Soon she'd be too old for such affections; she'd tell him not to muss her coiffure. But for now, he was taking all the hair ruffling he could get. He smiled down at her. "How do you know your mama so well?"

She looked up at him with an indulgent expression. They had had this conversation before. "Because I'm exactly like her."

"Exactly," he agreed. They held hands for a few more moments until something occurred to him. "Lucy or Lucinda?"

"Oh, Lucy," Katharine said, knowing instantly what he was talking about. "She's not *really* a Lucinda."

Gregory sighed and looked over at his wife, still sleeping in her bed. "No," he said quietly, "she's not." He felt his daughter's hand slip into his, small and warm.

"La la la Lucy," Katharine said, and he could hear her quiet smile in her voice.

"La la la Lucy," he repeated. And amazingly, he heard a smile in his own voice, too.

A few hours later Dr. Jarvis returned, tired and rumpled after delivering another baby down in the village. Gregory knew the doctor well; Peter Jarvis had been fresh from his studies when Gregory and Lucy had decided to take up residence near Winkfield, and he had served as the family doctor ever since. He and Gregory were of a similar age, and they had shared many a supper together over the years. Mrs. Jarvis, too, was a good friend of Lucy's, and their children had played together often.

But in all their years of friendship, Gregory had never seen such an expression on Peter's face. His lips were pinched at the corners, and there were none of the usual pleasantries before he examined Lucy.

Hyacinth was there, too, having insisted that Lucy needed the support of another woman in the room. "As if either of you could possibly understand the rigors of childbirth," she'd said, with some disdain.

Gregory hadn't said a word. He'd just stepped aside to allow his sister inside. There was something comforting in her fierce presence. Or maybe inspiring. Hyacinth was such a force; one almost believed she could *will* Lucy to heal herself.

They both stood back as the doctor took Lucy's pulse

and listened to her heart. And then, to Gregory's complete shock, Peter grabbed her roughly by the shoulder and began to shake.

"What are you doing?" Gregory cried, leaping forward to intervene.

"Waking her up," Peter said resolutely.

"But doesn't she need her rest?"

"She needs to wake up more."

"But—" Gregory didn't know just what he was protesting, and the truth was, it didn't matter, because when Peter cut him off, it was to say:

"For God's sake, Bridgerton, we need to know that she *can* wake up." He shook her again, and this time, he said loudly, "Lady Lucinda! Lady Lucinda!"

"She's not a Lucinda," Gregory heard himself say, and then he stepped forward and called out, "Lucy? Lucy?"

She shifted position, mumbling something in her sleep.

Gregory looked sharply over at Peter, every question in the world hanging in his eyes.

"See if you can get her to answer you," Peter said.

"Let me try," Hyacinth said forcefully. Gregory watched as she leaned down and said something into Lucy's ear.

"What are you saying?" he asked.

Hyacinth shook her head. "You don't want to know."

"Oh, for God's sake," he muttered, pushing her aside.

He picked up Lucy's hand and squeezed it with more force than he'd done earlier. "Lucy! How many steps are there in the back staircase from the kitchen to the first floor?"

She didn't open her eyes, but she did make a sound that he thought sounded like—

"Did you say fifteen?" he asked her.

She snorted, and this time he heard her clearly. "Sixteen."

"Oh, thank God." Gregory let go of her hand and collapsed into the chair by her bed. "There," he said. "There. She's all right. She will be all right."

"Gregory . . ." But Peter's voice was not reassuring.

"You told me we had to awaken her."

"We did," Peter said with stiff acknowledgment. "And it was a very good sign that we were able to. But it doesn't mean—"

"Don't say it," Gregory said in a low voice.

"But you must—"

"*Don't say it!*"

Peter went silent. He just stood there, looking at him with an awful expression. It was pity and compassion and regret and nothing he ever wanted to see on a doctor's face.

Gregory slumped. He'd done what had been asked of him. He'd woken Lucy, if only for a moment. She was sleeping again, now curled on her side, facing in the other direction.

"I did what you asked," he said softly. He looked back up at Peter. "I did what you asked," he repeated, sharply this time.

"I know," Peter said gently, "and I can't tell you how reassuring it is that she spoke. But we cannot count that as a guarantee."

Gregory tried to speak, but his throat was closing. That awful choking feeling was rushing through him again, and all he could manage was to breathe. If he could just breathe, and do nothing else, he might be able to keep from crying in front of his friend.

"The body needs to regain its strength after a blood loss," Peter explained. "She may sleep a while yet. And she might—" He cleared his throat. "She might not wake up again."

"Of course she will wake up," Hyacinth said sharply. "She's done it once, she can do it again."

The doctor gave her a fleeting glance before turning his attention back to Gregory. "If all goes well, I would think we could expect a fairly ordinary recovery. It might take some time," he warned. "I can't be sure how much blood she's lost. It can take months for the body to reconstitute its necessary fluids."

Gregory nodded slowly.

"She'll be weak. I should think she'd need to remain in bed for at least a month."

"She won't like that."

Peter cleared his throat. Awkwardly. "You will send someone if there is a change?"

Gregory nodded dumbly.

"No," Hyacinth said, stepping forth to bar the door. "I have more questions."

"I'm sorry," the doctor said quietly. "I have no more answers."

And even Hyacinth could not argue with that.

When morning came, bright and unfathomably cheery, Gregory woke in Lucy's sickroom, still in the chair next to her bed. She was sleeping, but she was restless, making her usual sleepy sounds as she shifted position. And then, amazingly, she opened her eyes.

"Lucy?" Gregory clutched her hand, then had to force himself to loosen his grip.

"I'm thirsty," she said weakly.

He nodded and rushed to get her a glass of water. "You had me so— I didn't—" But he couldn't say anything more. His voice broke into a thousand pieces, and all that came out was a wrenching sob. He froze, his back to her as he tried to regain his composure. His hand shook; the water splashed onto his sleeve.

He heard Lucy try to say his name, and he knew he had to get ahold of himself. *She* was the one who had nearly died; he did not get to collapse while she needed him.

He took a deep breath. Then another. "Here you are," he said, trying to keep his voice bright as he turned around. He brought the glass to her, then immediately realized his mistake. She was too weak to hold the glass, much less push herself up into a sitting position.

He set it down on a nearby table, then put his arms around her in a gentle embrace so that he could help her up. "Let me just fix the pillows," he murmured, shifting and fluffing until he was satisfied that she had adequate support. He held the glass to her lips and gave it the tiniest of tips. Lucy took a bit, then sat back, breathing hard from the effort of drinking.

Gregory watched her silently. He couldn't imagine she'd got more than a few drops into her. "You should drink more," he said.

She nodded, almost imperceptibly, then said, "In a moment."

"Would it be easier with a spoon?"

She closed her eyes and gave another weak nod.

He looked around the room. Someone had brought him tea the night before and they hadn't come to clean it up. Probably hadn't wanted to disturb him. Gregory decided that expeditiousness was more important than cleanliness, and he plucked the spoon from the sugar dish. Then he thought—she could probably use a bit of sugar, so he brought the whole thing over.

"Here you are," he murmured, giving her a spoonful of water. "Do you want some sugar, too?"

She nodded, and so he put a bit on her tongue.

"What happened?" she asked.

He stared at her in shock. "You don't know?"

She blinked a few times. "Was I bleeding?"

"Quite a lot," he choked out. He couldn't possibly have elaborated. He didn't want to describe the rush of blood he had witnessed. He didn't want her to know, and to be honest, he wanted to forget.

Her brow wrinkled, and her head tipped to the side. After a few moments Gregory realized she was trying to look toward the foot of the bed.

"We cleaned it up," he said, his lips finding a tiny smile. That was so like Lucy, making certain that all was in order.

She gave a little nod. Then she said, "I'm tired."

"Dr. Jarvis said you will be weak for several months. I would imagine you will be confined to bed for some time."

She let out a groan, but even this was a feeble sound. "I hate bed rest."

He smiled. Lucy was a doer; she always had been. She

liked to fix things, to make things, to make everyone happy. Inactivity just about killed her.

A bad metaphor. But still.

He leaned toward her with a stern expression. "You will stay in bed if I have to tie you down."

"You're not the sort," she said, moving her chin ever so slightly. He thought she was trying for an insouciant expression, but it took energy to be cheeky, apparently. She closed her eyes again, letting out a soft sigh.

"I did once," he said.

She made a funny sound that he thought might actually be a laugh. "You did, didn't you?"

He leaned down and kissed her very gently on the lips. "I saved the day."

"You always save the day."

"No." He swallowed. "That's you."

Their eyes met, the gaze between them deep and strong. Gregory felt something wrenching within him, and for a moment he was sure he was going to sob again. But then, just as he felt himself begin to come apart, she gave a little shrug and said, "I couldn't move now, anyway."

His equilibrium somewhat restored, he got up to scavenge a leftover biscuit from the tea tray. "Remember that in a week." He had no doubt that she would be trying to get out of bed long before it was recommended.

"Where are the babies?"

Gregory paused, then turned around. "I don't know," he replied slowly. Good heavens, he'd completely forgotten. "In the nursery, I imagine. They are both perfect. Pink and loud and everything they are supposed to be."

Lucy smiled weakly and let out another tired sound. "May I see them?"

"Of course. I'll have someone fetch them immediately."

"Not the others, though," Lucy said, her eyes clouding. "I don't want them to see me like this."

"I think you look beautiful," he said. He came over and perched on the side of the bed. "I think you might be the most beautiful thing I have ever seen."

"Stop," she said, since Lucy never had been terribly good at receiving compliments. But he saw her lips wobble a bit, hovering between a smile and a sob.

"Katharine was here yesterday," he told her.

Her eyes flew open.

"No, no, don't worry," he said quickly. "I told her you were merely sleeping. Which is what you were doing. She isn't concerned."

"Are you sure?"

He nodded. "She called you La la la Lucy."

Lucy smiled. "She is marvelous."

"She is just like you."

"That's not why she is marv—"

"It is exactly why," he interrupted with a grin. "And I almost forgot to tell you. She named the babies."

"I thought you named the babies."

"I did. Here have some more water." He paused for a moment to get some more liquid into her. Distraction was going to be the key, he decided. A little bit here and a little bit there, and they'd get through a full glass of water. "Katharine thought of their second names. Francesca Hyacinth and Eloise Lucy."

"Eloise . . . ?"

"Lucy," he finished for her. "Eloise Lucy. Isn't it lovely?"

To his surprise, she didn't protest. She just nodded, the motion barely perceptible, her eyes filling with tears.

"She said it was because you are the best mother in the world," he added softly.

She did cry then, big silent tears rolling from her eyes.

"Would you like me to bring you the babies now?" he asked.

She nodded. "Please. And . . ." She paused, and Gregory saw her throat work. "And bring the rest, too."

"Are you certain?"

She nodded again. "If you can help me to sit up a little straighter, I think I can manage hugs and kisses."

His tears, the ones he had been trying so hard to suppress, slid from his eyes. "I can't think of anything that might help you to get better more quickly." He walked to the door, then turned around when his hand was on the knob. "I love you, La la la Lucy."

"I love you, too."

Gregory must have told the children to behave with extra decorum, Lucy decided, because when they filed into her room (rather adorably from oldest to youngest, the tops of their heads making a charming little staircase) they did so very quietly, finding their places against the wall, their hands clasped sweetly in front of their bodies.

Lucy had no idea who *these* children were. *Her* children had never stood so still.

"It's lonely over here," she said, and there would have been a mass tumble onto the bed except that Gregory leapt into the riot with a forceful "Gently!"

Although in retrospect, it was not so much his verbal order that held the chaos at bay as his arms, which prevented at least three children from cannonballing onto the mattress.

"Mimsy won't let me see the babies," four-year-old Ben muttered.

"It's because you haven't taken a bath in a month," retorted Anthony, two years his elder, almost to the day.

"How is that possible?" Gregory wondered aloud.

"He's very sneaky," Daphne informed him. She was trying to worm her way closer to Lucy, though, so her words were muffled.

"How sneaky can one be with a stench like that?" Hermione asked.

"I roll in flowers every single day," Ben said archly.

Lucy paused for a moment, then decided it might be best not to reflect too carefully on what her son had just said. "Er, which flowers are those?"

"Well, not the rosebush," he told her, sounding as if he could not believe she'd even asked.

Daphne leaned toward him and gave a delicate sniff. "Peonies," she announced.

"You can't tell that by sniffing him," Hermione said indignantly. The two girls were separated by only a year and a half, and when they weren't whispering secrets they were bickering like . . .

Well, bickering like Bridgertons, really.

"I have a very good nose," Daphne said. She looked up, waiting for someone to confirm this.

"The scent of peonies is very distinctive," Katharine confirmed. She was sitting down by the foot of the bed with Richard. Lucy wondered when the two of them had decided they were too old for piling together at the pillows. They were getting so big, all of them. Even little Colin didn't look like a baby any longer.

"Mama?" he said mournfully.

"Come here, sweetling," she murmured, reaching out for him. He was a little butterball, all chubby cheeks and wobbly knees, and she'd really thought he was going to be her last. But now she had two more, swaddled up in their cradles, getting ready to grow into their names.

Eloise Lucy and Francesca Hyacinth. They had quite the namesakes.

"I love you, Mama," Colin said, his warm little face finding the curve of her neck.

"I love you, too," Lucy choked out. "I love all of you."

"When will you get out of bed?" Ben asked.

"I'm not sure yet. I'm still terribly tired. It might be a few weeks."

"A few *weeks*?" he echoed, clearly aghast.

"We'll see," she murmured. Then she smiled. "I'm feeling so much better already."

And she was. She was still tired, more so than she could ever remember. Her arms were heavy, and her legs felt like logs, but her heart was light and full of song.

"I love everybody," she suddenly announced. "You," she said to Katharine, "and you and you and you and you and you and you. And the two babies in the nursery, too."

"You don't even know them yet," Hermione pointed out.

"I know that I love them." She looked over at Gregory. He was standing by the door, back where none of the children would see him. Tears were streaming down his face. "And I know that I love you," she said softly.

He nodded, then wiped his face with the back of his hand. "Your mother needs her rest," he said, and Lucy wondered if the children heard the choke in his voice.

But if they did, they didn't say anything. They grumbled a bit, but they filed out with almost as much decorum as they'd shown filing in. Gregory was last, poking his head back into the room before shutting the door. "I'll be back soon," he said.

She nodded her response, then sank back down into bed. "I love everybody," she said again, liking the way the words made her smile. "I love everybody."

And it was true. She did.

23 June 1840
Cutbank Manor
Nr Winkfield, Berks.

Dear Gareth—

I am delayed in Berkshire. The twins' arrival was quite dramatic, and Lucy must remain in bed for at least a month. My brother says that he can manage without me, but this is so untrue as to be laughable. Lucy herself begged me to remain—out of his earshot, to be sure; one must always take into account the tender sensibilities of the men of our species. (I know you will indulge me in this sentiment; even you must confess that women are far more useful in a sickroom.)

It is a very good thing that I was here. I am not certain she would have survived the birth without me.

She lost a great deal of blood, and there were moments when we were not sure she would regain wakefulness. I took it upon myself to give her a few private, stern words. I do not recall the precise phrasing, but I might have threatened to maim her. I also might have given emphasis to the threat by adding, "You know I will do it."

I was, of course, speaking on the assumption that she would be too weak to locate the essential contradiction in such a statement—if she did not wake up, it would be of very little use to maim her.

You are laughing at me right now, I am sure. But she did cast a wary look in my direction when she awakened. And she did whisper a most heartfelt "Thank you."

So here I will be for a bit more time. I do miss you dreadfully. It is times like these that remind one of what it is truly important. Lucy recently announced that she loves everybody. I believe we both know that I will never possess the patience for that, but I certainly love you. And I love her. And Isabella and George. And Gregory. And really, quite a lot of people.

I am a lucky woman, indeed.

Your loving wife,
Hyacinth

Violet in Bloom

Romance novels, by definition, wrap up neatly. The hero and heroine have pledged their love, and it is clear that this happy ending will be forever. This means, however, that an author can't write a true sequel; if I brought back the same hero and heroine from a previous book, I'd have to put the previous happy ending in jeopardy before assuring them of another.

So romance series are instead collections of spin-offs, with secondary characters returning to star in their own novels, and previous protagonists popping by occasionally when needed. Rarely does an author get the chance to take a character and watch her grow over many books.

This was what made Violet Bridgerton so special. When she first appeared in *The Duke and I*, she was a fairly two-dimensional, standard Regency mama. But over the course of eight books, she became so much more. With each Bridgerton novel, something new was revealed, and by the time I finished *On the Way to the Wedding*, she had become my favorite character in the series. Readers clamored for me to write a happy ending for Violet, but I couldn't. Truly, I couldn't—I really don't think I could write a hero good enough for her. But I, too, wanted to learn more about Violet, and it was a labor of love to write "Violet in Bloom." I hope you enjoy it.

Violet in Bloom:
A Novella

Surrey, England
1774

"Violet Elizabeth! What on earth do you think you're doing?"

At the sound of her governess's outraged voice, Violet Ledger paused, considering her options. There seemed little chance she could plead complete innocence; she had been caught red-handed, after all.

Or rather, purple-handed. She was clutching a breathtakingly aromatic blackberry pie, and the still-warm filling had started to ooze over the lip of the pan.

"Violet . . ." came Miss Fernburst's stern voice.

She *could* say that she was hungry. Miss Fernburst knew well enough that Violet was mad for sweets. It was not entirely out of the realm of possibility that she might abscond with an entire pie, to be eaten . . .

Where? Violet thought quickly. Where *would* one go with an entire blackberry pie? Not back to her room; she'd never be able to hide the evidence. Miss Fernburst would never believe Violet was dumb enough to do that.

No, if she were stealing a pie in order to eat it, she would take it outside. Which was precisely where she'd been going. Although not exactly to eat a pie.

She might make a truth of this lie yet.

"Would you like some pie, Miss Fernburst?" Violet asked sweetly. She smiled and batted her eyes, well aware that despite her eight and a half years, she didn't look a day over six. Most of the time she found this vexing—no one liked to be thought a baby, after all. But she was not above using her petite stature to her advantage when the situation warranted.

"I'm having a picnic," Violet added for clarification.

"With whom?" Miss Fernburst asked suspiciously.

"Oh, my dollies. Mette and Sonia and Francesca and Fiona Marie and . . ." Violet rattled off a whole list of names, making them up as she went along. She did have a rather absurd number of dollies. As the only child in her generation, despite having a raft of aunts and uncles, she was showered with presents on a regular basis. Someone was always coming to visit them in Surrey—the proximity to London was simply too convenient for anyone to resist—and it seemed dollies were the gift *du jour*.

Violet smiled. Miss Fernburst would have been proud of her, thinking in French. It was really too bad there was no way to show it off.

"Miss Violet," Miss Fernburst said sternly, "you must return that pie to the kitchen at once."

"All of it?"

"Of course you must return all of it," Miss Fernburst said in an exasperated voice. "You don't even have a utensil with which to cut yourself a piece. Or consume it."

True. But Violet's ambitions for the pie had not required utensils of any kind. She was already in deep, though, so she dug herself further in by replying, "I couldn't carry it all. I was planning to go back for a spoon."

"And leave the pie in the garden for the crows to ravage?"

"Well, I hadn't really thought of that."

"Hadn't really thought of what?" came the deep, booming voice that could only belong to her father. Mr. Ledger walked closer. "Violet, what on earth are you doing in the drawing room with a pie?"

"Precisely what I am presently attempting to ascertain," Miss Fernburst said stiffly.

"Well . . ." Violet stalled, trying not to glance longingly at the French doors that led to the lawn. She was sunk now. She'd never been able to fib to her father. He saw through everything. She didn't know how he did it; it must have been something in her eyes.

"She said she was planning a picnic in the garden with her dollies," Miss Fernburst reported.

"Really." Not a question, a statement. Her father knew her far too well to make it a question.

Violet nodded. Well, a little nod. Or maybe more of a bob of the chin.

"Because you always feed actual food to your toys," her father said.

She said nothing.

"Violet," her father said sternly, "what were you planning to do with that pie?"

"Ehm . . ." Her eyes couldn't seem to leave a spot on the floor about six feet to her left.

"*Violet?*"

"It was only going to be a small trap," she mumbled.

"A small what?"

"A trap. For that Bridgerton boy."

"For—" Her father chuckled. She could tell he hadn't meant to, and after he covered his mouth with a hand and a cough, his face was once again stern.

"He's horrid," she said, before he could scold her.

"Oh, he's not so bad."

"He's dreadful, Father. You know that he is. And he doesn't even live here in Upper Smedley. He's only visiting. You'd think he would know how to behave properly—his father is a viscount, but—"

"Violet . . ."

"He is no gentleman," she sniffed.

"He's nine."

"Ten," she corrected primly. "And it is my opinion that a ten-year-old ought to know how to be a good houseguest."

"He's not our houseguest," her father pointed out. "He's visiting the Millertons."

"Be that as it may," Violet said, thinking that she'd very much like to cross her arms. But she was still holding that accursed pie.

Her father waited for her to finish the thought. She did not.

"Give the pie to Miss Fernburst," her father ordered.

"Being a good houseguest means that you don't behave horridly to the neighbors," Violet protested.

"The pie, Violet."

She handed it to Miss Fernburst, who, in all truth, didn't look like she much wanted it. "Shall I take it back to the kitchen?" the governess inquired.

"Please do," Violet's father said.

Violet waited until Miss Fernburst had disappeared

around the corner, then she looked up at her father with a disgruntled expression. "He put flour in my hair, Father."

"Flowers?" he echoed. "Don't young girls like that sort of thing?"

"Flour, Father! Flour! The kind one uses to bake cakes! Miss Fernburst had to wash my hair for twenty minutes just to get it out. And don't you laugh!"

"I'm not!"

"You are," she accused. "You want to. I can see it in your face."

"I'm merely wondering how the young fellow managed it."

"I don't know," Violet ground out. Which was the worst insult of all. He'd managed to cover her with finely ground flour and she still didn't know how he'd done it. One minute she'd been walking in the garden, and the next she'd tripped and . . .

Poof! Flour everywhere.

"Well," her father said matter-of-factly, "I believe he's leaving at the week's end. So you won't have to endure his presence for very much longer. If at all," he added. "We're not expecting to visit with the Millertons this week, are we?"

"We weren't expecting to visit with them yesterday," Violet replied, "and he still managed to flour me."

"How do you know it was he?"

"Oh, I know," she said darkly. As she was sputtering and coughing and batting at the flour cloud, she'd heard him cackling in triumph. If she hadn't had so much flour in her eyes, she probably would have seen him, too, grinning in that awful *boy* way of his.

"He seemed perfectly pleasant when he and Georgie Millerton came for tea on Monday."

"Not when *you* weren't in the room."

"Oh. Well . . ." Her father paused, his lips pursing thoughtfully. "I'm sorry to have to say it, but it's a lesson in life you'll learn soon enough. Boys are horrid."

Violet blinked. "But . . . but . . ."

Mr. Ledger shrugged. "I'm sure your mother will agree."

"But *you're* a boy."

"And I was horrid, I assure you. Ask your mother."

Violet stared at him in disbelief. It was true that her parents had known each other since they were small children, but she could not believe that her father would ever have behaved badly toward her mother. He was so kind and thoughtful to her now. He was always kissing her hand and smiling at her with his eyes.

"He probably likes you," Mr. Ledger said. "The Bridgerton boy," he clarified, as if that were necessary.

Violet let out a horrified gasp. "He does not."

"Perhaps not," her father said agreeably. "Perhaps he is simply horrid. But he probably thinks you're pretty.

That's what boys do when they think a girl is pretty. And you know I think you're uncommonly pretty."

"You're my father," she said, giving him a bit of a look. Everyone knew that fathers were required to think their daughters were pretty.

"I'll tell you what," he said, leaning down and touching her gently on the chin. "If that Bridgerton boy—what did you say his name was, again?"

"Edmund."

"Edmund, right, of course. If Edmund Bridgerton bothers you again, I shall personally call upon him to defend your honor."

"A duel?" Violet breathed, every inch of her tingling with horrified delight.

"To the death," her father confirmed. "Or perhaps just a stern talking-to. I'd really rather not go to the gallows for running through a nine-year-old boy."

"Ten," Violet corrected.

"Ten. You do seem to know a lot about young Master Bridgerton."

Violet opened her mouth to defend herself because, after all, it wasn't as if she could have avoided knowing a few things about Edmund Bridgerton; she'd been forced to sit in the same drawing room with him for two hours on Monday. But she could tell that her father was teasing her. If she said anything more, he'd never stop.

"May I go back to my room now?" she asked primly.

Her father nodded his assent. "But there will be no pie for pudding this evening."

Violet's mouth fell open. "But—"

"No arguments, if you please. You were quite prepared to sacrifice the pie this afternoon. It doesn't seem right that you should have some now that you've been thwarted."

Violet clamped her lips together in a mutinous line. She gave a stiff nod, then marched away toward the stairs. "I hate Edmund Bridgerton," she muttered.

"What was that?" her father called out.

"I hate Edmund Bridgerton!" she yelled. "And I don't care who knows it!"

Her father laughed, which only made her more furious.

Boys really were horrid. But especially Edmund Bridgerton.

London
Nine years later

"I tell you, Violet," Miss Mary Filloby said with unconvincing certitude, "it is a good thing we are not raving beauties. It would make everything so complicated."

Complicated how? Violet wanted to ask. Because from

where she was sitting (at the wall, with the wallflowers, watching the girls who *weren't* wallflowers), ravishing beauty didn't seem like such a bad thing.

But she didn't bother to ask. She didn't need to. Mary would take only one breath before imploring:

"Look at her. Look at her!"

Violet was already looking at her.

"She's got eight men at her side," Mary said, her voice an odd combination of awe and disgust.

"I count nine," Violet murmured.

Mary crossed her arms. "I refuse to include my own brother."

Together they sighed, all four of their eyes on Lady Begonia Dixon, who, with her rosebud mouth, sky blue eyes, and perfectly sloped shoulders, had enchanted the male half of London society within days of her arrival in town. Her hair was probably glorious, too, Violet thought disgruntledly. Thank heavens for wigs. Truly, they were the great levelers, allowing girls with dishwater blond hair to compete with the ones with the shiny, curly locks of gold.

Not that Violet minded her dishwater blond hair. It was perfectly acceptable. And shiny, even. Just not curly or gold.

"How long have we been sitting here?" Mary wondered aloud.

"Three quarters of an hour," Violet estimated.

"That long?"

Violet nodded glumly. "I'm afraid so."

"There aren't enough men," Mary said. Her voice had lost its edge, and she sounded somewhat deflated. But it was true. There weren't enough men. Too many had gone off to fight in the Colonies, and far too many had not come back. Add to that the complication that was Lady Begonia Dixon (nine men lost to the rest of them right there, Violet thought morosely), and the shortage was dire indeed.

"I have danced only once all night," Mary said. There was a pause, then: "And you?"

"Twice," Violet admitted. "But once was with your brother."

"Oh. Well, then that doesn't count."

"Yes, it does," Violet shot back. Thomas Filloby was a gentleman with two legs and all his teeth, and as far as she was concerned, he counted.

"You don't even *like* my brother."

There was nothing to say that wasn't rude or a lie, so Violet just did a funny little motion with her head that could be interpreted either way.

"I wish you had a brother," Mary said.

"So he could ask you to dance?"

Mary nodded.

"Sorry." Violet waited a moment, expecting Mary to

say, "It's not your fault," but Mary's attention had finally been ripped from Lady Begonia Dixon, and she was presently squinting at someone over by the lemonade table.

"Who's *that*?" Mary asked.

Violet cocked her head to the side. "The Duke of Ashbourne, I believe."

"No, not him," Mary said impatiently. "The one next to him."

Violet shook her head. "I don't know." She couldn't get a very good look at the gentleman in question, but she was quite sure she didn't know him. He was tall, although not overly so, and he stood with the athletic grace of a man who was perfectly at ease in his own body. She didn't need to see his face up close to know that he was handsome. Because even if he wasn't elegant, even if his face was no Michelangelo's dream, he would still be handsome.

He was confident, and men with confidence were always handsome.

"He's new," Mary said assessingly.

"Give him a few minutes," Violet said in a dry voice. "He'll find Lady Begonia in due course."

But the gentleman in question didn't seem to notice Lady Begonia, remarkable as that seemed. He loitered by the lemonade table, drinking six cups, then ambled over to the refreshments, where he gobbled down an astonishing amount of food. Violet wasn't sure why she was following his progress through the room, except that he was new, and she was bored.

And he was young. And handsome.

But mostly because she was bored. Mary had been asked to dance by her third cousin, and so Violet had been left alone in her wallflower's chair, with nothing to do besides count the number of canapés the new gentleman had eaten.

Where was her mother? Surely it was time to leave. The air was thick, and she was hot, and it didn't look as if she was going to gain a third dance, and—

"Hullo!" came a voice. "I know you."

Violet blinked, looking up. It was him! The ravenously hungry, twelve-canapé-eating gentleman.

She had no idea who he was.

"You're Miss Violet Ledger," he said.

Miss Ledger, actually, since she had no older sister, but she didn't correct him. His use of her full name seemed to indicate that he had known her for some time, or perhaps had known her quite a long time ago.

"I'm sorry," she murmured, because she'd never been good at faking an acquaintance, "I . . ."

"Edmund Bridgerton," he said with an easy grin. "I met you years ago. I was visiting George Millerton." He glanced around the room. "I say, have you seen him? He's supposed to be here."

"Er, yes," Violet replied, somewhat taken aback by Mr. Bridgerton's gregarious amiability. People in London weren't generally so friendly. Not that she minded friendly. It was just that she'd grown rather un-used to it.

"We were supposed to meet," Mr. Bridgerton said absently, still looking this way and that.

Violet cleared her throat. "He's here. I danced with him earlier."

Mr. Bridgerton considered this for a moment, then plopped down in the chair next to her. "I don't think I've seen you since I was ten."

Violet was still trying to recollect.

He grinned at her sideways. "I got you with my flour bomb."

She gasped. "That was *you*?"

He grinned again. "Now you remember."

"I'd forgotten your name," she said.

"I'm crushed."

Violet twisted in her seat, smiling despite herself. "I was so angry . . ."

He started to laugh. "You should have seen your face."

"I couldn't *see* anything. I had flour in my eyes."

"I was surprised you never exacted revenge."

"I tried," she assured him. "My father caught me."

He nodded, as if he had some experience with this particular brand of frustration. "I hope it was something magnificent."

"I believe it involved pie."

He nodded approvingly.

"It would have been brilliant," she told him.

He quirked a brow. "Strawberry?"

"Blackberry," she said, her voice diabolical with only the memory of it.

"Even better." He sat back, making himself comfortable. There was something so loose and limber about him, as if he fit smoothly into any situation. His posture was as correct as any gentleman's, and yet . . .

He was different.

Violet wasn't sure how to describe it, but there was something about him that put her at ease. He made her feel happy. Free.

Because he was. It took only a minute at his side to realize that he was the most happy and free person she would ever meet.

"Did you ever find the opportunity to put your weapon to use?" he asked.

She looked at him quizzically.

"The pie," he reminded her.

"Oh. No. My father would have had my head. And besides that, there was no one to attack."

"Surely you could have found a reason to go after Georgie," Mr. Bridgerton said.

"I don't attack without provocation," Violet said with what she hoped was a teasingly arch smile, "and Georgie Millerton never floured me."

"A fair-minded lady," Mr. Bridgerton said. "The very best kind."

Violet felt her cheeks turn ridiculously warm. Thank heavens the sun had nearly gone down and there wasn't much light coming through the windows. With just the flickering candles to light the room, he might not realize just how pink her face had gone.

"No brother or sister to earn your ire?" Mr. Bridgerton asked. "It does seem a shame to let a perfectly good pie go to waste."

"If I recall correctly," Violet replied, "it didn't go to waste. Everyone had some for pudding that night except me. And anyway, I don't have any brothers or sisters."

"Really?" His brow furrowed. "Strange that I don't remember that about you."

"Do you remember much?" she asked dubiously. "Because I . . ."

"Don't?" he finished for her. He chuckled. "Don't

worry. I take no insult. I never forget a face. It's a gift and a curse."

Violet thought of all the times—right now included—that she'd not known the name of the person in front of her. "How could such a thing be a curse?"

He leaned toward her with a flirtatious tilt of his head. "One gets one's heart broken, you know, when the pretty ladies don't remember one's name."

"Oh!" She felt her face flush. "I'm so sorry, but you must realize, it was so long ago, and—"

"Stop," he said, laughing. "I jest."

"Oh, of course." She ground her teeth together. Of course he was teasing. How could she have been such a dolt as to not realize it. Although . . .

Had he just called her pretty?

"You were saying you have no siblings," he said, expertly returning the conversation to its previous spot. And for the first time, she felt as if she held his full attention. He didn't have one eye on the crowd, idly scanning for George Millerton. He was looking at her, right into her eyes, and it was terrifyingly spectacular.

She swallowed, remembering his question about two seconds too late for smooth conversation. "No siblings," she said, her voice coming out too fast to make up for her delay. "I was a difficult child."

His eyes widened, almost thrillingly. "Really?"

"No, I mean, I was a difficult baby. To be born." Good heavens, where had her verbal skills gone? "The doctor told my mother not to have more." She swallowed miserably, determined to find her brain again. "And you?"

"And me?" he teased.

"Do you have siblings?"

"Three. Two sisters and a brother."

The thought of three extra people in her often lonely childhood suddenly sounded marvelous. "Are you close?" she asked.

He thought about that for a moment. "I suppose I am. I've never really thought about it. Hugo's quite my opposite, but I would still consider him my closest friend."

"And your sisters? Are they younger or older?"

"One of each. Billie's got seven years on me. She's finally got herself married, so I don't see much of her, but Georgiana's just a bit younger. She's probably your age."

"Is she not here in London, then?"

"She'll be out next year. My parents claim they're still recovering from Billie's debut."

Violet felt her eyebrows rise, but she knew she shouldn't—

"You can ask," he told her.

"What did she do?" she said immediately.

He leaned in with a conspiratorial gleam. "I never got all the details, but I did hear something about a fire."

Violet sucked in her breath—in shock *and* admiration.

"And a broken bone," he added.

"Oh, the poor thing."

"Not *her* broken bone."

Violet smothered a laugh. "Oh no. I shouldn't—"

"You can laugh," he told her.

She did. It burst out of her, loud and lovely, and when she realized people were staring at her, she didn't care.

They sat together for a few moments, the silence between them as companionable as a sunrise. Violet kept her eyes on the lords and ladies dancing in front of her; somehow she knew that if she dared to turn and look at Mr. Bridgerton, she'd never be able to look away.

The music drew to a close, but when she looked down, her toes were tapping. His, too, and then—

"I say, Miss Ledger, would you like to dance?"

She turned then, and she *did* look at him. And it was true, she realized; she wasn't going to be able to look away. Not from his face, and not from the life that stretched in front of her, as perfect and lovely as that blackberry pie from so many years ago.

She took his hand and it felt like a promise. "There is nothing I would rather do."

Somewhere in Sussex
Six months later

"Where are we going?"

Violet Bridgerton had been Violet Bridgerton for precisely eight hours and thus far she was liking her new surname very much.

"Oh, it's a surprise," Edmund said, grinning wolfishly at her from across the carriage.

Well, not exactly from across the carriage. She was practically in his lap.

And . . . now she *was* in his lap.

"I love you," he said, laughing over her squeal of surprise.

"Not as much as I love you."

He gave her his best look of condescension. "You only *think* you know what you're talking about."

She smiled. It was not the first time they had had this conversation.

"Very well," he allowed. "You may love me more, but I will love you *better*." He waited a moment. "Aren't you going to ask what that means?"

Violet thought of all the ways he had loved her already. They had not preempted their marriage vows, but they had not been precisely chaste.

She decided she had better not ask. "Just tell me where we are going," she said instead.

He laughed, letting one of his arms steal around her. "On our honeymoon," he murmured, his words falling warm and delicious over her skin.

"But *where*?"

"All in good time, my dear Mrs. Bridgerton. All in good time."

She tried to scoot back over to her own side of the carriage—it was, she reminded herself, the proper thing to do—but he was having none of it, and he clamped down with his arm. "Where do you think you're going?" he growled.

"That's just the thing. I don't know!"

Edmund laughed at that, big and hearty and so perfectly, splendidly warm. He was so happy. He made *her* happy. Her mother had declared that he was too young, that Violet should look for a more mature gentleman, preferably one who had already come into his title. But from that first shining moment on the dance floor, when her hand met his and she took her first true look into his eyes, Violet could not imagine a life with anyone but Edmund Bridgerton.

He was her other half, the spoon she was made to nestle into. They would be young together, and then they would grow old together. They would hold hands, and move to the country, and make lots and lots of babies.

No lonely households for her children. She wanted a passel of them. A gaggle. She wanted noise and laughter, and everything Edmund made her feel, with fresh air, and strawberry tarts, and—

Well, and the occasional trip to London. She was not so rustic that she did not wish to have her gowns made by Madame Lamontaine. And of course she could not possibly go a full year without a visit to the opera. But other than that—and a party here and there; she did like company—she wanted motherhood.

She craved it.

But she hadn't realized how desperately she wanted it until she'd met Edmund. It was as if something inside of her had been holding back, not allowing her to wish for babies until she'd found the only man with whom she could imagine making them.

"We're almost there," he said, peeking out the window.

"And that would be . . . ?"

The carriage had already slowed; now it ground to a halt, and Edmund looked up with a knowing grin. "Here," he finished for her.

The door swung open, and he alighted, holding out his hand to help her down. She stepped carefully—the last thing she wanted was to fall facedown in the dirt on her wedding night—then looked up.

"The Hare and Hounds?" she asked blankly.

"The very one," he said proudly. As if there weren't a hundred inns spread across England that looked precisely the same.

She blinked. Several times. "An inn?"

"Indeed." He leaned down to speak conspiratorially in her ear. "I suppose you're wondering why I've chosen such a spot."

"Well . . . yes." Not that there was anything *wrong* with an inn. It certainly looked well kept from the outside. And if he had brought her here, it must be clean and comfortable.

"Here's the rub," he said, bringing her hand to his lips. "If we go home, I shall have to introduce you to all of the servants. Of course there are only six, but still . . . their feelings will be terribly injured if we do not lavish the appropriate amount of attention on them."

"Of course," Violet said, still a little awed by the fact that she would soon be mistress of her own home. Edmund's father had given him a snug little manor house but one month earlier. It wasn't large, but it was theirs.

"Not to mention," Edmund added, "that when we don't come down to breakfast tomorrow, or the next . . ." He paused for a moment, as if pondering something terribly important, before finishing with "or the next . . ."

"We won't be coming down to breakfast?"

He looked her in the eye. "Oh no."

Violet blushed. Right down to the tips of her toes.

"Not for a week, at least."

She swallowed, trying to ignore the heady curls of anticipation that were unraveling within her.

"So you see," he said with a slow smile, "if we spent a week, or really, perhaps two—"

"Two weeks?" she squeaked.

He shrugged endearingly. "It's possible."

"Oh my."

"You'd be so terribly embarrassed in front of the servants."

"But not you," she said.

"It's not the sort of thing men find embarrassing," he said modestly.

"But here at an inn . . ." she said.

"We can remain in our room all month if we wish, and then never visit again!"

"A month?" she echoed. At this point she could not be sure if she had blushed or paled.

"I'll do it if you will," he said devilishly.

"Edmund!"

"Oh, very well, I suppose there might be a thing or two for which we will have to show our faces before Easter."

"Edmund . . ."

"That's Mr. Bridgerton to you."

"So formal?"

"Only because it means I get to call you Mrs. Bridgerton."

It was remarkable, how he could make her so ridiculously happy with a single sentence.

"Shall we head inside?" he asked, lifting her hand as a prompt. "Are you hungry?"

"Er, no," she said, even though she was, a little.

"Thank *God*."

"Edmund!" she laughed, because by now he was walking so quickly she had to skip to keep up with him.

"Your husband," he said, drawing up short for the express purpose (she was sure) of making her crash into him, "is a very impatient man."

"Is that so?" she murmured. She was beginning to feel womanly, powerful.

He didn't answer; they'd already reached the innkeeper's desk, and Edmund was confirming the arrangements.

"Do you mind if I don't carry you up the stairs?" he asked once he was done. "You're light as a feather, of course, and I'm manly enough—"

"Edmund!"

"It's just that I'm rather in a rush."

And his eyes—oh, his eyes—they were filled with a thousand promises, and she wanted to know every one of them.

"I am, too," she said softly, placing her hand in his. "Rather."

"Ah, hell," he said hoarsely, and he scooped her into his arms. "I can't resist."

"The threshold would have been enough," she said, laughing all the way up the stairs.

"Not for me." He kicked open the door to her room, then tossed her onto the bed so that he could shut and lock it behind them.

He came down atop her, moving with a catlike grace she'd never seen in him before. "I love you," he said, his lips touching hers as his hands came under her skirt.

"I love you more," she gasped, because the things he was doing—they ought to be illegal.

"But I . . ." he murmured, kissing his way down to her leg and then—good heavens!—back up again. "I shall love you *better*."

Her clothes seemed to fly away, but she felt no modesty. It was astounding, that she could lie beneath this man, that she could watch him watching her, seeing her—*all* of her—and she felt no shame, no discomfort.

"Oh God, Violet," he groaned, positioning himself awkwardly between her legs. "I have to tell you, I don't have a whole lot of experience with this."

"I don't, either," she gasped.

"I've never—"

That got her attention. "You've never?"

He shook his head. "I think I was waiting for you."

Her breath caught, and then, with a slow, melting smile, she said, "For someone who's never, you're rather good at it."

For a moment she thought she saw tears in his eyes, but then, just like that, they were gone, replaced by a wicked, wicked twinkle. "I plan to improve with age," he told her.

"As do I," she returned, just as slyly.

He laughed, and then she laughed, and they were joined.

And while it was true that they both did get better with age, that first time, up in the Hare and Hounds's finest feather bed . . .

It was bone-crackingly good.

Aubrey Hall, Kent
Twenty years later

The moment Violet heard Eloise scream, she knew something was dreadfully wrong.

It wasn't as if her children never yelled. They yelled all the time, generally at each other. But this wasn't a yell, it was a scream. And it wasn't born of anger or frustration or a misplaced sense of injustice.

This was a scream of terror.

Violet ran through the house, with speed that ought to have been impossible eight months into her eighth pregnancy. She ran down the stairs, across the great hall. She ran through the entry, down the portico stairs . . .

And all the while, Eloise kept screaming.

"What is it?" she gasped, when she finally spied her seven-year-old daughter's face. She was standing at the edge of the west lawn, near the entrance to the hedgerow maze, and she was still screaming.

"Eloise," Violet implored, taking her face in her hands. "Eloise, please, just tell me what is wrong."

Eloise's screams gave way to sobs and she planted her hands over her ears, shaking her head over and over.

"Eloise, you must—" Violet's words broke off sharply. The baby she was carrying was heavy and low, and the pain that shot through her abdomen from all the running hit her like a rock. She took a deep breath, trying to slow her pulse, and placed her hands under her belly, trying to support it from the outside.

"Papa!" Eloise wailed. It was the only word she seemed able to form through her cries.

A cold fist of fear landed in Violet's chest. "What do you mean?"

"Papa," Eloise gasped. "Papapapapapapapapapa—"

Violet slapped her. It would be the only time she would ever strike a child.

Eloise's eyes went wide as she sucked in a huge breath of air. She said nothing, but she turned her head toward the entrance to the maze. And that was when Violet saw it.

A foot.

"Edmund?" she whispered. And then she screamed it.

She ran toward the maze, toward the booted foot that was sticking out of the entrance, attached to a leg, which must be attached to a body, which was lying on the ground.

Not moving at all.

"Edmund, oh Edmund, oh Edmund," she said, over and over, something between a whimper and a cry.

When she reached his side, she knew. He was gone. He was lying on his back, eyes still open, but there was nothing of him left. He was gone. He was thirty-nine years old, and he was gone.

"What happened?" she whispered, frantically touching him, squeezing his arm, his wrist, his cheek. Her mind knew she could not bring him back, and her heart even knew it, too, but somehow her hands would not accept it. She could not stop touching him . . . poking, prodding, yanking, and all the while sobbing.

"Mama?"

It was Eloise, come up behind her.

"Mama?"

She couldn't turn around. She couldn't do it. She couldn't look at her child's face, knowing that she was now her only parent.

"It was a bee, Mama. He was stung by a bee."

Violet went very still. A bee? What did she mean, a bee? Everyone was stung by a bee at some point in their lives. It swelled, it turned red, it hurt.

It didn't kill you.

"He said it was nothing," Eloise said, her voice trembling. "He said it didn't even hurt."

Violet stared at her husband, her head moving from side to side in denial. How could it not have hurt? It had *killed* him. She brought her lips together, trying to form a question, trying to make a bloody sound, but all she could get out was, "Wh-wh-wh-wh——" And she didn't even know what she was trying to ask. *When* did it happen? *What* else did he say? *Where* had they been?

And did it matter? Did any of it matter?

"He couldn't breathe," Eloise said. Violet could feel her daughter's presence growing close, and then, silently, Eloise's hand slipped into her own.

Violet squeezed it.

"He started making this sound"——Eloise tried to imitate, and it sounded awful——"like he was choking. And then . . . Oh, Mama. Oh, Mama!" She threw herself against Violet's side, burying her face where there had once been a curve of a hip. But now there was just a belly, a huge, massive belly, with a child who would never know its father.

"I need to sit down," Violet whispered. "I need to——"

She fainted. Eloise broke her fall.

When Violet came to, she was surrounded by servants. All wore masks of shock and grief. Some could not meet her gaze.

"We need to get you in bed," the housekeeper said briskly. She looked up. "Have we a pallet?"

Violet shook her head as she allowed a footman to assist her into a sitting position. "No, I can walk."

"I really think—"

"*I said I can walk*," she snapped. And then she snapped on the inside, and something burst inside of her. She took a deep, involuntary breath.

"Let me help you," the butler said gently. He slid his arm around her back, and carefully helped her to her feet.

"I can't—but Edmund . . ." She turned to look again, but she couldn't bring herself to do it. *It wasn't him*, she told herself. *That's not how he is.*

That's not how he *was*.

She swallowed. "Eloise?" she asked.

"Nanny has already brought her up," the housekeeper said, moving to Violet's other side.

Violet nodded.

"Ma'am, we must get you to bed. It's not good for the baby."

Violet placed her hand on her belly. The baby was kicking like mad. Which was par for the course. This one kicked and punched and rolled and hiccupped and never, ever stopped. It was quite unlike the others. And it was a good thing, she supposed. This one was going to have to be strong.

She choked back a sob. They were both going to have to be strong.

"Did you say something?" the housekeeper asked, steering her toward the house.

Violet shook her head. "I need to lie down," she whispered.

The housekeeper nodded, then turned to a footman with an urgent stare.

"Send for the midwife."

She didn't need the midwife. No one could believe it, given the shock she'd had and the late state of her pregnancy, but the baby refused to budge. Violet spent three more weeks in bed, eating because she had to, and trying to remind herself that she must be strong. Edmund was gone, but she had seven children who needed her, eight including the stubborn one in her belly.

And then finally, after a quick and easy birth, the midwife announced, "It's a girl," and placed a tiny, quiet bundle in Violet's arms.

A girl. Violet couldn't quite believe it. She'd convinced herself it would be a boy. She would name him Edmund, the A-G alphabetization of her first seven children be damned. He would be called Edmund, and he would *look* like Edmund, because surely that was the only way she would be able to make sense of all this.

But it was a girl, a pink little thing who hadn't made a sound since her initial wail.

"Good morning," Violet said to her, because she didn't know what else to say. She looked down, and she saw her own face—smaller, a bit rounder—but definitely not Edmund's.

The baby looked at her, straight into her eyes, even though Violet knew that could not be true. Babies didn't do that so soon after birth. Violet should know; this was her eighth.

But this one . . . She didn't seem to realize she wasn't supposed to stare her mother down. And then she blinked. Twice. She did it with the most startling deliberation, as if to say, *I'm here. And I know* exactly *what I'm doing.*

Violet caught her breath, so totally and instantly in love she could hardly bear it. And then the baby let out a cry like nothing she had ever heard. She wailed so hard the midwife jumped. She screamed and screamed and screamed and even as the midwife fussed, and the maids came running in, Violet could do nothing but laugh.

"She's perfect," she declared, trying to latch the tiny banshee onto her breast. "She is absolutely perfect."

"What shall you name her?" the midwife asked, once the baby had busied herself trying to figure out how to nurse.

"Hyacinth," Violet decided. It was Edmund's favorite flower, especially the little grape hyacinths that popped up each year to greet the spring. They marked the new birth of the landscape, and this hyacinth—her Hyacinth—she would be Violet's new birth.

The fact that as an H, she would follow perfectly after Anthony, Benedict, Colin, Daphne, Eloise, Francesca, and Gregory . . . Well, that simply made it all the more perfect.

There was a knock at the door, and Nanny Pickens poked her head in. "The girls would love to see Her Ladyship," she said to the midwife. "If she's ready."

The midwife looked at Violet, who nodded. Nanny ushered her three charges inside with a stern "Remember what we talked about. Do not tire your mother."

Daphne came over to the bed, followed by Eloise and Francesca. They possessed Edmund's thick chestnut hair—all of her children did—and Violet wondered if Hyacinth would be the same. Right now she possessed just the tiniest tuft of peachy fuzz.

"Is it a girl?" Eloise asked abruptly.

Violet smiled and changed her position to show off the new baby. "It is."

"Oh, thank heavens," Eloise said with a dramatic sigh. "We needed another one."

Beside her, Francesca nodded. She was what Edmund had always called Eloise's "accidental twin." They shared a birthday, the two of them, a year apart. At six, Francesca generally followed Eloise's lead. Eloise was louder, bolder. But every now and then Francesca would surprise them all and do something that was completely her own.

Not this time, though. She stood beside Eloise, clutching her stuffed doll, agreeing with everything her older sister said.

Violet looked over at Daphne, her oldest girl. She was nearly eleven, certainly old enough to hold a baby. "Do you want to see her?" Violet asked.

Daphne shook her head. She was blinking rapidly, the way she did when she was perplexed, and then all of a sudden she stood up straighter. "You're smiling," she said.

Violet looked back down at Hyacinth, who'd dropped off her breast and fallen quite asleep. "I am," she said, and she could hear it in her voice. She'd forgotten what her voice sounded like with a smile in it.

"You haven't smiled since Papa died," Daphne said.

"I haven't?" Violet looked up at her. Was that possible? She hadn't smiled in three weeks? It didn't feel awkward.

Her lips formed the curve out of memory, perhaps with just a little bit of relief, as if they were indulging in a happy memory.

"You haven't," Daphne confirmed.

She must be right, Violet realized. If she hadn't managed to smile for her children, she certainly hadn't done so in solitude. The grief she'd been feeling . . . it had yawned before her, swallowed her whole. It had been a heavy, physical thing, making her tired, holding her down.

No one could smile through that.

"What is her name?" Francesca asked.

"Hyacinth." Violet shifted her position so the girls could see the baby's face. "What do you think?"

Francesca tilted her head to the side. "She doesn't look like a Hyacinth," Francesca declared.

"Yes, she does," Eloise said briskly. "She's very pink."

Francesca shrugged, conceding the point.

"She'll never know Papa," Daphne said quietly.

"No," Violet said. "No, she won't."

No one said anything, and then Francesca—little Francesca—said, "We can tell her about him."

Violet choked on a sob. She hadn't cried in front of her children since that very first day. She'd saved her tears for her solitude, but she couldn't stop them now. "I think—I think that's a wonderful idea, Frannie."

Francesca beamed, and then she crawled onto the bed,

squirming in until she'd found the perfect spot at her mother's right side. Eloise followed, and then Daphne, and all of them—all the Bridgerton girls—peered down at the newest member of their family.

"He was very tall," Francesca began.

"Not so tall," Eloise said. "Benedict is taller."

Francesca ignored her. "He was tall. And he smiled a great deal."

"He held us on his shoulders," Daphne said, her voice starting to wobble, "until we grew too large."

"And he laughed," Eloise said. "He loved to laugh. He had the very best laugh, our papa . . ."

London
Thirteen years later

Violet had made it her life's work to see all eight of her children happily settled in life, and in general, she did not mind the myriad tasks this entailed. There were parties and invitations and dressmakers and milliners, and that was just the girls. Her sons needed just as much guidance, if not more. The only difference was that society afforded the boys considerably more freedom, which meant that Violet did not need to scrutinize every last detail of their lives.

Of course she tried. She was a mother, after all.

She had a feeling, however, that her job as mother would never be so demanding as it was right at this moment, in the spring of 1815.

She knew very well that in the grand scheme of life, she had nothing about which to complain. In the past six months, Napoleon had escaped Elba, a massive volcano had erupted in the East Indies, and several hundred British soldiers had lost their lives at the Battle of New Orleans—mistakenly fought *after* the peace treaty with the Americans had been signed. Violet, on the other hand, had eight healthy children, all of whom presently had both feet planted on English soil.

However.

There was always a *however*, wasn't there?

This spring marked the first (and Violet prayed, the last) season for which she had two girls "on the market."

Eloise had debuted in 1814, and anyone would have called her a success. Three marriage proposals in three months. Violet had been over the moon. Not that she would have allowed Eloise to accept two of them—the men had been too old. Violet did not care how highly ranked the gentlemen were; no daughter of hers was going to shackle herself to someone who would die before she reached thirty.

Not that this couldn't happen with a young husband.

Illness, accidents, freakishly deadly bees . . . Any number of things could take a man out in his prime. But still, an old man was more likely to die than a young one.

And even if that weren't the case . . . What young girl in her right mind wanted to marry a man past sixty?

But only two of Eloise's suitors had been disqualified for age. The third had been just a year shy of thirty, with a minor title and a perfectly respectable fortune. There had been nothing wrong with Lord Tarragon. Violet was sure he'd make someone a lovely husband.

Just not Eloise.

So now here they were. Eloise was on her second season and Francesca was on her first, and Violet was *exhausted*. She couldn't even press Daphne into service as an occasional chaperone. Her eldest daughter had married the Duke of Hastings two years earlier and then had promptly managed to get herself pregnant for the duration of the 1814 season. And the 1815 one as well.

Violet loved having a grandchild and was over the moon at the prospect of two more arriving soon (Anthony's wife was also with child), but really, sometimes a woman needed help. This evening, for example, had been an utter disaster.

Oh, very well, perhaps *disaster* was a bit of an overstatement, but really, who had thought it a good idea to host a masquerade ball? Because Violet was certain it had not been she. And she had definitely not agreed to attend as Queen Elizabeth. Or if she had, she had not agreed to the crown. It weighed at least five pounds, and she was terrified it would go flying off her head every time she snapped it back and forth, trying to keep an eye on both Eloise and Francesca.

No wonder her neck hurt.

But a mother could not be too careful, especially at a masquerade ball, when young gentlemen (and the occasional young lady) saw their costumes as a license to misbehave. Let's see, there was Eloise, tugging at her Athena costume as she chatted with Penelope Featherington. Who was dressed as a leprechaun, poor thing.

Where was Francesca? Good heavens, that girl could go invisible in a treeless field. And while she was on the subject, where was Benedict? He had *promised* to dance with Penelope, and he had completely disappeared.

Where had he—

"Ooof!"

"Oh, my pardon," Violet said, disentangling herself from a gentleman who appeared to be dressed as . . .

As himself, actually. With a mask.

She did not recognize him, however. Not the voice nor the face beneath the mask. He was of average height, with dark hair and an elegant bearing.

"Good evening, Your Highness," he said.

Violet blinked, then remembered—*the crown*. Although how she might forget the five-pound monstrosity on her head, she'd never know.

"Good evening," she replied.

"Are you looking for someone?"

Again, she wondered at the voice, and again, she came up with nothing. "Several someones, actually," she murmured. "Unsuccessfully."

"My condolences," he said, taking her hand and leaning over it with a kiss. "I myself try to restrict my quests to one someone at a time."

You don't have eight children, Violet almost retorted, but at the last moment she held her tongue. If she did not know this gentleman's identity, there was a chance that he did not know hers, either.

And of course, he *could* have eight children. She wasn't the only person in London to have been so blessed in her marriage. Plus, the hair on his temples was shot through with silver, so he was likely old enough to have sired that many.

"Is it acceptable for a humble gentleman to request a dance with a queen?" he asked her.

Violet almost refused. She hardly ever danced in public. It wasn't that she objected to it, or that she thought it unseemly. Edmund had been gone for more than a dozen years. She still mourned him, but she was not *in* mourning. He would not have wanted that. She wore bright colors, and she maintained a busy social schedule, but still, she rarely danced. She just didn't want to.

But then he smiled, and something about it reminded her of the way Edmund had smiled—that eternally boyish, ever-so-knowing tilt of the lips. It had always made her heart flip, and while this gentleman's smile didn't quite do *that*, it woke something inside of her. Something a little bit devilish, a little carefree.

Something *young*.

"I would be delighted," she said, placing her hand in his.

"Is Mother *dancing*?" Eloise whispered to Francesca.

"More to the point," Francesca returned, "who is she dancing *with*?"

Eloise craned her neck, not bothering to hide her interest. "I have no idea."

"Ask Penelope," Francesca suggested. "She always seems to know who everyone is."

Eloise twisted again, this time searching the other side of the room. "Where *is* Penelope?"

"Where is Benedict?" Colin asked, ambling over to his sisters' sides.

"I don't know," Eloise replied. "Where is Penelope?"

He shrugged. "Last I saw her, she was hiding behind a potted plant. You'd think with that leprechaun costume she'd camouflage better."

"Colin!" Eloise smacked his arm. "Go ask her to dance."

"I already did!" He blinked. "Is that Mother dancing?"

"That's why we were looking for Penelope," Francesca said.

Colin just stared at her, his lips parted.

"It made sense when we said it," Francesca said with a wave. "Do you know who she's dancing with?"

Colin shook his head. "I hate masquerades. Whose idea was this, anyway?"

"Hyacinth," Eloise said grimly.

"*Hyacinth?*" Colin echoed.

Francesca's eyes narrowed. "She's like a puppet master," she growled.

"God save us all when she's grown," Colin said.

No one had to say it, but their faces showed their collective *Amen.*

"Who *is* that dancing with Mother?" Colin asked.

"We don't know," Eloise replied. "That's why we were looking for Penelope. She always seems to know these things."

"She does?"

Eloise scowled at him. "Do you notice anything?"

"Quite a lot, actually," he said affably. "Just not generally what *you* want me to notice."

"We are going to stand here," Eloise announced, "until the dance is finished. And then we shall question her."

"Question whom?"

They all looked up. Anthony, their eldest brother, had arrived.

"Mother is dancing," Francesca said, not that that technically answered his question.

"With whom?" Anthony asked.

"We don't know," Colin told him.

"And you plan to interrogate her about it?"

"That was Eloise's plan," Colin replied.

"I didn't hear you arguing with me," Eloise shot back.

Anthony's brows came together. "I should think it is the gentleman who warrants an interrogation."

"Has it ever occurred to you," Colin asked of none of them in particular, "that as a woman of fifty-two years, she is perfectly capable of choosing her own dance partners?"

"No," Anthony replied, his sharp syllable slicing across Francesca's: "She's our *mother*."

"Actually, she's only fifty-one," Eloise said. At Francesca's sour glare, she added, "Well, she *is*."

Colin gave one baffled look at his sisters before turning to Anthony. "Have you seen Benedict?"

Anthony shrugged. "He was dancing earlier."

"With someone *I don't know*," Eloise said with rising intensity. And volume.

All three of her siblings turned to her.

"None of you find it curious," she demanded, "that both Mother and Benedict are dancing with mysterious strangers?"

"Not really, no," Colin murmured. There was a pause as they all continued to watch their mother make her elegant steps on the dance floor, and then he added, "It occurs to me that this might be why she never dances."

Anthony quirked an imperious brow.

"We've stood here for the past several minutes and done nothing but speculate about her behavior," Colin pointed out.

Silence, and then, from Eloise, "So?"

"She's our *mother*," Francesca said.

"You don't think she deserves her privacy? No, don't answer that," Colin decided. "I'm going to look for Benedict."

"You don't think *he* deserves his privacy?" Eloise countered.

"No," Colin replied. "But at any rate, he's safe enough.

If Benedict doesn't want to be found, I won't find him." With wry salute he wandered off toward the refreshments, although it was really quite obvious that Benedict wasn't anywhere near the biscuits.

"Here she comes," Francesca hissed, and true enough, the dance had ended, and Violet was walking back to the perimeter of the room.

"Mother," Anthony said sternly, the moment she reached her children.

"Anthony," she said with a smile, "I haven't seen you all evening. How is Kate? I'm so sorry she wasn't feeling up to attending."

"Who were you dancing with?" Anthony demanded.

Violet blinked. "I beg your pardon?"

"Who were you dancing with?" Eloise repeated.

"Honestly?" Violet said with a faint smile. "I don't know."

Anthony crossed his arms. "How is that possible?"

"It's a masquerade ball," Violet said with some amusement. "Secret identities and all that."

"Are you going to dance with him again?" Eloise asked.

"Probably not," Violet said, glancing out over the crowd. "Have you seen Benedict? He was supposed to dance with Penelope Featherington."

"Don't try to change the subject," Eloise said.

Violet turned to her, and this time her eyes held a light gleam of reproof. "Was there a subject?"

"We are merely looking out for your best interests," Anthony said, after clearing his throat several times.

"I'm sure you are," Violet murmured, and no one dared to comment on the delicate undertone of condescension in her voice.

"It's just that you so rarely dance," Francesca explained.

"Rarely," Violet said lightly. "Not never."

And then Francesca voiced what they had all been wondering: "Do you like him?"

"The man with whom I just danced? I don't even know his name."

"But—"

"He had a very nice smile," Violet cut in, "and he asked me to dance."

"And?"

Violet shrugged. "And that's all. He talked a great deal about his collection of wooden ducks. I doubt our paths will cross again." She nodded at her children. "If you will excuse me . . ."

Anthony, Eloise, and Francesca watched her walk away. After a long beat of silence, Anthony said, "Well."

"Well," Francesca concurred.

They looked expectantly at Eloise, who scowled back at them and finally exclaimed, "No, that did *not* go well."

There was another long unfilled silence, and then Eloise asked, "Do you think she will ever remarry?"

"I don't know," Anthony said.

Eloise cleared her throat. "And how do we feel about that?"

Francesca looked at her with obvious disdain. "You're speaking about yourself in the plural now?"

"No. I honestly want to know how *we* feel about it. Because I don't know how *I* do."

"I think . . ." Anthony began. But several seconds went by before he slowly said, "I think we think that she can make her own decisions."

None of them noticed Violet standing behind them, hidden by a large decorative fern, smiling.

Aubrey Hall, Kent
Years later

There weren't very many advantages to growing older, but *this*, Violet thought with a happy sigh as she watched several of her younger grandchildren frolicking on the lawn, had to be one of them.

Seventy-five. Who would have ever thought she'd

reach such an age? Her children had asked her what she wanted; it was a huge milestone, they said, she should have grand party to celebrate.

"Just family," had been Violet's reply. It would still be very grand. She had eight children, thirty-three grand-children, and *five* great-grandchildren. Any family gath-ering would be grand!

"What are you thinking, Mama?" Daphne asked, coming to sit next to her on one of the comfortable chaises Kate and Anthony had recently purchased for Aubrey Hall.

"Mostly how happy I am."

Daphne smiled wryly. "You always say that."

Violet gave a one-shouldered shrug. "I always am."

"Really?" Daphne didn't sound as if she quite believed her.

"When I'm with all of you."

Daphne followed her gaze, and together they watched the children. Violet wasn't sure how many were out there. She'd lost count when they had started playing a game that involved a tennis ball, four shuttlecocks, and a log. It must have been fun, because she would have sworn she saw three boys drop from trees to take part.

"I think that's all of them," she said.

Daphne blinked, then asked, "On the lawn? I don't think so. Mary's inside, I'm certain of that. I saw her with Jane and—"

"No, I mean I think I'm done with grandchildren." She turned toward Daphne and smiled. "I don't think my children are going to give me any more."

"Well, *I'm* certainly not," Daphne said, with an expression that clearly said, *Perish the thought!* "And Lucy *can*not. The doctor made her promise. And . . ." She paused, and Violet enjoyed simply watching her face. It was so entertaining to watch her children think. No one ever told you that when you became a parent, how much fun it was to watch them do the quietest things.

Sleeping and thinking. She could watch her progeny do those forever. Even now, when seven of the eight had passed the age of forty.

"You're right," Daphne finally concluded. "I think we're all done."

"Barring surprises," Violet added, because truly, she wouldn't mind if one of her children managed to produce one last grandchild.

"Well, yes," Daphne said, with a rueful sigh, "I know all about those."

Violet laughed. "And you wouldn't have it any other way."

Daphne smiled. "No."

"He just dropped from a tree," Violet said, pointing toward the lawn.

"A tree?"

"On purpose," Violet assured her.

"Of that I have no doubt. I swear that boy is part monkey." Daphne looked out over the lawn, her eyes moving swiftly from side to side, looking for Edward, her youngest son. "I'm so glad we're here. He needs siblings, poor thing. The other four hardly count; they are so much older."

Violet craned her neck. "He appears to have got into an altercation with Anthony and Ben."

"Is he winning?"

Violet squinted a bit. "It looks as if he and Anthony are working together . . . Oh, wait, here comes Daphne. Little Daphne," she added, as if it were necessary.

"That should even things out," Daphne said, grinning as she watched her namesake box her son's ears.

Violet smiled and let out a yawn.

"Tired, Mama?"

"A bit." Violet hated to admit to such things; her children were always so quick to worry about her. They never seemed to understand that a seventy-five-year-old woman might like naps for no other reason than she'd liked them all her life.

Daphne didn't press the matter, though, and they lounged on their chaises in companionable silence until, quite out of the blue, Daphne asked, "Are you *really* happy, Mama?"

"Of course." Violet looked at her with surprise. "Why would you ask such a thing?"

"It's just . . . well . . . you're *alone*."

Violet laughed. "I'm hardly alone, Daphne."

"You *know* what I mean. Papa has been gone for nearly forty years, and you never . . ."

With considerable amusement, Violet waited for her to finish the sentence. When it was apparent that Daphne could not bring herself to do so, Violet took pity on her and asked, "Are you trying to ask if I've ever taken a lover?"

"No!" Daphne burst out, even though Violet was quite sure she'd wondered.

"Well, I haven't," Violet said matter-of-factly. "If you must know."

"Apparently I must," Daphne mumbled.

"I never wanted to," Violet said.

"Never?"

Violet shrugged. "I did not make a vow, or anything so formal. I suppose that if the opportunity had arisen, and the right man had come along, I might have——"

"Married him," Daphne finished for her.

Violet gave her a sideways look. "You really are a prude, Daphne."

Daphne's mouth fell open. Oh, this was fun.

"Oh, very well," Violet said, taking pity on her. "If I'd

found the right man, I probably would have married him, if only to spare you from expiring from the shock of an illicit affair."

"Might I remind you that you are the one who could hardly bring herself to speak to me about the marriage bed the night before my wedding?"

Violet waved that off. "I'm long past that awkwardness, I assure you. Why, with Hyacinth——"

"I don't want to know," Daphne said firmly.

"Well, yes, probably not," Violet conceded. "Nothing is ordinary with Hyacinth."

Daphne didn't say anything, so Violet reached out and took her hand. "Yes, Daphne," she said with great sincerity, "I am happy."

"I can't imagine if Simon——"

"I couldn't imagine it, either," Violet cut in. "Yet it happened. I thought I should die of the pain."

Daphne swallowed.

"But I didn't. And you wouldn't. And the truth is, eventually it does become easier. And you think that perhaps you could find happiness with someone else."

"Francesca did," Daphne murmured.

"Yes, she did." Violet closed her eyes for a moment, recalling how terribly worried she'd been for her third daughter during those years of her widowhood. She'd been so terribly alone, not shunning her family precisely, but not truly reaching out to them, either. And unlike Violet, she'd had no children to help her find her strength again.

"She is proof that one can be happy twice," Violet said, "with two different loves. But, you know, she's not the same kind of happy with Michael as she was with John. I would not value one higher than the other; it's not the sort of thing one can measure. But it's different."

She looked ahead. She was always more philosophical when her eyes were on the horizon. "I wasn't expecting the *same* kind of happiness I had with your father, but I would not settle for less. And I never found it."

She turned to look at Daphne, then reached out and took her hand. "And as it happened, I didn't need it."

"Oh, Mama," Daphne said, her eyes filling with tears.

"Life hasn't always been easy without your father," Violet said, "but it has *always* been worth it."

Always.